Red Sea Escape

Caesarion Lives!

By

ADHAM SAFWAT

Dedication

My father, Adham Safwat, who is struggling today with Parkinson's disease, dedicated this novel to his family, particularly his grandchildren, to encourage them to appreciate and enjoy the many splendors of the sea. In addition, he would have recalled the wise old sailors in the Red Sea who taught him about their culture and their craft, and his close friends from his early adulthood who often accompanied him on his extended stays on the Egyptian Red Sea coast.

In bringing this novel to publication, special thanks must be given to my father's good friend Dr. Edward Dawkins of Winters, California, who also had a passion for exploring in his own right, who encouraged me to pursue the publication of my father's novel, and who directed me to Jennifer Ann Gordon, who has provided guidance in bringing about its publication.

—Adam Safwat
November 2017

About the Author

Born in 1932 in Cairo, Egypt, and raised in the Cairo suburb of Maadi, Adham Safwat rejected the formality of the legal training that his father, an eminent jurist, had hoped he would pursue and instead spent many years exploring the beauty of the Red Sea and its then-rich coral and marine life. His adventures brought him closer to the fishermen and sailors of the Red Sea, and he learned about their ancient craft of navigating the waters of that great body of water. It was during this time that he also discovered his other passions, Roman and Arabic military history and astronomy, which he studied as an amateur later in life.

In the late 1960s, while in his early thirties, Safwat left his beloved Red Sea and his many friends in Cairo and immigrated to the United States, disillusioned with the turn of events in Egypt. Eventually he moved with his family to Northern California after his wife, Amira Safwat, was offered a position on the medical faculty at Stanford University. It would not be long before he discovered Hawaii, especially its Big Island, and his love of the sea and its people turned to Polynesian culture. In the late 1980s, he turned to building several Polynesian outrigger canoes, fashioned as faithfully as possibly on those from Tahiti. He even brought a special carpenter from Bora Bora to carve out the canoes from entire Koa logs in Hawaii.

Safwat loved the sea and its lore and believed that every child should experience its wonders and pleasures and learn of its majesty. He brought his family to the sea often and passed on his experiences to them and numerous friends. Later in life, when he returned to the Egyptian coast of the Red Sea for brief visits, he saw the demise of some of its coral and marine life due to pollution, tourism, and rising temperatures. Eventually, in the early 2000s, he penned this novel to tell the tale of Caesarion's flight from Alexandria, which also takes the reader along the voyage to discover the people and places of the Red Sea and the stars in the night sky that guided its sailors for centuries. Safwat and his wife currently reside in Glen Allen, Virginia.

Contents

INTRODUCTION

Much has been researched, written, and imagined about the relationship of Egypt's last Ptolemaic ruler, Cleopatra VII, with Julius Caesar and, later, Mark Antony, and the dramatic final act of both Antony and Cleopatra. Strangely, however, there has not been much popular interest in the fate of Cleopatra's son by Julius Caesar, known as Caesarion (Ptolemy XV, the last heir of the Ptolemaic dynasty in Egypt), whom, when he was still very young, Cleopatra installed as a co-ruler of Egypt after Caesar was murdered. After defeating Mark Antony's forces at Actium in 30 BC, Octavian advanced on Alexandria and secured Egypt as a province of the Roman Empire. With Antony dead by his own hand and her rule over, and to avoid eventual humiliation by Octavian, Cleopatra committed suicide. As the son of Caesar, Antony had promoted Caesarion as a potential successor to the Roman throne in his rivalry with Octavian, and the young Caesarion was indeed believed to resemble his noble father.

The fate of Caesarion is not clear, and it is believed he was ultimately murdered by Roman captors at Octavion's order, who undoubtedly viewed him as a threat. Whether in fact he was murdered is still in historical doubt (though the consensus appears to be that he was), but it is believed he attempted to escape at the direction of his mother, Cleopatra, and may have reached the Red Sea coast or gone further to India. Various historical accounts claim that Caesarion was either intercepted on his flight from Egypt in or near Ethiopia, later discovered at the Red Sea Port of Berenice, or coaxed out of hiding from elsewhere by Octavian's false assurances that he would be allowed to return safely as ruler of Egypt. In any event, Octavian declared himself ruler of Egypt after Caesarion's murder and eventually emperor of Rome.

In this novel, the narrator, the fictional Hiro Nearchus, a captain in Cleopatra's navy, recounts Caesarion's flight from Alexandria but with a twist. Rather than being caught, Caesarian assumes a different identity and eventually finds a new destiny for himself among the tribes of the southern Arabian coast.

CHAPTER 1: The Harbor Lights of Alexandria

A fast runner delivered a message to me in the shipbuilding yard. Brief and urgent, it was from Galen, the queen's physician: "Wait for me in the yard near the light tower."

The lighthouse stood at the western end of a circular harbor. The land from the base of the light tower to the water was reserved for shipbuilders. Activity here never stopped. I often spent long hours watching the construction of new ships, talking to other captains in the queen's navy and the craftsmen of these ships. From the shipyard, through the sometimes hazy dusk sky, I could see across the harbor to Cleopatra's palace, built on a rocky promontory at the eastern end of the harbor.

A wide avenue paved with slabs of granite connected the light tower to Cleopatra's palace, skirting the edge of the sea. Every day, hundreds of citizens strolled by the sea on this wide avenue to see their friends and to be seen; to enjoy the clean, cool sea breeze; and to watch the sun setting into the sea. When darkness fell, a huge fire was lit on top of the light tower. The orange-red glow would last all night, guiding the ships to Alexandria. Lights from every house along the harbor and every ship in the harbor shimmered on the calm waters. The children, strolling with their parents, carried small lanterns of glass with a candle inside. In the calm summer sea, more than a hundred small fishing boats were busy catching fish just outside the breakwater, even after dusk had fallen. Each boat had a glass box hanging over the side holding two oil lamps. Attracted by the light, the fish rose to the surface. Above it all, as if to not be outshined, a thousand oil lamps glittered in the queen's palace.

I did not know it at the time, but as I watched the changing colors at sunset, Cleopatra and her physician, Galen, stood on her balcony, silently admiring the beautiful city. When the fire was lit on top of the light tower, the queen turned to Galen and said, "My wise friend, we have talked about this before. The time has come. Caesar and Antony are dead. Humiliation is now my only suitor. Emperor Octavian hopes to drag me to Rome in chains. His legions are three days from our city. I wish to die a quick and painless death. You must help me, Galen. You are my only true friend."

Galen went to the nomads who lived to the west of Alexandria. They were desert people who knew how to capture the horned viper of Egypt. They also grew the sweetest figs. Cleopatra's physician bought three baskets filled with ripe figs, and in each basket there was one horned viper. Galen returned to the queen's palace. He found her waiting for him on a large balcony overlooking the sea. Galen approached the queen and said, "I have done what you have ordered me to do."

Cleopatra called one of her slave girls, the one she liked least, and ordered her to eat a fig from the basket. The girl reached for a fig, and the viper struck her on the arm. She screamed once and then sank to the ground. The look of terror on her face gave way to the pallor of death. In a few moments, she lay dead on the marble floor.

Cleopatra nodded her approval. "She did not suffer greatly."

Galen said, "My queen, the desert trackers tell me that if this viper strikes a man, even though the sun may be low on the horizon, he will not see the sun set."

She answered him, "Sunsets . . . they are so beautiful here on the sea. I would like to see just one more. I shall eat the figs after sunset today. My burial place must be a secret. You know where Alexander was buried. Have some slaves bury me there." The queen spoke with sadness in her voice. "Alexandria, most beautiful of all cities, will fall into the dirty hands of Octavian. Caesarion, my beloved son, will no longer be safe here. Octavian will never allow Julius Caesar's son to live, and surely he has already tasked his forces to assassinate him as soon as they conquer our city."

After a pause to ensure that no one could hear our conversation, the queen charged Galen with her final wish: "Please, Galen, help my son flee from Alexandria. Go see Hiro Nearchus, captain of my navy, and tell him that I have asked you to take Caesarion to the island of

Serendib[1] at the southern tip of India. The governor of the harbor there is a good friend. He will allow Caesarion to grow up in safety. You must be at the harbor of Myos Hormos before the news of my death reaches the people of Upper Egypt.[2] Take all the gold and silver coins you need and a few good men to guard you. May all the gods be kind to you, my friend."

And so it was that the queen's physician came to me in the shipyard near the lighthouse after dark three days before the Emperor Octavian entered Alexandria.

I watched Galen walking toward me with the natural grace his body possessed. The gods had given him a noble head with black curly hair, now speckled with grey, which covered his ears and neck. His lofty brow and sincere brown eyes commanded respect. His face had strong features, yet his smile showed extreme kindness. He was a man who found it difficult to hide his emotions. Now he was fifty years of age and a famous physician. He always dressed in the finest cloaks made of the best linen. He was extremely clean in body and clothes. I never saw him wear any jewelry. He admired the Roman virtue of *gravitas* and believed that the higher the civilization, the less jewelry men wore. Aristocrats and the poor alike sought his advice. He radiated massive authority, and people turned to him in times of trouble.

My dear friend sat next to me, his face grave and his voice filled with emotion. "Hiro, before her suicide, the queen entrusted her son to me. I promised her that I would take Caesarion beyond the Red Sea to safety. I cannot do this without your help. My wife and children will stay with her family. I hope I can return to Alexandria in less than a year. Will you go?"

I thought about this dangerous voyage for a long time, Galen looking at me with his piercing eyes.

---

[1] *Serendib* is the Arabic name for the island of Sri Lanka (formerly called Ceylon). Horace Walpole coined the word *serendipity*, which means "unexpected good fortune," from the fairy tale "Three Princes of Serendib."

[2] *Upper Egypt* is the name given to southern Egypt. The Nile River originates in the south and flows north to Alexandria and the Mediterranean. Thus, it is necessary to travel "up" the Nile to reach southern Egypt.

"Hiro, there is no time to waste. Egypt is no longer a friend and ally of Rome. Egypt will soon be a province, and the Romans will send a governor. Our people will be slaves of her empire. The young men you see laughing around you now will be forced by the lash to work harder and harder. Rome will want more grain. No woman will be safe, and no man will live in dignity."

I found it hard to believe, but I replied in a soft voice, "We could go to the fort at Myos Hormos. The officers know me there. But we will need gold. There will be many men to pay."

Galen said, "And to bribe. Hiro, I have more gold coins than you can count. Word of Cleopatra's death has not reached the people outside Alexandria. The country is still safe for us as long as we travel faster than the news. Tell your sons to get their weapons and meet me at the queen's palace at moonrise."

At my house my two sons, sixteen and eighteen years of age, met me with their usual smiles just as if the whole city were not in danger and there was no invading army marching toward us. I told my sons of Cleopatra's death. "We are leaving the city. We must carry many bags of gold and silver coins, but our safety depends on keeping that a secret. Bring your short swords, sharp knives, and an extra cloak. We are going to the coast of the Red Sea, to the port of Myos Hormos."

I had struggled in the last few years to fill the void in my sons' lives after the death of their mother. I could not help but wonder whether taking them from Alexandria would be good for them, but I told myself that they would do well to travel and to have a change of scenery. And perhaps this was true and not just my own way of justifying turning our lives upside down in service to the queen and Caesarion.

At moonrise we moved quickly to Cleopatra's palace. The sounds of crying women and wailing slave girls had not stopped. Just inside the main gate we found Galen with three of his trusted servants, gigantic Nubians with honest faces and dark brown skin. Without saying a word, he rode on a mule while his servants walked behind, armed with swords and knives like ourselves. Each also had a long whip made of hippopotamus hide. With their whips they could keep the crowds away from us. My sons walked on either side of the gold-laden mule, and I took the bridle and led them out of the city.

I was wearing my red cape and Greek helmet with red feathers. People in the streets recognized these as signs of high rank in the queen's army and navy, and they stepped silently out of our path. There was no panic in the city, just silent fear.

One of Galen's faithful young Nubian servants was Adoo, who walked by his side. He was talking to Galen in a respectful and melodious voice. He had the charming habit of sprinkling his conversation with proverbs he learned in his childhood. His full name was Adoo Bahar, which means "slave of the river god." His parents thought this name might protect him from evil crocodiles. I looked at Adoo with his oval, humorous, strong-jawed face. He was the most typical Nubian man I had ever seen with his serene brown eyes, shining dark brown skin, and shaved head, as with all of his people protected by a fine white turban. Adoo was a tall man, about twenty-five years old. Unlike many tall people who have shoulders too narrow for their bodies, he had broad, muscular shoulders and long limbs. Looking at him, I could guess the stamina and strength in his magnificent body. Three scars on each side of his face radiated from the corners of his eyes to the hairline, and on his right thigh a dark blue tattoo of geometrical pattern encircled his leg. He walked with the loping gait of a man born and raised in the open spaces of his country, Nubia, a desert land to the south between Egypt and Sudan.

And so it came to pass that four citizens and three Nubians arrived at the pier where riverboats were tied.

Egypt is blessed with steady northwesterly winds that allow riverboats to sail up the Nile against the current. Floating down from Upper Egypt is sometimes aided by a few days of south wind or calm. One branch of the Nile feeds Alexandria, and we found many boats of all sizes tied at the pier, waiting for cargo to go to Upper Egypt.

The riverboat captains observed our group and recognized an opportunity, so they gathered around. Galen asked which of them had a completely empty boat. One of the captains stepped forward, a wiry man, barefoot and tanned by the sun, with green eyes and a pleasant grin on his face. "Great ones, I have no cargo and will take you where you want to go."

"What is your price for taking us to Upper Egypt? We want to leave now." The short, wiry man laughed and said that he would be willing to sail now and would be content with whatever pay he received, for he knew by the looks of this distinguished party that he would get more than he expected.

We stepped into the empty boat. Galen ordered his servants to bring the mule into the boat without unloading the bags of gold coin. I was sure he did not want people to notice what we were carrying. He looked at the boat owner and said, "I need this mule. My old legs cannot walk far. You may raise sail now."

The great white lateen sail was raised by two crewmen with our help, and the wind filled it and pushed the boat to the center of the river. The banks were visible in the light of the half moon. If we ran onto a sandbar in the river, it would be easy to push this boat free—it had no cargo and no ballast. It was drawing little water, and because of its wide beam, it was quite stable.

Now the people on the docks could no longer see or hear us. The Nubians took the bags of gold coins off the mule, stowed them in the covered area under the foredeck, and sat down, fully relaxed, on the giant wooden beams holding the mast. From that point, only one at a time would sleep while the other two kept their eyes on the treasure. At night they would take turns, six hours each, and in the afternoon heat, they would sleep in turn, two hours each.

Galen motioned me to follow him, and he stepped up to the foredeck. We sat down under the great sail. With the wind following us, nobody else could hear a word of what he said.

"Hiro, I could not speak freely when we were on land. Please keep this secret between just you and me. If one of us dies, the other must complete this journey. Cleopatra asked me to take Caesarion to the island of Serendib. There is a strong Greek garrison in the harbor there, and the governor was a good friend of Caesar. Hopefully, the boy will be safe there."

"Where is Caesarion?" I asked Galen.

He said, "He is disguised as a boy of the desert traveling on camelback with some loyal Bedouins. These people will keep their oath when they are well paid. If anybody hears that the boy is traveling in the western desert of Egypt with Bedouins, they will think he is going to North Africa, and the search for him will be diverted there. But after a couple of days, the Bedouins will turn to the south and travel three more days to meet us near the Great Pyramid. We shall take the boy across the river and across the Eastern Desert, and we will go to the port of Myos Hormos on the Red Sea coast. There, you, my friend, will select the best boats and the best crew, and we shall sail down the Red Sea into the Indian Ocean and on to Serendib."

I said, "It will be a great adventure for my sons, and they will learn much about the world. You have the gold; I have the authority. Yes, we shall take the best ships, and we will go."

But Galen added, "Always say, 'May the gods help us.' You never know what fortune or misfortune awaits us."

We spent the rest of the night talking. Memories stirred in the depths of our souls. I was proud to call Galen my friend. As young boys growing up together in Alexandria, we had spent many happy times playing in the sea. When the weather was calm, fishing was our main goal in life, and when the weather was rough, we played endlessly in the surf. Love of the sea was a great bond between us, strengthened by many shared adventures.

Galen's family was rich. They had sent him to the school of the Stoics, and he found pleasure in learning from the great teachers. The best minds of the Roman world were drawn to Alexandria by the generosity of the Ptolemies, and Galen would spend nearly all his evenings listening to their discourses. During the days he would spend time with me in the shipyard watching the boatbuilders. After I became a captain in the navy commanding many ships, he would often join me on voyages throughout the Mediterranean. He visited Rome, Athens, and all of the cities where he could meet philosophers, astronomers, and mathematicians. Wherever we stopped, he would gather medicinal plants to try to cure our sick sailors. Galen was a born leader of men. He could have been a great general, even a lawgiver and a statesman, but he chose to be a physician.

The first rays of daylight showed over the horizon, and from the warm darkness of the river came the sounds of the water against the hull and hundreds of waterfowl that would not sleep.

CHAPTER 2: The River

In the twilight I could see a village ahead of us built on high ground to protect it from the annual flood. Every summer the Nile would rise, flooding all the lands around its course. The brown water laden with silt would surround all the villages and wash away their trash. The villagers would have nothing to do except when their lord gathered them for forced labor on projects such as building pyramids or temples. The young people would spend their days fishing or catching waterfowl, and since mud was near at hand, they would repair their houses or build new ones. Bundles of reeds thick as a man's leg would serve instead of wood beams. Summer was a great time for the young; they did much useful work, but nobody was ordering them around. They wanted to play in the water and catch fish or birds. They built simple rafts from bundles of reeds, and on two or more bundles, they would lash a platform made from more reeds. On these rafts the boys stood with their homemade harpoons and fowling sticks, which they used to stun the birds. Life was all around them. Millions of migrating birds were flying over the Mediterranean Sea to rest and winter in the Nile Delta. Some would fly on to southern lands, but millions would stay until spring.

The two crewmen were awake and rubbing their eyes. The captain was standing in the stern controlling the tiller with his foot. The rudder was huge but did not dig deep into the water. The submerged part was only about as deep as a forearm, but the area was large and could control the boat easily. One word from the captain and the sail was down. Pushing the boat with long poles, every man stuck the end of a wooden pole into the muddy bottom and pushed hard until the boat grounded near the shore. The captain did not want to use his sail to ground the boat because the power would be too much, and they might get stuck in the shallows for a long time.

There was on board a great earthenware jar, high as a man's waist. This jar was filled with river water. Water oozed out of the pores and trickled down the sides, which was then collected in a second glazed pot. Thus was clean water filtered out of the big jar.

The crew had secured the boat and built a small fire. They had a round clay pot about an arm's length across. The potter had fashioned clay to look like ropes and had laid these ropes one over the other in a circle to make the pot. It was full of sand, on top of which they built the fire with dry wood stored in the boat. This is where they did their cooking. Three stones were near the fire area, on which they placed the jug of clean filtered water until it boiled. The captain put some honey in the boiling water. Then he gave each a wooden cup filled to the brim and a dry piece of bread. He smiled and said, "We call this sun bread because it is baked in the shape of a disk and then left in the strong sun all day to dry. It can be stored many days. Dip it in your hot drink; it is good."

After breakfast, Galen called Adoo and said, "Take the two crewmen and go to the village. Load the mule with provisions and come back as quickly as you can."

The boat captain had on board a smaller sail for rough weather, which he used to make shade on the boat. We stretched out under it and went to sleep. My sons were wide awake after a good night's sleep, and they watched over us. Before falling asleep, Galen told the boys, "Don't swim here. It is dangerous. I will explain later." I wanted to ask him what dangers lurked in this river other than crocodiles, but I was too tired and went to sleep. I knew the boys would obey him. They respected the old man's wisdom.

The sun was high in the sky when Adoo returned, the mule heavy with bags and baskets. The two crewmen were steadying the load, one man on each side. They wanted to make sure the mule didn't slip and fall in the mud. A group of young children from the village followed because they were curious, and this looked like good entertainment—a mule, a tall Nubian with a long whip in his hand like some devil from far away, and two normal men trying to keep the baskets from falling off the mule. The crew extended a long wooden plank from the boat to shore. My sons stood on the plank while the crewmen unloaded the baskets of food and handed them one by one to Adoo, who passed them to the boys. The work of unloading was done quickly and silently. The only noise was the laughter of the children watching. Then Galen looked at the children.

"Do you like this mule?"

"Yes, yes, we like him."

"He is yours."

He gave the bridle to the tallest boy, who smiled and said nothing. He did not walk away but waded into the river and dragged the willing animal behind him for a bath. All the children jumped into the river. They swam around the mule and tried to stand on his back for a good jump. Their laughter could be heard for a long time. We were sailing once again, the north wind pushing us south against the current. The men were stowing the provisions under the covered foredeck.

Galen was sitting in the shade of the sail, and he motioned the boys to come sit next to him. I joined them in the shade. He was saying, "See how happy these children are. All they need is water, mud, and a mule to play with. But we know there is something in the water that will make some of them sick. Not all of them, mind you, but more than half. We don't know what it is; however, when they grow up, they will be pale and tired. They will not die, but they will be weak, and the strangest thing of all is that their penises will drip blood."[3]

Galen continued to entertain us with captivating conversation. He was a rare and marvelous teacher. I could see how my sons enjoyed talking to him. He never talked down to them, but he talked *to* them as if they were his equals in knowledge and wisdom.

---

[3] We now understand this disease thanks to a German scientist, Bilharz, who discovered the life cycle of a river fluke, a microscopic worm that penetrates human skin and travels in the bloodstream to lay eggs in the urinary bladder, irritating it so much that blood will flow down the urinary tract. Some young children seem to develop a tolerance for this parasite. *Schistosomiasis*, as this disease is known, can be cured, but the children go back into the river and canals and get reinfected. Upper Egypt and Nubia are free from this parasite, and people there are strong and healthy, mainly because they have no irrigation ditches and drainage canals, which harbor a water snail necessary to complete the life cycle of the parasite. Even in ancient times, Herodotus, the historian and traveler, noticed the symptoms of urinary bleeding in some Egyptian men.

The sun was low on the horizon. Other riverboats were anchored, and as we passed, they would hail us loudly, "Come and join us for dinner!"

Our captain would wave back and laugh. "A 'boatman's invitation!' They know we will not stop."

Soon we were served a delicious meal on deck in a large wooden bowl. I could see surprise on everyone's face. The food was truly delicious, as good as anything I ever tasted in Alexandria. Of course, it had been cooked on land and delivered to our boat. The women in that village knew how to keep their men happy.

The boat captain ate his meal with us, then took the tiller. He would steer for at least ten hours until sunrise. His crewmen would sleep, and we tried to stay awake to keep him company and to help him remain alert. On a fast-moving boat in the middle of the river, there were no mosquitoes. That was another pleasant surprise.

My younger boy, Justin (his full name is Justinianus), asked me how the boat captain could steer at night without running aground on a sandbar or crashing into a drifting log.

I said, "You know how you can walk in our home at night without crashing into things? The river is this captain's home. Every village, every large tree, any possible landmark at all is fixed in his memory. He probably started sailing up and down the Nile with his father. Now the light of the half moon is enough for him. A boy who fails to develop this skill will never become a boat captain. As for logs drifting in the Nile, you will never see one, day or night. Egypt has no forests. A log is so valuable, it will be salvaged as soon as somebody spots it. Since the time of the Great Kings, wood was shipped to Egypt as tribute to Pharaoh. As long as he was powerful, cedar wood came from Phoenicia and ebony and other dense hardwoods from Africa. The Egyptians had a large fleet in the Red Sea and another in the White Sea, which the Romans call the Mediterranean Sea."[4]

We spread our clean mats on deck and covered ourselves with cloaks. We were silent and relaxed, all of us looking at the stars

---

[4] Even now, the Egyptians call the Mediterranean the White Sea because of its white sand beaches and white sand bottom, which extend for miles west of Alexandria. The Romans called it Mediterraneus, referring to the fact that it was surrounded by land.

moving slowly from east to west. One who has never traveled in a dry desert cannot imagine what the skies of Egypt are like, and it is impossible to describe. It is so beautiful, it robs you of sleep, and when you wake up in the middle of the night, you are amazed again. No wonder the desert people were our first astronomers. The days were hot and the nights cool, so they traveled at night and gave a name to every bright star in the heavens.

Galen asked in a soft voice, "Did you name your son Ari after the great astronomer Aristarchus of Samos?"[5]

"Yes," I replied. "He had the courage to propose a theory contrary to the beliefs of all mankind. Aristarchus believed the stars and the sun do not move around the earth from east to west. We will observe the same rising and setting of sun and stars if we move around ourselves because the earth spins around its axis, and he was the first astronomer to say so."

Galen said, "It may take centuries, thousands of years even, before all common men believe this. New ideas sink slowly into the minds of men."

We drifted into restful sleep looking at the heavens and listening to the sounds of the Nile against the hull. A song came to my mind, the "Song of the Old Fisherman of Lohaye":

My sailboat was built on the Island of Lohaye,
But her colors today look strange to me.
Her crew said, "Come aboard, hagee Ali."
And I said, "Bring me my share, boys.
I shall rest here, in the shade under this tree."

At sunrise, we were out of the Nile Delta. Our boat was sailing south, and on the western horizon we saw the three Great Pyramids, which was our appointed meeting place. The nomads were to be waiting for us with Cleopatra's son. There was a sudden change in scenery. The riverbanks were covered with high date palms, thousands of them planted close together, shading the land and the villages.

---

[5] Samos is a Greek Island near the coast of Turkey. The famous astronomer Aristarchus lived there and was the first to declare that the earth and planets revolve around the sun. To honor him, a crater on the moon is named after him.

Without this vast shade, the people would not be able to tolerate the summer sun of Egypt.

In this man-made garden there was a tremendous production of food, and that is how Pharaoh could feed the army of soldiers he needed to force his neighbors to pay tribute, the army of shipbuilders to maintain his fleet, and another of stonemasons who did nothing all their lives but build monuments for the glory of their king. When they died, their sons followed in their footsteps, building temples and pyramids for Pharaoh, hoping they could join him after death in another and better life.

There were two small towns on the banks of the river, one on each bank. Small ferryboats sailed back and forth all day long, moving people and livestock between these towns. The town on the west bank was called the Ferries West. I asked the boat captain if he knew someone in this town who would rent horses. He said, "There is an old man here, an Arabian sheikh, who lives at the edge of the desert. I will lead you to his house."

We followed him to the town. My sons were walking by my side.

Justin asked, "What is the meaning of *sheikh*?"

"*Sheikh* means a chief, and it also means an old man. All the tribal leaders are old men, respected for their wisdom and their accomplishments. The story of a sheikh's life is well known to his tribe, and that is why they honor him."

It was a long walk to the edge of the town, not far from the desert. The last house had a wall around it and in the courtyard a few date palms and pomegranate trees.

I told my sons, "When we go into the sheikh's house, do not speak to him unless he speaks to you first. If he shakes your hand, do not show the strength of your grip; squeezing is considered bad manners. If they offer us food or drink, always use your right hand. It is extremely vulgar to touch food or drink with your left hand, a sure sign of bad upbringing. The left hand is reserved for private, unclean tasks. I know you are both hungry right now, but if we eat here, restrain yourselves."

Justin asked, "But if we eat very little, won't that insult our host? Won't he think we dislike his food?"

"That would be true only if we were *invited* guests."

We stood by the door. Instead of knocking, the boatman clapped his hands loudly.

"Remember, my sons, this sheik is not expecting us."

A small boy opened the door and said, "Who are you looking for?"

The boatman replied, "Some travelers want to talk to your sheikh."

The boy went back into his house, and a few moments later, a young man, handsome and energetic, walked out of the door. "You are all welcome to our house." Without waiting for an answer, he led us around the house to a sizable room built outside the wall, with a wide door and three windows. This was the guest room, always built outside the main house, a wise arrangement if your guests are strangers. We sat down on clean mats and leaned on leather pillows stuffed with straw. The sheikh walked into the room and said, "Welcome, welcome!"

He sat down slowly. His son came in with a generous tray of sweet melons and dates, and another boy walked in carrying three small earthenware *ollas*[6] filled with cool water. They had a well in the courtyard. Almost every house in this town had one. The groundwater was near the surface, seeping from the Nile but filtered through the soil. Jugs filled with this clean water hung in the shade to be cooled by the breeze.

We exchanged a few polite phrases; then I explained why we had come to his house. The sheikh told me, "I always keep my horses and camels in the desert. When I bring them into the Nile Valley, they get ill. Horses are healthier in the dry desert. My sons will bring horses for you."

I let the boatman return to his boat. He seemed eager to go back. I realized later on that I had made a blunder. I should never have let him out of my sight.

After a short wait, the boys returned with six horses. The boys were smiling and happy. Obviously, they enjoyed getting out into the

---

[6] A bulging wide-mouthed pot or jar.

open desert and riding the superb Arabian horses. I am sure the sheikh sent his sons to watch and protect his horses. He did not want anyone riding them too hard in the heat of the day. I liked his three sons; they were wiry, energetic boys with intelligent eyes. I told them to take us to the Sphinx first, and they led the way at a fast pace.

As soon as we came to that great statue, we dismounted and walked up to it. We moved slowly because the Sphinx was surrounded by soft, windblown sand, and our feet sank deep into it. When we came up to the statue, we laid our hands on its great body, that of a reclining lion with the head of a man, a very Egyptian face, looking straight ahead to the horizon. The Sphinx was carved out of limestone. The nearby pyramids were built on higher ground on a rocky plateau swept clean of sand by the constant wind. Much of that fine sand piled high around the Sphinx. My two sons were busy climbing onto the forearms of the lion with a human head.

I was asking myself, *Why would the ancient Egyptians place the Sphinx right in the middle of the easy road to their Great Pyramids? Why would Pharaoh want this huge statue with the body of a lion and the head of a man to block this approach? Was it to frighten the common people and keep them away from his tomb? Or was it to show his people that Pharaoh is still here with them, guarding the Nile Valley from evil?* These were pleasant but idle speculations.

CHAPTER 3: The Pyramids

We rode up to the tomb of Pharaoh Khufu. I sat in the shade with Galen and asked the young men to climb the Great Pyramid all the way to the top and sweep the northern horizon to see if they could spot any riders coming toward us. Sitting in the shade of this great tomb built by Pharaoh Khufu,[7] I wondered whether Khufu believed he would come back to life and join the great sun god, Ra. He probably did, for some of the most effective leaders are those who believe their own religion.

In less than one hour, the boys were back. I asked them, "Have you seen a caravan in the desert?"

The nomad boy answered, "No, no caravan, but a few camels are moving fast toward us."

I told him, "I wish to meet them. You lead the way."

We rode our horses and galloped toward the setting sun. There was a group of riders on camelback. As we approached them, I could see a dozen men and two youths. They were riding hybrid camels, especially bred for speed. Some of them were pure white, an unusual color for camels.

They saw us, stopped, and dismounted. The group looked like a raiding party. Every man was leaning on a spear. Each one of them had a wide leather belt around his waist with a long, curved dagger. On their camels, I could see unstrung bows and quivers full of arrows. These were men of the desert. Determined not to be captured by any pursuers, they could see any suspicious force when it was still far enough for them to escape. These were the last free men on earth. They didn't pay taxes, and their sons didn't serve in the army.

They greeted me politely and offered us their hands as a gesture of friendship. We sat down, and one of them opened his bag and came back with some dry bread and salt. He broke the bread into small

---

7 Khufu's father, Sneferu, greatly advanced the architecture of pyramids through his own pyramids, including the Bent Pyramid of Sneferu.

pieces, then put the salt in the palm of his right hand. We dipped the bread in the salt and ate it. This ritual meant that we could trust each other. If a desert nomad offered to share his bread and salt with you, you never could refuse, and you could be certain that he would not harm or betray you for at least three days. These were their sacred laws of hospitality.

I exchanged a few polite phrases with the man who offered me the salt, and then I told him, "I came here to meet you, to conduct these two boys to safety."

He answered, "You speak the truth." Then he motioned to Caesarion and another young boy to come forward. They both looked to be about seventeen years old. Though they were sunburnt and dusty like the nomadic boys, the softness of their hands indicated that they had not spent much time in the desert.

Caesarion greeted me in Greek and introduced his companion. "This is Marcus. He is my best friend."

The leader of the Arabs said, "The young man acknowledges you. That is good, but I must talk to the physician."

Galen dismounted and walked directly toward the nomads. Their leader and two others rose to greet him, and he talked to them in their own dialect. He offered the leader a small leather pouch filled with gold coins. The man refused it three times, and thrice Galen thrust it into his palm. The man said, "We have already been rewarded generously."

Galen replied, "This is a small gift for you, my friend."

"And what gift can I give to you in return?"

"Four spears and four daggers."

Galen took four leather belts with long, curved daggers and four spears. The spear shafts were made of a strong and flexible wood and the sharp points of bronze. He saluted the desert men and turned to Caesarion and his friend Marcus. "Here, these are your weapons now. Wear the belt around your waist. Keep your spear near your hand at all times." Then, to Ari and Justin, he gave the same gifts, a spear and a dagger for each. Now the young men were well armed and could defend themselves.

We rode our horses back toward the boat. I was riding next to Galen.

"Galen, where did you meet those nomads?"

"Oh, I often buy rare plants from them—medicinal plants—and they once sold me some snakes."

"Snakes? What can snakes cure?"

"Humiliation."

That last answer he whispered to the desert, not to me, so I just let my dear friend be.

We returned to our boat before sunset. I thanked the Arab boys and praised their horses. They saluted us and left. We pushed our boat away from the riverbank to get a good rest away from the mosquitoes. Ari and Justin were talking to Caesarion and Marcus. I felt sure they would become good friends. Shared adventure would create a strong bond of friendship among these young men. Already they were calling Caesarion "Caesare," pronouncing it "SHEZZ-ah-ray."

We were trying to fall asleep. The sound of music coming from the village was loud. There was much clapping of hands and singing. As the moon got bigger and brighter, the villagers had their weddings and celebrations. For three nights before the full moon, they danced and sang and celebrated their feasts. I could hear one of their songs loud and clear:

O sad young Prince with a crown on your head,
Your beautiful loved one has left you and fled.
How will the wound in your heart ever heal
When you keep her perfume in your bed?

We got up early the next morning. Small boats were already busy ferrying people between the two banks of the Nile. I asked the boat captain to take us to the small town of Ferries East.

As we approached the eastern bank of the river, I saw a large group of people, more than thirty peasants. They were silent and standing still. This was unusual. When we came closer, I could see at the edge of the water a man beating a woman with repeated blows to her head and body. She was not screaming, but her head was on the ground between her arms. No one in the crowd was trying to stop the savage beating. Anger welled up inside me, and I ordered the boatman, "Take me there as quickly as you can go." The man moved his boat and rammed the bow in the mud. The crowd was still and silent. I jumped off the boat, and I could see Adoo follow me with his whip in his hand.

Quickly, I put my arms around the man who was beating the woman. I was surprised that his body instantly went limp, and there was no resistance. I looked around me. The crowd was surging toward the boat, but the mud on the riverbank slowed them down a little. Adoo understood immediately that this was an attack, a trap laid for us by thieves. He gave a loud yell to alert his friends to the danger, a bloodcurdling yell that would strike fear into the heart of any coward. The other two Nubian giants exploded into action with their whips of hippopotamus hide. They were aiming at the thieves' heads. Every time they took out a man's eye or took off his ear, there was a loud cry of pain and terror that discouraged the whole gang. Adoo, with his whip, was opening a way for us to get back to the boat. I was protecting his back, following him closely with my short sword in my hand. Anyone who dared to come close would have felt the sharp point of the blade.

We reached the boat and stood together shoulder to shoulder, heaving mightily to free it from the mud, with the two Nubian giants standing above us, their long whips singing in the air to protect us from the crowd. With one leap, we were in the boat, and it was drifting away from the bank. I looked at Galen. He was smiling and shaking his head from side to side. "We fell into a trap, Hiro." The boat captain and his two crewmen had joined the thieves. The four young men, Ari, Justin, Caesare, and Marcus, stood there, the spears m their hands dripping blood, their young chests heaving with excitement, their eyes wild and large. They now knew fear, but they did not panic. They had faced a hostile mob and stood up to defend themselves without hesitation. For the first time in their young lives, they had learned that anger can overcome fear.

Every boat captain who unloads cargo in Ferries East knows the local gang of thieves, and if he is a prudent man, he will pay them to leave his boat alone and not steal his cargo. Now, after the attack, it was obvious that I should never have let the captain out of my sight, but I had allowed him to go into town. The temptation of all the bags filled with gold coins was too much for him, and now he was left without coins and without a boat of his own.

We sailed the boat many miles south of the accursed town to a small island covered with reeds, and we anchored there. It was a good anchorage, and we sat on deck after dinner, talking for a long time in the moonlight.

Galen spoke to his three Nubian servants. "You have served me well. Tomorrow I will give you two rewards: this boat and your freedom. Sail back to Nubia and rejoin your families as free men."

They thanked Galen over and over again. He gave each one of them enough gold coins to start a new life. In their tribe, every male wishing to get married would get a plot of land, and his fellow tribesmen would help him build a house of mudbrick. It would be up to his wife and her female relatives to decorate it with intricate designs and furniture.

The three faithful Nubians slept like happy men, but the next morning the youngest, Adoo, came to Galen and said, "Hakeem, I wish to stay with you. You need a servant, and I need to see the world." Then Adoo took his leather purse filled with gold coins and gave it to his two friends saying, "When you reach our land, give this to my mother and father. If they are not alive, give it to my brothers and sisters."

Galen said to the young man, "Adoo, you can stay if you wish. You are right. I need a servant on this trip. The first service I want from you is to walk with your friends to the nearest town and buy seven camels for us. Choose well. She-camels are best for traveling."

Caesare asked, "Do you think his friends will give the gold coins to his mother, or will they keep them for themselves?"

Galen told us, "These Nubians are the most honest people you will ever find. Trust me, if you need to employ someone who will not be tempted to steal, hire a Nubian. Without a doubt, the coins will be given to Adoo's family. Nubians grow up in a small tribe surrounded by a stony, arid desert where visitors are few. If you know everybody around you and they all know you, then that makes your honor your most valuable possession. If a Nubian boy or girl does something wrong, any adult may discipline him or her immediately. The punishment is not harsh, but it is quick and certain. To live happily, a child soon learns to obey the rules. The children and adults alike have clung tightly to their honor under Egyptian rule. The Nubians call their land Nooba. It means 'Land of Gold, Noob.' The pharaohs kept Nooba under their control for the gold and the emerald mines."

"Now, young men," I said, "prepare for a three-day journey across the Eastern Desert."

We bathed and oiled our skins. We put on the new clothes Galen had bought for us, which were robes of Egyptian linen with wide sleeves and one deep pocket on the chest. The sleeves were so big, a man could roll them up to bare his arms and shoulders and keep cool. The boys proudly tied their leather belts with their curved daggers around their waists. I did not wear my military helmet or red cape because our plan was to join a trading caravan, and we would have to look like traders or ordinary travelers.

Adoo returned with seven healthy camels for us to ride. The preparations did not take long. We had to travel a few miles to reach a place in the desert called Gandal, where the camel caravans assembled. All traders and travelers who wanted to go to Palestine or Syria gathered there. The tribesmen who live in the Desert of Sinai worked as guides and provided camels for the traders. That gave them a steady income, better than robbing caravans.

CHAPTER 4: The Desert

Gandal, the meeting place, would be about a three-hour ride from the river. I showed the young men how to ride a camel, with their legs crossed in front of the saddle pommel in the fashion of nomads. Each rider had a flexible thin stick to guide his camel. These camels were well trained; a light touch on the side of the neck would make them turn. I was leading because I knew the way. Anyone meeting us would have no doubt that we were desert travelers. We were all armed except Galen, who would not carry weapons. His faithful servant, Adoo, always at his side, was ready for anything.

On the way, we rode through a flat plateau strewn with flint. Then, all around us, there was wood in the sand. We picked up a few pieces. It was stone that looked exactly like wood. We admired these pieces of colorful stone-wood and rode on. In less than three hours, we covered about twenty miles.

We could see ahead of us the small settlement known as Gandal. There was a well with a good supply of fresh water all year round. The people who lived there had built troughs around this well so the camels could drink, and they made a living selling supplies to travelers. A caravan of camels was there, ready to start. We hoped to join them.

We stopped and dismounted not far from the well, and I told Adoo, "I will look for the leader of this caravan. You and the boys water the camels. Stay together."

It was easy to find the leader. Everybody knew him. He was sitting in the shade, under a shelter made of palm fronds. There were many of these shelters all around. Vendors were selling everything a traveler might need. I saluted the caravan leader in his own dialect and told him that we had our own camels, but we needed a guide and three of his camels to carry water, skins, and provisions. We quickly agreed on the price. He called one of his men and ordered him to accompany me. Then the leader said to me, "We leave tomorrow before sunset.

Tonight, you and your party will be our guests at our customary feast. Hadi, your guide, will join you now and help you get ready."

I introduced the guide to our party. Then I told Adoo, "Go with Hadi. I rented three camels. They should be in good shape, but examine them thoroughly. Then buy new waterskins, oil, dry fruit, fresh melons, and flour, enough for ten people. Buy barley and millet for the camels. We shall wait for you here."

Galen was resting in the shade, and I joined him. Adoo, Hadi, and the boys returned with three camels laden with provisions and three fat sheep. I asked, "What are the sheep for?"

Adoo smiled and said, "Hadi advised us that three sheep would be a proper gift for tonight's party. We also bought some cloth to make a shade."

"Well done," I said. "Now, sit down in the shade and start oiling the waterskins. First, you blow them up full of air to be sure there are no holes. Then tie the end and rub the oil into the leather. There will be three waterskins for each of you. You can drink only one a day, and there will be some water for you to wash your faces in the morning."

Hadi spread a piece of cloth on the ground in front of each of our camels. Then Adoo helped him carry a bag of barley to pour a good portion for each animal on the piece of cloth. Then our guide said, "We must eat well tonight, like our camels! And tomorrow they must drink their fill, for they will not have water for three days. If they finish this barley, give them more. I must go now."

"Wait," I said. "Take these three sheep to your sheikh. This is our gift to him."

Suddenly there appeared a line of camels loaded with goods. When they reached us, there was utter confusion. It is hard to describe the noise, the shouting, and the biting and bellowing of the camels. They were huge white Syrian dromedaries, and the servants unloading them were Egyptian peasants. The owners sat on their mules, cursing their men. Owners did not travel with the caravan (*kafila*, as the Arabs call it). They sent a trusted man to deliver their loaded camels to the merchants awaiting them.

Just before sunset, calm and quiet returned, and we gathered around a huge fire for the customary feast before departure. All around this fire were flat stones close to the flames. When the stones became properly heated, the meat would be cooked on them.

A magician stepped into the ring to entertain the crowd. He leaned on a walking stick and dramatically surveyed his audience. He bellowed, "Fellow travelers, I am confident that you have not survived and prospered all these years without all of you developing a keen eye for detail. With that in mind, please observe that I have nothing hidden in my humble clothes. Now, prepare to behold what wonders I can do." Then he said, in a low voice, "Come closer if you dare, all of you who doubt my magic powers!" The boys, Ari, Justin, Caesare, and Marcus, moved closer to the magician. The man uttered a loud cry and then threw his stick on the ground. Instantly it became a snake. The snake felt the heat of the fire and was trying to move away.

Ari asked me, "How can the magician turn a stick into a snake?"

I told him, "He can't. This is an old trick of the Egyptians. I will explain it to you tomorrow morning."

The *Badu*[8] brought in baskets filled with mutton and goat meat mixed with crushed onions. They quickly laid the thin sliced meat on the hot stones. One man stood with a sharply pointed stick about six feet long. He picked up cooked meat with his stick and offered it to one of the seated men, who took it with his right hand and started eating. This way of cooking meat was preferred by the Arabs to cooking on charcoal. The meat did not touch the hot embers, only the hot stone. The man serving with his long, sharp stick did not stop. His helpers added more meat. Everybody ate in silence. As he finished, each man rubbed his hands with soft sand to take the grease off his fingers, and a young man gave them wet towels to rub their hands. Then came slices of sweet melons of all kinds, and they were good to eat after the grilled meat.

Now the meal was over and the dancing began. In the Nile Valley, there would be loud drums and dancing girls. Not in the desert! Here the dancing was done by horses, and the men watched, clapping hands

---

[8] *Badu* is the Arabic word underlying the English word *Bedouin*, referring to the nomadic people of the Egyptian deserts.

27

rhythmically. Six musicians were playing—flutes of different sizes and shapes, and one small drum beating a simple rhythm.

Three white horses were led into the ring. One had a young rider on its back; the other two were held by a head rope in the hands of their owners. These white horses were moving their forelegs to the rhythm of the music. Obviously, they were still learning, and the owners would touch them lightly on the knee with a thin stick to make the horse lift it up with the rhythm of the music. After a while, the white horses retired, and a black stallion with a white star on his forehead was led into the ring by his owner. The horse was richly caparisoned with silver bells and silk tassels with threads of gold. I had never seen such a beautiful animal. No wonder a desert Arab would lay down his life rather than surrender his horse to brigands! The horse tossed his head. The large, fine eyes alight with intelligence and the noble lines of his face and neck blended gracefully into his powerful body. When the music started, the horse danced by himself for some time, then danced again with his proud owner in the saddle. At the end of the dance, the owner dismounted and, with a resonant voice, recited a poem praising his horse:

> *Black stallion with a star on your forehead,*
> *Unbeatable on the battlefield or the chase,*
> *Like a rock driven by a flash flood!*
> *Thundering down the steep mountain's face.*

Poetry and eloquence: *these* are the arts in which the Arabs excel. They do not care for painting and sculpture. Every tribe wishes for a great poet to praise the courage of their men and the virtue of their women, and also to insult with verse their hated enemies.

In Arabia, there is an ancient city called Mecca, and in this city there is a room built of stone in the form of a cube. Called the *Kaba*, the Arabs assert that it was built by Abraham. Today there are seven poems hanging on the walls. The Arabs hold these seven hanging poems in great esteem. Every year, there is a trade fair near Mecca and a poetry contest. The greatest poems are written down, and people will memorize as much as they can and recite them from generation to generation.

When reciting Arabic poetry, the delivery is all-important. If a poet does not have a resonant voice, he will select a friend to read his poetry. The music and rhythm must be correct, but there is no harm in substituting one word for another if you forget. One of the traders in the caravan was a man in his fifties with a beard dyed brown, fine clothes, and ugly features. He wanted to recite some poetry, so he rose, walked to the center, leaned on his stick, and began to recite famous lines by one of the greatest ancient poets. The man's accent was horrible. We could tell he was Greek. It was painful to the Arabs and sounded ridiculous to me. Hadi, our guide, walked quickly up to him and said, "Please stop. That is enough." His two hands were outstretched in a gesture that meant *stop*.

The Greek slapped Hadi once across his face and said, "Go back to your place, dog!" I could see Hadi's face. Every muscle was twitching uncontrollably, and his body froze. Then he turned his back to the trader slowly and deliberately—a grave insult when done by an Arab—and walked slowly away.

Galen said to me, "This is not good. These Badu of the desert weigh the insult, not the injury. That man could lose his life."

We slept late and were up early. After breakfast, I told Ari and Justin, "Go find the magician's helper. Give the boy a few coins and bring him here with his snake."

When they returned, I opened the pouch and took the snake out. A magician's snake can be handled without danger. Usually they are not venomous, but if they are, the magicians pull the fangs out. The young men gathered around. They were eager to find out how the magician changed a stick into a live, moving snake. I told them, "Most snakes have a heart in the middle of their body, so if you hold the head up, the snake will faint because blood is not going to his brain."

I put the snake's head in the palm of my hand, well hidden. The snake fainted, and with my left hand I picked up some dust and sprinkled it on the snake. I told them, "If you decide to become magicians, do not use a tree-climbing snake. They don't faint because their hearts are closer to their heads. Now, watch carefully. You must keep the head well hidden in your hand. Pretend you are leaning on a stick, let the tail touch the ground, and keep distracting the people with your left hand so they don't see what the right hand is doing." I moved my left arm in expansive gestures and said in a low, resonant voice, "Behold my magic powers." I let the snake fall to the ground. It revived and moved in a most impressive manner.[9]

The boys were laughing. They picked up the snake and tried the trick themselves. I enjoyed watching their magician's gestures. Caesare was the best, a born orator like his father.

---

[9] See the Bible, King James Version (hereinafter KJV Bible), Exodus 7:11–12: "Then Pharaoh also called the wise men and the sorcerers: now the magicians of Egypt, they also did in like manner with their enchantments. For they cast down every man his rod, and they became serpents."

CHAPTER 5: The Caravan

Today, late in the afternoon before the sun set, the caravan would be on its way, moving slowly all night long. About two hundred camels were in this *kafila*. The owners were urging their servants to water the camels, to make them drink as much as they could. The camels were more interested in each other, biting, growling, and kicking. Finally, the owners, with their servants and children, rode their mules back to the Nile Valley.

The nomads were busy loading their camels. Once loaded, they had to move because a fully loaded camel standing in one place would suffer pain in its feet. For every ten camels there was one guide. They started moving ahead at a slow pace, every camel tethered to the tail of the one in front of him. We had three camels loaded with food and waterskins for ourselves, and each one of us was riding a fast dromedary. We could move at four times the speed of the loaded camels, so we told our guide, Hadi, that we would ride ahead and join the caravan at sunset.

After sitting all day inactive in the shade, we were pleased to get out and survey the wild scene from the backs of our dromedaries. The sun was behind us, and we were headed east toward the Red Sea. It was easy riding with the sun behind us and no glare in our eyes. The young men were excited and urged the dromedaries to go faster. Their ride turned into a race. Then they turned around, came back, and rode their camels next to mine. They were having a pleasant conversation, and in the silence of the desert, it was easy to hear each other, even at a distance.

Ari asked me, "How can the Badu live in this arid desert?"

"In the low deserts, where there is no rainfall, you will not find any nomads. There is no pasture for their animals. They will look for a high plateau that is cool in the summer and catches some rain. Every fifteen or twenty years, there is unusual weather with many thunderstorms. When this happens, the flash floods are strong enough to erode the sides of the mountains. You will see many dry riverbeds carved by water. They are strewn with smooth pebbles and large, round boulders. The Arabs call these canyons *wadi*. The flash flood they call *seyl*. The seeds of hardy trees and bushes grow, and their roots follow the water down through the gravel. So the Badu dig wells wherever they see some green trees."

Justin said, "What about normal years, when there is no heavy rain?"

I told him that every year in the fall and winter, there will be some thunderstorms and rainfall. The high mountains will catch this rain, and the Badu can see it from afar. They drive their flocks of goats and camels to the mountains that catch the rain. A hundred small canyons will drain this water into a bigger canyon, and this is where the Badu will graze their flocks. That is why every tribe has to defend a large area of land, so they can move around following the rain and pasture. Tribal wars are never-ending. The powerful keep the weak out of their land, and all tribes agree on four months of truce in every year to allow the trade caravans to pass safely. Traders pay taxes in the port of Alexandria. In the desert, they also have to pay or else their caravans will be plundered. We could have found the way to the Red Sea by ourselves, but then we would have risked attack by the wild men of the desert.

The sun was setting. We rode back and joined the caravan. The camels were moving slowly, about two miles an hour. In one night they could cover twenty or more miles, and in the day they rested. The men were walking. They rode only late at night, when they were tired.

Galen was walking near his camel. Adoo, his servant, and Hadi, the guide, were close to him. We dismounted and joined them. Hadi said, "Come, walk with us. Riding a camel all night is more tiring than walking."

I asked Hadi, "Can we see wild animals?"

Hadi said, "A short distance to the south of this flat plain, there are many wadi. There you can hunt gazelle, and on the mountain you will find the wild goat, ibex, and the wild sheep with great horns."

Galen said, "You know, Hiro, this plain is the easiest route from the Nile Valley. A canal once connected the River Nile to the Red Sea."

Caesare asked, "Who built that canal?"

Galen said, "A pharaoh called Necho started it, but then the Persian invasion of Egypt ended the rule of the pharaohs. The canal was later completed under the Persian king Darius the First, about five hundred years ago."

Justin said, "What happened to the canal? Can we see it?"

"The canal was neglected," I explained. "Only the desert sands fill it. Nobody wanted to take the trouble to keep it clear."[10]

We were entertaining ourselves with pleasant conversation. But our guides, the Badu, were not conversing with each other; they were singing, sometimes loudly and sometimes softly, to themselves. Hadi was singing:

> *I am known to the wilderness, to the sword and the steed.*
> *I am known to the night, to my guest, and to paper and reed.*

Without using the word *courage*, the poet boasts that he is a bold warrior, and without using the word *generous*, he says that he is a generous host. He boasts that he is a poet whose words deserve to be written down with paper and reed without mention of the words *poet* or *poetry*. For those who do not know their language and have not spent much time in the desert, it is impossible to understand Arabic poetry and why it moves them so powerfully. Poetry and eloquence are the arts of the desert people, not painting and sculpture.[11]

---

[10] The Roman emperor Trajan reopened this canal; then it was filled with sand once more, until the Arab general Amr Ibn Al-'as, who conquered Egypt from the Romans around 640 AD, reopened it again for the shipments of grain from the Nile to the Red Sea to Arabia.

[11] The ancient Greeks believed poets and other artists needed help from the Muses, a group of nine goddesses. They inspired musicians, sculptors, and poets. Their mother was Mnemosyne (Memory). She gave powerful memory to great poets. The Arabs, too, believed that great poets recited great poetry with the help of a friendly *Jinn* who whispers in his ear.

Apart from the pomp of words and the music of the sound, there is a dreaminess of idea. The Arab poet sets before you the grand outlines of a picture with a few masterful touches, and the rest of this picture must be filled in by the listener. Arabic has rich and varied synonyms, illustrating the finest shades of meaning; moreover, they have a richness of rhyme, which leaves the poet unfettered to choose.

Galen asked Hadi, "Do you have more poetry to sing for us?"Hadi raised his voice, singing:

Ruined is my village and deserted my halting place.
Wild beasts roam the hills, and floods have left their trace,
Time-worn marks, like ancient glyph and writ
That scratches our mountain's flinty face.

I turned to Hadi. "The poet is referring to old inscriptions on the rocks. Have you ever seen any such drawings?"

"Yes," he said. "In fact, there is a wadi nearby that has many rock drawings. Tomorrow afternoon I will take you there if you wish."

We had been walking for some hours in the moonlight and were getting tired. We mounted our dromedaries. Adoo arranged rolls of cloth on the camel saddle to make Galen more comfortable. I was riding near Galen, and he said to me, "Poetry is the language of love, war, and all things exciting. I think the nomads will never cease to sing."

Two nomads joined Hadi. I looked at these wild men of the desert. They were proud without insolence. Their walk was almost a swagger, but there was nothing offensive in it. They were singing songs, praising their own tribe, boasting of their courage and generosity, describing the beauty of the desert and the night sky. Hour after long hour, I sat in the saddle. When there was light in the eastern horizon, the caravan stopped.

All the camels were unloaded quickly. The work had to be finished before sunrise. Once the sun is above the horizon, it burns the face and eyes and makes a person very tired. Our three pack dromedaries were lightly loaded with only waterskins and our clothes. A loaded camel does not like to couch itself. They protested loudly as the Arab guides forced them to kneel down, repeating the command,

"*Nekh, nekh.*" There was loud noise over the plain as all camels were forced to couch, and the operation of unloading was skillfully completed by practiced hands.

Every guide lighted a fire with dry wood he carried on his camel. The young men gathered around Hadi. He was busy cooking crushed millet in a pot of boiling water. Adoo was kneading a large ball of dough to make bread. There was a pleasant smell rising from the fire. I asked Hadi, "Which wood are you burning in this fire? The aroma is so good."

He showed me a dry branch in his hand and said, "This bush, when green, it is good food for the camels, and when dry, it makes the best fire for cooking bread."[12]

The crushed millet was cooked. Hadi made large balls of it and set them on flat stones to cool. Then he gave them to the camels. Adoo spread the dough into the shape of a large disc, about the thickness of two fingers. He swept the hot red embers aside and put down the bread loaf in the hot sand. The red hot embers were pushed back over the bread and around it.

The sun was still below the horizon, and the desert air was cool. We sat down, tired and hungry, waiting for breakfast. Adoo pushed away the embers, lifted up a large loaf of hot bread, and put it over a flat stone. Hadi gave him a brush made of camel hair, which he used to sweep away the ashes stuck in our bread. We had a good breakfast— hot bread with sweet, sticky dates compressed into blocks, followed by melons. After the meal, Hadi offered us twigs to clean our teeth. These twigs had a sweet flavor and a pleasant smell like fresh-baked bread.

I asked Hadi, "Which bush gives you this *miswak* [toothpick]?"

He said, "It is the *arak*[13] bush. But it's most important use comes in when we are forced to drink brackish water. We crush the twigs and

---

[12] *Marakh* (*Leptadenia pyrotechnica*) is a shrub common in the *wadi*, or valleys, of the Eastern Desert of Egypt. It grows to nine feet high, with a yellow trunk up to six inches thick.

[13] *Arak* (*Salvadora persica*): The Arabs still make natural toothpicks and toothbrushes from it. See KJV Bible, Exodus 15:24: "And the people murmured against Moses, saying, 'What shall we drink?' And he cried unto the Lord, and the

put them in the waterskins, making the water taste good enough to drink."

We made temporary shelters using spears and cloth to protect us from the sun during the day. I prepared a place for myself to sleep and used my cloak as a pillow. The sun rose quickly over the horizon, and I was thankful for the shade. All the camels slowly turned and faced the hot disc of the sun. I was wondering why the camels always face the sun when resting. I thought, *Maybe if their sides are not exposed to the rays, they will receive less heat.*

As I was thinking these idle thoughts about the camels and the heat, I heard loud shrieks and shouting not far from our resting place. Adoo got up immediately and went to the source of the noise. He came back and said, "The Greek merchant is beating his servants and cursing them because he did not like his breakfast."

Galen said, "He is tired after last night and cannot control his temper." Soon we were all sleeping deeply. When I woke up in late afternoon, the camels were still facing the sun, looking at the western horizon. One by one, our party rose from their sleep. They sat in the shade while Hadi and Adoo prepared a meal of bread and fruit. On a march in the desert, food has to be simple and light.

We mounted our dromedaries and followed our guide, moving fast to the south of the caravan route. We reached a range of hills gradually rising to volcanic mountains. The young men, Ari, Justin, Caesare, and Marcus, followed Hadi into one of the canyons. Galen, Adoo, and I were at some distance behind them. Our camels were choosing the easiest route into this wadi, the dry bed of the flash floods. Now we were riding on white, soft sand. Then the ground sloped upward, and marvelous colors streaked the white sides of the canyon: reddish brown, streaks of yellow and red, and blue patches on the ground and on the walls of the wadi.

Another turn and we saw green vegetation. The dromedaries could smell water, and they hurried to a small spring in the rock trickling down and getting lost in the dry gravel. There were trees and green

---

Lord showed him a tree, which when he had cast into the waters, the waters were made sweet."

bushes for the camels to eat, but they wanted to drink. We couched the animals and dismounted. The boys were drinking from the rock spring and washing their faces. "Come taste this water. It is very sweet," said Justin. We all had our fill, and then Hadi picked up a flat stone and started building a little dam to hold the water. The boys joined him, and soon they had a pool of water about a foot deep.

Hadi called the camels. "*Hobe, hobe.*" This is a command the nomads use when they want their camels to drink. The thirsty animals came running to this little pool. We all stood around smiling. We were riding these beasts hard and felt sorry for them because we knew they were so thirsty. There was not enough water here for the caravan, but for a small number of people and their animals, the spring was enough.

Our camels had their fill. Hadi ordered them, "*Nekh, nekh,*" and they sat down among the green bushes, nibbling at the leaves. Hadi took the head rope of each animal and tied it around the camel's knee. That way they will stay couched in one place. Hadi looked at me, smiling, and said, "Now we can walk around. Let me show you the rock drawings."

We followed our guide to a cliff with plentiful shade. This must have been the resting place for a group of prehistoric hunters. There were many drawings on the rock depicting animals and people hunting with spear and bow—primitive drawings but easy to understand.

Then Caesare said, "I see a cave up there! Shall we climb up to it?" The young men started moving up the hillside. This cave was about eight hundred feet up.

I told Adoo, "Go with them. Teach them how to be careful of snakes and scorpions."

I walked with Galen to a large *Tundub*[14] tree, and we sat down in the shade, silently admiring the beauty of the small oasis. We could see a variety of birds flying in this place, obviously drawn to the water. There were many feathers under the tree. I asked Hadi, "Why so many feathers in this place?"

He replied, "This must be the favorite tree of a falcon. He catches smaller birds and eats them here." True enough, in a short while, a

---

[14] *Tundub* is Arabic for the *Capparis decidua* tree.

sooty falcon alighted on the tree. It had a slate blue body, yellow legs, and yellow at the base of the bill.

Galen remarked, "These many birds provide this falcon with quite a banquet."

Hadi said, "Yes, he has a good life until the day comes when he makes a mistake and breaks a wing. I often see them in pairs. They will attack a bird on the wing, which tries desperate maneuvers to evade them, and when the bird is tired, it will dive to earth. If it is lucky, it will find a small hiding place among the stones where the falcons cannot reach it."

"Do you see much wildlife?" asked Galen.

"Yes, in places where there is some water, a small spring like this one or rock pools in the higher mountains. Some of these pools will hold water for an entire year after a thunderstorm. If you are patient, you will see gazelles, ostriches, and an occasional leopard. Nearer to the Nile Valley, there are many hyenas and jackals."

Our boys were descending from the cave. They walked over and sat in the shade. "What did you find?" asked Galen.

Ari said, "The cave has two openings and is cool inside."

"And we found these," said Justin, presenting Galen with some flint arrowheads.

"You can see the sea from up there," said Marcus.

"When we mounted our camels, I looked back at this beautiful, lonely oasis. There were some hares eating the flower balls that fell from the *seyat* tree."

Hadi said, "The sun is setting. Time to join the caravan."

As soon as we reached the sandy alluvial fan at the mouth of the wadi, the boys raced their refreshed dromedaries with their sticks, shouting like wild men of the desert and riding with legs crossed around the pommel of the saddle. Galen looked at me, smiling, and said, "They are learning fast. You must be proud." I looked at these lads silhouetted against the setting sun. Yes, I was proud.

Later, we were riding slowly. With the sun low on the horizon, every small thing threw a long shadow on the ground. Hadi saw some dry gourds in a spreading vine and picked some. They were the size of pomegranates. He said, "These *hanzal*[15] are useful for making a fire."

Galen said, "I know this plant. It is a well-known purge, but I have never seen anybody use it to make fire."

"I will show you tomorrow morning," said Hadi.

The caravan was moving on the flat plateau. We joined them and walked along in the clear moonlight. There was a fresh breeze blowing, which made us cool and strong. Galen said, "It is better to walk for a few hours. Sitting on the camel's back all night makes my back ache." Then he looked at the young men and said, "Do you know the story of the famous priest Moses and his brother, Aaron?"

Ari said, "Yes, we know it."

Galen continued, "We are now walking their same route. This is the easiest way out of the Nile Valley, and a multitude of people with animals, carts, and children would certainly choose the easy way."

Caesare asked, "This exodus of the tribe called Israelites, when did it happen?"

"About one thousand two hundred years ago," said Galen. "There is a *stela* from the time of Pharaoh Mer-Ne-Ptah with a song of victory in battle inscribed on it, and it ends with these words: 'Israel is desolated and has no seed.'" This pharaoh was the thirteenth son of King Ramses the Second.

Justin asked, "What made the Israelites leave Egypt?"

Galen shrugged. "There must have been many reasons, but I imagine that had there been no famine, no pestilence, and no drought, that tribe would never have followed Moses out of Egypt."[16]

Caesare asked, "Since the ancient Egyptians were such mighty builders, why did they not build a dam on the Nile so as to have a reservoir of water?"

Galen said, "The pharaoh built one with blocks of limestone. It had no gates. The floodwaters could flow over I, and boats could sail

---

[15] Hanzal: This useful gourd is Citrullus colocynthis.

[16] See KJV Bible, Exodus 7:21: "And the fish that was in the river died, and the river stank, and the Egyptians could not drink of the water of the river, and there was blood throughout all the land of Egypt."

over it. It was used only when the level of the Nile was very low. Then this dam would hold the water back until the river rose once again."

Adoo spoke up. "I have never seen this dam."

Galen said, "There is an island in the Nile opposite the Great Pyramid. The dam was built about one thousand years ago. It runs from one side of the river to the island, and from the island to the other bank. But the Nile carries so much silt now, it is almost useless. You can see it only in winter when the river is very low."[17]

We were getting tired of walking, so we mounted our dromedaries. The moon was almost full. Tomorrow night there would be a full moon, and now the wind was blowing stronger. Around the time of the full moon, the winds blow harder in the open desert and the open sea.

Adoo and Hadi were riding next to each other. They took turns singing to entertain themselves. Adoo knew songs of the Nile Valley, and Hadi knew the songs of his tribe. Adoo sang in a strong, clear voice:

Look, high up in the sky. There is a silver bed for Isis,[18]
Hanging with ropes of pearls between the moon and the Pleiades.
Here she rests, the goddess with a thousand names,
Mother of our god Horus, beautiful, beloved Isis.

After Adoo finished his song, there was silence for a while. Then Hadi raised his voice in a plaintive, sad melody:

I hope all those who blame me,
And all who believe me impure,
I hope a she-viper strikes them,
And may they never find a cure!

I asked Hadi, "Who composed that song?"

---

[17] When the Arabs invaded Egypt, this dam was still there, opposite the old city of Fustat, and was called Dam of the Pagans *(Sadd-El-Kaffara)*.

[18] Isis, a goddess of ancient Egypt. She was associated with the star Sirius. From Alexandria, her cult spread to all Mediterranean cities, including Rome, and some of the mythology and practices surrounding Isis's cult may have been assimilated by the early Christians.

He laughed and said, "A young girl hated the man her father chose for her. She wanted to marry the boy she loved. When her father heard this song, he said, 'I had no idea she was so unhappy,' and arranged for her to marry the one she wanted. The women of our tribe express their wishes in short songs. In both sadness and in happiness, they sing."

The wind was blowing stronger by the hour. At first light, we stopped the caravan, couched the animals, and unloaded bags and boxes. Hadi called us politely and asked us to please sit around the fireplace to make a windbreak. He dug a hole in the sand and built a fire bigger than usual. After our bread was cooked, he produced from his bag all the hanzal gourds he had collected yesterday and put them in the hot embers. When they were black, he spread a piece of wet cloth on a flat rock. Then he took the hot blackened gourd, put it on the wet cloth, and wrapped the cloth around it. Next he beat this gourd with a stone and crushed it inside the wet cloth. This cloth was saturated with a black, oily liquid. Hadi spread it to dry and told us, "When it is dry, I cut a small piece of this cloth, put it on the flint, and strike it with the iron. The spark will start a fire easily."

Justin asked him, "What will you do if you cannot find these gourds?"

Hadi told him, "Take some fresh charcoal, crush it on a flat stone, then put a piece of wet cloth on the powder. Make sure your cloth is impregnated with charcoal dust, let it dry, and with this you can start a fire."

We finished breakfast before sunrise and were busy erecting a shade tent for the day. Loud cries and screams interrupted our work. Hadi walked toward the source of this noise, and I followed him. We found the Greek trader beating his two servants with his camel stick. I asked him, "Why do you beat these boys?"

Without stopping his blows, he said, "They don't feed the camels."

I took the stick out of his hand, broke it in half, and said, "We want peace and quiet."

Hadi turned to him. "Listen to me! The camels will not eat as long as the wind is blowing so hard. Leave these poor boys alone. You overload your camels, you beat your servants, and you disturb us."

The Greek trader picked up half his broken stick and raised his arm to strike Hadi. I gripped his forearm and forced him to drop the stick. The ugly Greek did not stop his curses and insults. His small eyes were like black buttons darting between me and Hadi. Rage covered his face. He shouted at me, "I know who you are! Many times have I seen you in Alexandria, and the queen's physician is with you . . . and her son, too! What are you all up to?"

I ordered his two servants to go and take a walk in the desert and also said, "Leave your master alone until he calms down."

I walked back to our shade and told Galen all that had happened. "This man recognized you and Caesare. I fear he will spread the news."

Galen assured me, "Don't worry, Hiro. Who will hear him in the open desert?"

I walked into our shade. It was a long time before I went into deep sleep.

When I got up, everyone was awake. The temperature had cooled remarkably because of the strong north wind. It was time to load the camels and move. Everybody was working quickly to get the caravan moving. Suddenly the Greek trader's two servants came running toward me.

"What is the matter?" I asked them.

They said, "Our camels are loaded. It is time to move, but we cannot find our master. We looked everywhere."

I called Adoo, and we both went with the servants to their camels. "Show us his footprints." The two boys showed us the man's footprints in the sand. I turned to Adoo and said, "You are a good tracker. Take one of these boys with you and find the Greek. He probably walked into the desert to do things I would rather not think about." Then I ordered the other servant to start moving with the caravan because his master's camels were fully loaded and they could not stand still. The boy obeyed without hesitation. Then I called to Adoo, "When you find him, come back to our shade."

I walked back, wondering what could have happened to the obnoxious Greek. Did he step on a snake, or did he break his ankle?

When I reached our shade, I told the boys and Galen that "we have to wait here for Adoo. He is now following the missing man's tracks."

Galen said, "Adoo grew up in the desert of Nubia. He is a relentless tracker. He will find him."

Our boys were relaxed in the shade. Since our baggage was very light, we did not have to worry about loading the camels. Adoo returned, walking at his normal pace. He sat down, silent in our shade. Galen asked him, "Well, Adoo, did you find the man?"

"Yes, Hakeem. He was sitting in a shallow hole in the ground, his eyes looking up to the sky, and his belly open from one side to the other."

Galen looked at Hadi and said, "Did you hear what Adoo said?" Hadi nodded his head. "Do you know who did it?" asked Galen,

The answer was, "Life is short. His time had come. But ours has not yet come. Time for us to move on." And we all rose to our feet and walked silently to the caravan.

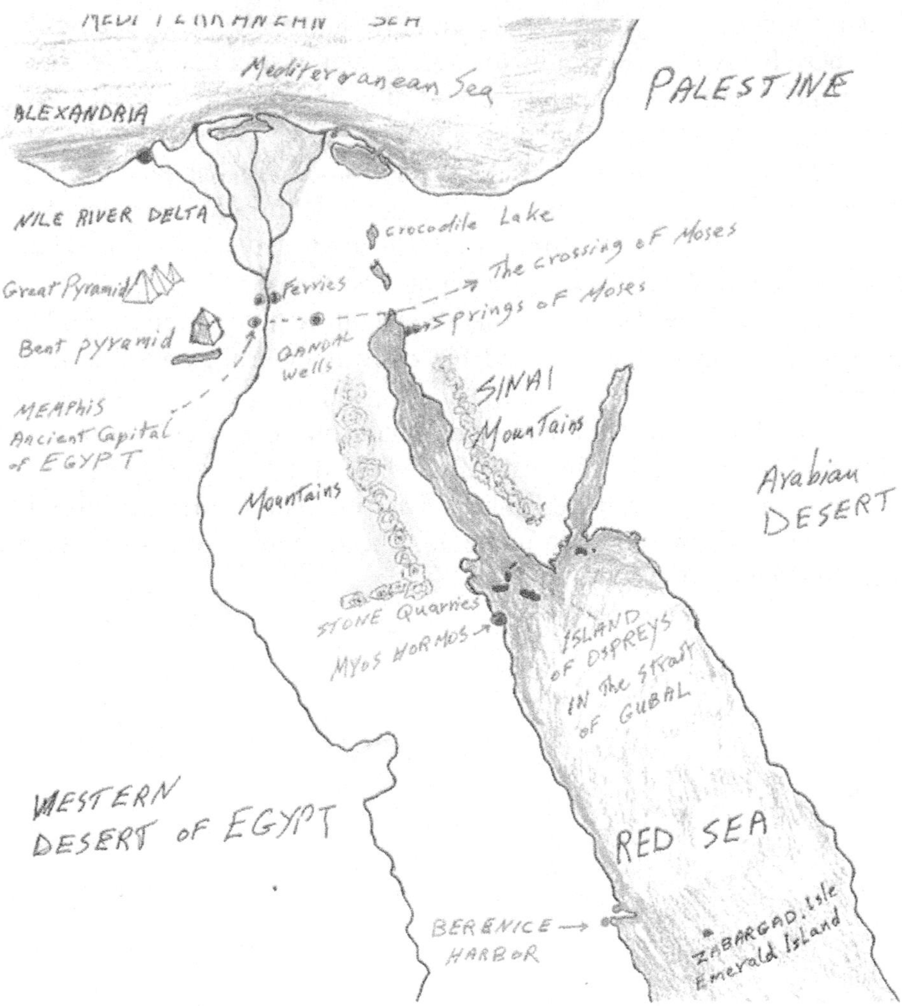
Mediterranean Sea
PALESTINE
ALEXANDRIA
NILE RIVER DELTA
Crocodile Lake
The crossing of Moses
Great Pyramid
Ferries
Springs of Moses
Bent pyramid
QANDAL
wells
SINAI
Mountains
MEMPHIS
Ancient Capital
of EGYPT
Mountains
Arabian
DESERT
STONE Quarries
MYOS HORMOS
ISLAND
OF OSPREYS
IN the Strait
of GUBAL
WESTERN
DESERT of EGYPT
RED SEA
BERENICE
HARBOR
ZABARGAD Isle
Emerald Island

CHAPTER 6: Crossing the Red Sea

The colors were changing, and the wild desert was beautiful at this time of day. We were all silent for a long time. Then Galen spoke to the young men: "These Arabs of Sinai are good-humored people, as long as you treat them with kindness and courtesy. But beware—if you misunderstand their points of honor, they will quickly take offense and turn vengeful. The Arab townspeople are different, and the Badu despise them. But the true sons of the desert have a chivalrous spirit. Your guide will defend you against brigands with sword and spear, and he expects you to do the same for him. Theirs is a leonine society, ruled by the sword. Yet if one of these nomads swears by the honor of his tribe, this oath should not to be taken lightly."

We walked silently until we got tired of walking; then we rode our fast dromedaries. There was a full moon in the sky. It rose over the eastern horizon just after the sun set in the west. The cool north wind was blowing hard, and it made us feel energetic and refreshed. Riding in the night at the end of summer with the bright light of a full moon illuminating the wild scene, the traveler's senses are quickened, ready for danger. After becoming accustomed to the rhythm of travel in the desert, the morale improves, and one's disposition becomes frank and accommodating. The hypocrisy of civilization is left behind. And if your tastes acclimate to this way of life, then you suffer real pain when you return to the noise and haste of the city. From the well of Gandal to the Red Sea, the distance is about sixty miles—two nights for a fast dromedary, three nights for a slow caravan.

The Red Sea is long and narrow, with an opening only at the southern end, a narrow strait about twenty miles wide connecting the sea to the Ocean of India. In the north, the Red Sea has two gulfs, or two arms. Between them is the desert of Sinai. The western gulf ends in a bay, and on the north side of this bay is a shallow, smaller bay

45

called the Mud Flats because the bottom is all sticky mud. We camped at the edge of the sea near this bay.[19]

The north wind was near gale force. However, there was no sand blowing into our eyes because the wind was coming from the northeast over the water. I told Hadi, "The wind will not let you build a fire."

He said, "I will use the camels as a windbreak." He couched the camels close to each other and started his fire. There was no use making millet cakes for them today because they would not eat with the wind howling.

We walked into the sea, our feet sticking in the muddy bottom, and we had a refreshing swim. The sun was rising in the east while at the same time the full moon was setting in the west. This was the hour of high water. For six hours there would be an ebb tide. By noon the small bay would be dry. Then the tide would flow in again for six hours, and at moonrise the water would be over five feet deep. After our swim, breakfast tasted better than ever, and we fell asleep, exhausted with fatigue.

At noon I woke up, and my sons were awake having lunch with dry fruits and melons. I pointed to the mud flats, now almost completely dry, and told them, "When there is a full moon, the low tide is at its lowest, especially when there is a powerful north wind pushing the waters to the south, and the low water mark at midnight will be lower than this daytime low tide."

We were sitting in the shade, watching the seabirds feeding on the mud flats, when Galen spoke to us. "I believe we are camping in the same place chosen by Moses for the Israelites when the Egyptian chariots caught up with them on their way out of Egypt."

Caesare asked, "Why was Pharaoh chasing them after he gave them permission to leave?"

Galen replied, "Before leaving Egypt, they stole much silver and gold jewelry."

Justin asked, "Why would the Israelites steal from the Egyptians?"

---

[19] To this day on Egyptian maps, it is named Sahl-Al-Tina, referring to a vast, flat plain. On a day of dead calm, this bay will be flat and oily, like a mirror, colored red from shore to shore with the reflection of the rising and setting sun. This effect may explain how the Red Sea got its name.

Galen said, "Because Moses was sure the wild men of the desert would plunder the Israelites unless they had something of value to pay for safe passage, and so they stole jewelry from their neighbors, who naturally complained to Pharaoh."[20]

Ari asked Galen, "What happened?"

Galen said, "The Israelites were terrified when they saw chariots and foot soldiers camped near them, and they shouted at Moses, 'Why did you bring us to die here? Are there no graves in Egypt?' Moses knew the Egyptian army would attack at sunrise, so at midnight, at maximum low water, he led his people over the mud flats under a brilliant full moon.

"Before sunrise the Egyptians saw the Israelites crossing the bay and chased them. The wheels of their chariots got stuck in the mud. Then the tide, a wall of water five feet high, rushed back into this narrow bay. They were not tall people, and they were burdened with heavy armor and were ignorant of how to swim, so most of the soldiers drowned."[21]

Ari asked Galen, "So you believe this story is true?"

Galen replied, "The essence of the story is true, but the explanation is magical, which may be why the story has survived for two thousand years."

I told them, "It is quite possible a scribe who lived in the Nile Valley and never saw salt water in his life wrote the story."

Caesare said, "After many years, some Israelites returned to Egypt because they were persecuted by other Israelites. They now live just outside the city of Alexandria, near Lake Mareotis. I saw them when I

---

[20] See the KJV Bible, Exodus 11: 2, 35: "Speak now in the ears of the people, and let every man borrow of his neighbor, and every woman of her neighbor, jewels of silver and jewels of gold. . . . And the children of Israel did according to the word of Moses; and they borrowed of the Egyptians jewels of silver and jewels of gold, and raiment. "

[21] See the KJV Bible, Exodus 14:21, 27: "And Moses stretched out his hand over the sea; and the Lord caused the sea to go back by a strong east wind all that night, and made the sea dry land, and the waters were divided. . . . And Moses stretched forth his hand over the sea and the sea returned to his strength when the morning appeared; and the Egyptians fled against it; and the Lord overthrew the Egyptians in the midst of the sea."

was bird hunting at the lake. They live together and are fervent in their beliefs."

"And these Israelites of Mareotis are always quarreling with the Greeks," Marcus added. "They insult our Greek gods. We, on the other hand, respect the gods of other people, even those strange gods of Egypt with heads of a hawk or a jackal."

Adoo, who was listening carefully, said, "It is a good story. Every day I learn more."

Galen was standing beside me looking grave. We were watching the caravan move away. They had about fifteen slow miles to go before reaching the Springs of Moses, where the Israelites stopped to drink and water their animals. "Hiro," he said, "six days have passed since we left Alexandria. Now Octavian controls the city, and his messengers are on their way to notify all the military governors to arrest Caesarion." He was silent for a moment. "Octavian is cunning. I would not be surprised if he chose as his messengers Greek soldiers who know the looks of Caesarion and would be able to recognize him on sight."

I nodded. "This has always been the way of the ruler, to eliminate all who have a claim to his throne. What should we do?"

Galen spoke softly. "If we can't keep our enemies from finding Caesarion, we must make sure they don't recognize him when they do."

"How will you change Caesare's appearance?"

"I will make his skin brown and give him the same scars Adoo has on his face. He will pose as my second Nubian servant." We were sitting around a small fire. Galen called Caesare and asked him to sit down next to Adoo. He said, "Caesare, do you see these scars on Adoo?" He touched three scars going from the corner of Adoo's eye to the hairline. "This procedure is quick and almost painless. Will you let me do this?"

Caesare, knowing why Galen was proposing to scar him, answered in a soft voice, "All right. Do it now."

Galen produced a very sharp knife that he always carried in his belt. He put the knifepoint in the fire and asked Adoo to hold the boy's head perfectly still. With a steady hand, Galen made three cuts in the skin, the first cut from the corner of the eye to the hairline, the second below it and a little shorter, the third above the first and sloping upwards. Then he rubbed cool ashes onto the cuts to stop the bleeding. He repeated the same on the other side of Caesare's face. The boy remained calm and motionless, flinching only slightly from the pain.

With some relief that the procedure was over, I asked, "What is next, Galen?"

"I can make his skin as dark as Adoo's. The Arabs use a plant they call henna. They mix it with oil and rub the feet and hands of all young virgins when they are ready for marriage. They also give them very attractive tattoos on the back side of their hands and fingers. We can obtain some henna from the Bedouins. In a few days, Caesare will be as brown as a Nubian."

We slept a few hours and then got up after midnight. The Pleiades were high in the sky. I told the boys, "The Arabs call this group of seven stars *Al-Thuraya*, which means 'the chandelier.' Looking toward the east, there is *Al-Debran*, which means 'the follower' because this bright star rises after the Pleiades stars and follows them across the sky to the western horizon. Then, moving down in the great dome of the night sky, there is the belt of Orion. The Arabs call Orion 'the giant.' The first star in the belt to rise above the horizon they call *Al-Mintaka*, 'the belt.' The second star they call *Al-Nitham*, the one that holds the other two in line. We pronounce it *Nilam*. The third star is *Al-Nitak*, 'the girdle,' and from this star you can imagine the giant's sword hanging down. The star that is the point of the sword is known to the Arabs as *Saiph*, 'the sword.' The bright one on the other side is called *Rigel*, or 'leg' in Arabic."[22]

Ari interrupted gently, "Did you notice Orion is a left-handed giant? His sword is hanging on his right side!"

We all looked at the constellation of Orion, and I said, smiling, "You are right. I never heard that before! Remember that Orion's belt rises in the true east and sets in the true west, and these three stars forming the belt will give you exact directions when they are low on

---

[22] These Arabic names for these stars in the constellation of Orion are still used today: *Alnetak, Mintaka, Alnilam, Saiph,* and *Rigel.*

the horizon." The sky was perfectly clear, and I said, "From Orion, move down toward the east and you can see the brightest star in the sky, Sirius. The Arabs call it *Shaera*. The Greeks could not pronounce the Arabic name, so they changed it to Sirius. When Sirius is visible just before sunrise and low on the eastern horizon, we know that the hot days of summer are over. We call this the heliacal rising of Sirius—rising before Helios, the sun. About twenty-five days later, Canopus, the second-brightest star in the sky, can be seen low on the horizon before sunrise. The Arabs call Canopus *Suhail*."

I was pleasantly surprised to hear Caesarion and Marcus singing youthfully:

Orion, mighty warrior in the sky, powerful and free,
What are we, little men on the battlefields to thee!!
Your sword and your belt of light will shine eternally
While we foolish men kill and fight and claim we are free!!

CHAPTER 7: The Springs of Moses

We reached the Springs of Moses about an hour before sunrise. The air was cool in our faces, and we were enjoying the night ride, probably our last on camelback. I was watching Suhail (Canopus), and as the rays of the rising sun lit up the eastern horizon, the star was flashing gold and red before disappearing, indicating the beginning of the cool weather season and the end of summer.

There was a natural anchorage not far from here, sheltered from the north wind. I hoped we would find a fast sailing boat in that harbor to take us to the port of Myos Hormos on the Red Sea. There we could join the fleet sailing to India, which was a regular annual voyage. Sometimes a hundred or more ships would go to the Malabar Coast and Serendib to bring back pearls, rubies, ivory, feathers, and animal skins to be shipped to Rome from Alexandria. A few Roman senators made speeches complaining that the silver coming from the mines in Spain was shipped to India to bring back pearls and other trifles to adorn the ladies in Rome. However, the Roman ladies ultimately won the battle.

Our caravan stopped at the Springs of Moses to water their camels. The water was plentiful but too bitter for humans to drink.[23] From the Arabs, the people bought waterskins filled with sweet, fresh water from a spring in the mountains a few miles away. They also obtained fresh goat milk in exchange for gifts. The nomads consider it a disgrace to sell milk for money, but if they have plenty, they will give you some, and you are expected to give them a gift such as a piece of cloth, a knife, or even some grain.

On a nearby hill was a settlement of nomads. They lived in large black tents made from the hair of their black goats, woven so tightly

---

[23] See the KJV Bible, Exodus 15: 23: "And when they came to Marah, they could not drink of the waters of Marah, for they were bitter: therefore the name of it was called Marah." *Morah* in Arabic means "bitter" or "brackish." These springs, near the coast of the Red Sea, are known today as *Ain Musa* (the Springs of Moses).

that the tents kept rainwater out even in a thunderstorm. We headed for this settlement and camped nearby. A lone figure came toward us. It was Hadi, our guide. He sat down and had breakfast with us. We told him that we would be parting here.

Hadi was a proud and simple man of the desert. He had all that he needed to survive: tremendous endurance, knowledge of where the water holes were, experience in tracking, and familiarity with the breeding of camels and horses. Secure in the knowledge that his tribe would back him against all comers, he felt safe in his wild land. I liked Hadi, and when I gave him three camels as a parting gift, he smiled and thanked me, then went to join his caravan. Not for him the pleasures of philosophy and the theater. For him and his people, the excitement of war, the chase, and the pleasures of poetry and song were enough.

A young boy about ten years old walked out of the black tents and came toward us. He stood about twenty feet away and looked at us with large, intelligent eyes. He had a handsome face and clear skin. My son Justin walked toward him and greeted him in his own tongue, but the boy would not answer. He just stood there looking us over, silent and relaxed. Ari walked to him and gave him some fruit. The boy took his gift but did not say a word. He came closer but remained silent.

Galen was smiling. "These nomadic tribes teach their young sons never to talk to a stranger. The origin of this custom is their terrible blood feuds, which go on from generation to generation. A boy will be safe if no one knows his family name, safe from enemies seeking revenge."

The silent Bedouin boy came closer to us, all curiosity. He held the fruits we gave him but would not eat. Suddenly a flock of blue-green birds flew over our heads, hundreds flying low and swift, making yelping sounds like a hundred puppy dogs. The birds were bee-eaters, flying west to winter in the Valley of the Nile. They migrate regularly in the cool season after the heliacal rising of

Canopus.[24] The desert people call them dogs of Canopus because of the sound they make during flight. In the Nile Valley they are called birds of paradise because of their beautiful plumage. The small boy looked up, smiling, and said, "*Kilab Suhail*" *(Kilab* means dogs; *Suhail* is the star Canopus).

"We know you can talk," Galen said to the boy. "Now, take us to your father."

Soon we met his father, a dignified old man with a white beard. A curved dagger in his belt, he was leaning on a walking stick, waiting for us to enter his tent. Once inside the black tent, we saw a Greek soldier reclining on some pillows and sipping wine. He was obviously agitated. The old Arab explained that this soldier was a messenger who had arrived there on horseback, and since he could not find a fast sailboat to take him to Myos Hormos, he had no choice but to wait and rest until the sailboats arrived.

I wanted to find out if this soldier knew the contents of the message he was carrying, so I invited him to come with us when we rode to the spring in the nearby valley to obtain fresh, sweet water. The soldier readily agreed to join us.

The old Arab said, "I and my youngest son will accompany you."

I thanked him and said, "I shall go back to my friends. We will be ready in an hour."

I hurried back to my companions, and they noticed the urgency in my voice. "There is a messenger in the tent. He is carrying orders for the military commander at Myos Hormos."

Galen said, "I will not be surprised if these orders are to arrest us and Caesarion. To be safe, let the young men stay here. . . . No, wait. They should go to the edge of the sea. Tell them to just take a swim and wait for us."

With camels and empty waterskins, Adoo, Galen, and I went back to the black tents. The boy was teasing his sister, and the little girl was crying. I touched the boy lightly on his head. "Tell your father we are ready."

---

[24] The nomads look for the stars before sunrise because the air is colder and clearer. The heliacal rising of a known star means that star is visible above the eastern horizon before the sun (Helios) rises.

The old man had six donkeys carrying empty waterskins. The Greek soldier joined us on horseback. We followed the Arab and his son into a wide valley, and after riding for an hour or so, we entered a steep, narrow canyon. Our guide showed us the rock springs. The old Arab stopped and dismounted.

"Let us fill the waterskins. The animals can drink in the rock pools below the spring." We quickly filled our waterskins and then sat down in the shade to rest. The Greek soldier sat next to me, and I engaged him in pleasant conversation. I tried to find out as much as possible about him and his mission.

A group of about thirty sand grouse flew into the canyon. They flew round and round, came down low over the water pools, and then swiftly flew up again, as if suspecting some hidden danger, and all of the time they cried, "*Kata, kata, kata.*" When they alighted by the water pool, their calling ceased and they drank quickly, then stood, preening themselves in silence.

The old Arab and his son joined us in the shade. The boy was excited. "I will go hunt the *kata*." Arabs call the desert sand grouse "kata" in imitation of their quick calls.

The sheikh gently told his son, "Leave the birds alone. We don't need any." But the boy would not listen.

"He is a little devil and bothers his sister all the time."

"Well, why don't you punish him?" asked the Greek soldier.

The old man replied, "I cannot punish him. Nor can his mother. That is our custom. It keeps children from hating their parents."

The Greek soldier was aghast. "So your son receives no discipline at all?"

"Oh, of course he does! As soon as his uncle returns, he will punish him."

The old sheikh looked at Galen. "*Hakeem* [which means *wise man* or *doctor*], can you explain this to me? It is about my young boy. He tells me stories every night before sleeping, stories of grand adventures he has with a band of twenty warriors. He is their leader, of course, and he has named them all. And he can describe every imaginary friend in great detail."

Galen comforted the old man. "Do not worry, *ya sheikh* [old man]. Send your boy to the mountains to the rest of your tribe. He will find other boys to play with. They will teach him hunting and tracking. Imaginary warriors are no match against real friends."

The old man nodded but said, "But I cannot send him away yet. He is the son of my youngest wife, more dear to her than her eyes. She would be miserable. I will have to wait at least a year."

Galen said, "This is just human nature. Even grown, rational men have imaginary friends. We give them names like Apollo and Artemis. Don't we talk to them and call upon them for help in time of need?"

The sheikh was silent for a moment and then said to Galen, "Your words have calmed my troubled soul, Hakeem. I have a gift for you. Many balsam trees grow on these stony hills. Would you like to collect some?"

Galen replied graciously, "That will be a gift I value. Balsam makes good medicine for burns." Galen turned toward me. "Hiro, we should collect some of this balm, which our Arab friend calls 'balsam.' We Greeks call it 'balsamon.' Queen Cleopatra once ordered hundreds of these bushes to be planted in Heliopolis. They produce a marvelous perfume and the best balm for wounds and burns."

The Arab sheikh produced from his pockets short pieces of rope made from camel's hair and told us, "You have to wear this *hibas*[25] because vipers abound in these bushes. I don't know why. Maybe the smell attracts mice, and the hungry vipers follow." He proceeded to tie pieces of rope around our wrists, above our elbows, below the knees, and around the ankles. "You all have sharp knives. If a viper strikes you, do not hesitate. Cut off the finger full of venom, and tighten the hibas to stop the blood flow." Then he told his son sternly, "Do *not* come with us. Stay here and hunt the kata."

He led the way up the sides of the wadi and pointed out the balsam trees to us, large shrubs, really, that love stony, dry soil. We approached the shrubs with great care, then cut the bark with sharp knives. A soft yellowish-brown gum trickled out of these incisions. I collected the gum in the palm of my left hand and kept rubbing it to

---

[25] *Hibas* means "tourniquet, " from the word *habs,* to stop or arrest.

make sticky round balls. The Greek soldier was doing the same. Greed made him hasty, for he knew balsamon was worth its weight in silver. Suddenly, he uttered a loud cry, shattering the silence of the desert. We hurried to his aid. He had tightened the hibas around his right wrist. His hand was swelling rapidly. The Arab sheikh commanded him, "Cut your hand off now, or you will die!"

"I cannot. Please! You cut it off." The sheikh pulled out his curved dagger, told the Greek soldier to lie down on the ground, then told me to pin him down so he couldn't move. He grabbed the man's hand, pulled it away from the forearm, went around it with his curved dagger, and with one powerful circular cut, he severed the Greek's wrist and cut his hand away. The soldier did not utter a cry, but his face was pale like death, and his whole body was shaking uncontrollably.

I carried him down the hillside and let him rest in the shade, and all he mumbled was, "Water. Give me some water." Galen stopped the bleeding with pieces of cloth, then spread some of the balm on the wound and covered it neatly with cloth, which we cut from our clothes.

Galen said, "Let him rest here in the shade. I need some more balsam. Come with me, Hiro."

So we went back up the hillside and collected more gum.[26] When we returned after a few hours, the Greek soldier was capable of walking, and he mounted his horse. We loaded our camels with waterskins and went back to the campsite by the sea.

Galen went straight to his medicine box and picked out a small ball of raw opium. Back in the black tent, he gave the opium to the Greek soldier. We sat down near the wounded man. Galen was feeling his pulse. "He will be all right. The opium will ease his pain. It is truly a gift from the gods. A physician's duty is to ease pain and suffering, not to fight mortality. No one wins against death."

---

[26] The Europeans used balsam to anoint their kings in coronation ceremonies. It was worth its weight in silver. Known as the "balm of Gilead," it was used to dress wounds. In the seventeenth century, some trees were still alive in Heliopolis, the City of the Sun, in Egypt. Pliny, the Roman writer, noted that vipers are always found near these bushes.

The Greek soldier was relaxed. The opium was easing his pain. I asked him why he was here all alone. He told us his story.

"I was present the day the two Roman armies were arrayed against each other in battle order. Octavian and his generals were ready to crush the forces of Marcus Antonius. There was silence before the battle. Octavian, young, brave, and cunning, rode out between the two armies accompanied by a centurion, who repeated every word Octavian said in a loud and powerful voice: 'Roman citizens, Roman soldiers! There must be an end to civil war. We must all fight the barbarians on our frontiers. Do not raise your swords against your brothers. Step forward without fear and embrace your fellow soldiers of Rome.'"

The Greek continued, "Marcus Antonius saw death staring him in the face. His centurions rode toward Octavian, shouting, 'Hail, Octavianus Imperator,' and the soldiers on foot went to his enemy while Antonius fled to Alexandria.

"I was among the auxiliary Greek forces, and we had no desire to battle the Octavian's legions. Soon after Antonius's death, Octavian invaded Alexandria. He sent messengers to all the ports of Egypt with orders to arrest Caesarion, the son of Queen Cleopatra. I am one of those messengers." He stopped, closed his eyes, and was silent for a moment. Then he continued, "I was riding with two other soldiers. The wild men of the desert attacked us; they wanted our horses. I alone escaped." He was silent for a moment. "My two companions were wounded and left to a terrible fate. Hungry jackals and hyenas do not bother to wait for men to die."

"Are you carrying the orders, or did you lose them?" I said in a low voice, trying not to show my emotion.

"I have the orders with me, and I must deliver them to the commander in Myos Hormos."

"I am a naval officer, and I am on my way to join the Red Sea fleet. You can trust me with the message. When I get to the port, I will give it to the governor."

Galen turned to the Arab sheikh. "Please keep this soldier comfortable. Let him join the caravan coming from Syria so he can return to Alexandria and his family." The old Arab readily agreed and also gave us a bag of henna, which Galen had requested. I gave the man a few gold coins and thanked him.

On my way out of the tent, the Greek soldier called me. "Captain, don't forget the message." He handed me a papyrus scroll in a hollow bamboo. I tried not to show the immense relief I felt.

"Take care of yourself. We might meet again someday." I had the orders in my hands without having to kill this innocent man.

I walked down the hill toward our camp at the edge of the sea. Galen, walking slowly by my side, seemed worried. The lines on his handsome face were deeper than usual. "How on earth did he get here so quickly?"

"Most probably the order to arrest Caesarion was given on the battlefield right after Antony's suicide. And the messengers rode south in a straight line, passing near Crocodile Lake, and got here before us."

"I wonder if the news will reach the governor of the Red Sea port before we get there."

"That is highly improbable. Anyway, the boys will live aboard the ship like crew and never step on land in Egypt anymore."

"We are far enough from the tents," said Galen. "Open the message, Hiro."

I read the papyrus scroll and was not surprised. It was a straightforward order from Octavian to all military governors to arrest Caesarion, son of Queen Cleopatra, and to bring him to Octavian alive.

I showed the orders to Galen. "Why does Octavian want Caesarion alive? Do you think he wants to raise the boy in Rome and let him inherit the empire? After all, Julius Caesar was Octavian's uncle, and Caesarion is Caesar's son. Could it be that Octavian wants to preserve the Julian line to rule the empire?"

Galen looked at me with disbelief. "Hiro, princes who are kind are rare. Octavian wants to see the boy. If he looks like a prince, he will kill him. If he looks like a fool, he will let him live. He wants to avoid the shame of killing Caesar's son. We must get the boy out of the Roman Empire as quickly as possible."

Adoo was relaxed in the shade. The boys, Ari, Justin, Marcus, and Caesare, were having a friendly contest on the beach. They found a stone smoothed by the waves in the shape of a perfect ball and another stone like a perfect discus and tossed them as far as they could, running from one end of the beach to the other, their young muscles glistening with sweat. Finally they plunged into the sea to cool down and then came out to enjoy the shade. How could I tell these happy young men that that we were all in danger? I left the talking to Galen.

He showed them the orders and described how this message fell into our hands. The urgency of our situation dawned on them and wiped away the carefree expressions they had had only moments before. Then Galen said in a low voice, "Now you know that Caesarion the prince has become Caesarion the fugitive, and all of us, as his companions, are also wanted men. Beware that many people will be anxious to turn us in for the reward. From this moment, do not call Caesarion by his name. Call him 'Che,' even when we are alone." Then Galen said to Che, "I want you to expose your body to the sun every day, Che." He gave him a mixture of oil and henna to darken his skin. In a few days he would be bronzed and tanned like Adoo.

During our traveling across the desert from the Nile Valley to the Red Sea, I had watched Caesarion. There were thousands of young men like him, but he seemed to embody the best qualities of the civilized Greek youth. He was tall, big-limbed, and handsome. He had inherited the green eyes of his mother and the brown hair of his father. You could read intelligence, curiosity, and humor in his eyes. He had looked eternally carefree, but today the words he heard from Galen made him somber and serious. His manner of speech was polite and restrained; he never raised his voice when talking to his friends. I was impressed by his rational arguments and his sharp mind. There was no trace of self-pity in his character.

The gods love men like Che, who sway effortlessly before the storms of fate and spring back with a smile, looking upon life with lighthearted optimism. Here was a born leader, fortified by his early training. Like all aristocratic youth in Greece and Rome, his body had been trained in the open air and toughened with athletics and military exercises. He had the best teachers, who instructed him in mathematics, music, laws, and oratory, and he grew up listening to the stories of heroes and kings, their victories and their defeats. The ideals of self-control and moderation were instilled in his character: never to gloat over a fallen enemy and not to show much sadness in the face of defeat. There would always be another chance to win and another battle to fight.

Che's friend Marcus was the born follower. He followed his friend Che everywhere, and many times I saw him step into dangerous situations, oblivious to the risks and dangers. He was of medium height and strong with a good layer of fat distributed all over his body, unlike weak fat men, who carry their body fat around their waist. Marcus had an attractive, good-natured face that people liked immediately. His brown eyes shone in his sunburnt face, and his smile showed perfect white teeth. He liked to play practical jokes, and when he succeeded, his grin developed into a great infectious peal of laughter. His voice was impressively powerful. It could be heard from one end of the ship to the other. The thing I remember best about him was his total fearlessness. It took me a long time to understand that this was not bravery; he just could not see the dangers ahead. He followed Che blindly, with complete faith in his friend's leadership. Many times I watched Che start on some foolhardy adventure and Marcus follow him without question. Then when Che realized how dangerous it was, he would change his mind and turn back. Marcus, his faithful friend, would turn around without asking why.

CHAPTER 8: The Fish Eaters

Late in the afternoon, about ten boats appeared sailing close together, heading for the safe anchorage where we were. Knowing the men of the Red Sea, I guessed they were having a race just for the fun of it.

"Let us go and meet them on the beach," I said. "Watch the sailors and listen. You will have to learn their dialect and their jargon quickly. You will notice the difference between our sailors in the Mediterranean and these men of the Red Sea."

The young men here are sons of fishermen. They grew up on small boats, fishing with nets and handheld lines, learning all the time from their fathers about winds and currents, reefs and dangers. They memorize the name of every anchorage, every pass, and every break in a reef that leads to a safe lagoon. They are truly men of the sea. There is little of the desert left in them. The Greeks call them *ichthyofagi*—fish eaters.

The sailors in the Mediterranean, on the other hand, are like laborers. Many are slaves and prisoners of war. They work on the ships without understanding the sea. Of course, the officers know how to navigate and the carpenters know how to repair, but the sailors are the ignorant dregs of society.

The boats were in the bay, still moving fast but sheltered from the waves. We walked down to the beach to meet them and to watch how they maneuvered and anchored. The first boat to approach the beach did not slow down. However, at the proper distance, they dropped a stem anchor and let the line out. Just before hitting the beach, they pulled down the yard and folded the sail. Their boat had enough momentum to rest her bow on the sand.

Two young men jumped out and hurried up the slope of the beach. When the proper distance away from the water, they fell to digging a deep hole in the sand with their bare hands, laughing and chattering all the time. A strong young man threw a heavy stone anchor out of the

61

boat. It fell on the beach with a thud. He jumped after the stone with the anchor rope held in his hand, tied it around the anchor stone, then lifted the stone up and walked quickly toward the two boys. Every few steps, he dropped the heavy stone. The sound of *thud, thud* was loud and clear until he reached the hole, dropped the anchor stone into, it and filled it with sand. They use large stones because iron anchors are too expensive. Their boat is secure with two anchors, one holding the bow, the second holding the stem. The sailors call the stone anchor *fed* because of the sound it makes when falling on sand. Every moving part on these boats is named after the sound it makes.

Another boat came alongside and anchored in the same way, and then a third and fourth boat. Now the latecomers were arriving at top speed. They didn't anchor in the same way as the early arrivals. Instead, they rushed between two boats. The crews on the secure boats were expecting this. As the fast-moving boat squeezed into the narrow space between the other two, the crew smartly threw lines to the men on the moving boat. In a flash they tied the ends to the proper cleats, and the boat stopped as if by the hand of a giant. You would never see such a display of seamanship in the harbor of Alexandria.

The Arab sheikh saw the ten boats approaching, and now he was on the beach with his donkeys carrying waterskins, fresh sweet water for the crews. His children stood by his side, smiling and full of curiosity. He watched the boats being unloaded by energetic crewmen who carried small boxes out of their boats and piled them neatly on the beach, all the while chanting rhythmically, "*Ya mal, Ya mal, hey Ya mal*" (Oh, wealth and riches). When this was done, I watched the sheikh's children sweep the sand around the pile of boxes with brooms made of palm fronds.

I asked him, "Why do the children sweep the sand around those boxes?"

He smiled and said, "If anyone approaches these boxes, we will know him by his footprints. But we have never had any thefts here. These boxes are full of mother-of-pearl shells and some large pearls. The caravan coming from Syria will take these boxes to the Nile Valley and deliver them to their owners."

Galen approached the Arab sheikh and said, "Tomorrow we sail with these boats. You may keep our camels as a gift. I hope you will accept."

The sheikh thanked Galen and turned to his son. He whispered something in his ear. The boy quickly grabbed the head rope of a camel, pulled the head down, put his foot on the camel's neck, and gracefully let the camel lift him up to the saddle. He urged the camel with a thin stick to go as fast as possible to their black tents.

The boy was back in no time. He handed his father a small bag. The sheikh presented it to Galen. Smiling benignly, he said, "And this is my gift for you, Hakeem."

Galen opened the bag and turned his noble head toward me. "This is balsam," Galen said, "the best balm for burns." He was silent for a moment. "I need to procure more medicine for our long voyage. How can I obtain more opium?"

I told Galen, "We will stop in the land of Ethiopia for fresh water and supplies. There lives a slave trader near the coast, a repulsive man rich enough to fund his own small private army. He also supplies all Black Africa with opium. We can buy some from him "

That night we slept on the beach. The north wind blowing from the desert was dry and warm, the clear sky full of stars.

Before sunrise, Adoo whispered to me, "I see the tail of the fox. Time to get up."[27] I sat up and looked at the eastern horizon. It was covered with beautiful red, orange, and gold clouds that did look like the bushy tail of a fox. In the northern part of the Red Sea, there are no grey days. When you sleep in the open on a boat or a sandy beach, you wake up surrounded by the beauty of nature. I felt fortunate to be here and happy to be sailing in this coral sea once again.

We walked down the sloping beach toward the sailboats. At night the crewmen had pulled their boats away from the beach to sleep in deeper water. Now they all pulled back until their bows touched the sand so they could retrieve their stone anchors. We jumped on the foredeck of our chosen boat. Adoo handed us our few belongings.

---

[27] A reference to nacreous clouds (*nacre* is mother-of-pearl) that may be seen only before sunrise and sometimes after sunset. They are wonderfully colored, made of dust and water droplets.

Then, with a powerful, graceful leap, he was on deck, smiling and excited. I asked him, "Adoo, is this your first time on the sea?"

"Yes, my first taste of salt water!"

I introduced the crew of three brothers. The oldest, Salama, was the captain. Tall, wiry, self-assured, and with a pleasant smile on his face, he was not over twenty-five years old. His two younger brothers, about twenty years old, were Maui and Heysha. Heysha, the youngest, had red, inflamed eyes. I guessed he was in charge of lighting the fire. His long shirt smelled of smoke, and he was looking at us and laughing out loud all the time. He was not used to strangers, and to him we looked funny.

I told Salama, "Let us sail early. We need at least twelve hours to reach the Strait of Jubal."[28]

Salama smiled. He looked like a friendly, honest man, and said, "Good. The wind is sharrow this morning," which means almost gale force. He pointed out two large coral heads reaching almost to the surface of the sea. "We will row between these two coral heads. Then we will raise sail."

The sailors in the Red Sea have a curious way of preparing themselves for action. They stand on deck, clapping hands forcefully and rhythmically, all the while stomping their feet on the wooden decks. The whole boat vibrates and sounds like a giant's drum. The captain ordered our boys, "Come join us. Wake up your arms and your feet." The boys stood on deck, laughing and stomping their feet and clapping hands. Maui and Heysha set the pace, faster, faster, and still faster, until they all broke out laughing.

Che requested of Salama, "Tell us how to row with these long oars."

The captain laughed. "Just sit near Maui and do what he does. There are six ways of rowing, all of them right. If you sweat and your arms ache, then you are doing it well."

In the middle of the boat, a strong beam of wood holds the mast in place. Rowers sit on this beam. Che and Maui sat on one side of the mast, Ari and Heysha on the other side. Two men pulled on one long,

---

[28] The Strait of Jubal is the entrance of the Red Sea from the Gulf of Suez.

sweeping oar with one man in front of them, standing and pushing the same oar to control the recovery at the end of each stroke. I stood in front of Ari and Heysha; Adoo helped Che and Maui. We had the long oars in place, our hands gripping the wood, warmed up and ready.

The captain had a satisfied look on his face—more hands to work than he'd expected. He ordered Marcus and Justin to pull the stem anchor out. They eagerly pulled on the rope and lifted the anchor stone with some difficulty. As soon as the anchor cleared the surface, our captain gave a loud yell, which made our hearts beat faster. "*Gorrr!*" (pull). The long, sweeping oars struck the water lustily and in unison. That was the secret of good rowing—perfect rhythm.

The two brothers, Maui and Heysha, would glance at each other and sing out, "Your side, Brother Maui."

The answer came back, "Your side, Brother Heysha."

We joined in this chant. "Pull, Maui. Pull, Heysha. *Gorr, gorr.*"

We were enjoying the rowing because we knew it would not last long. We would have the pleasure of the sport without reaching the point of pain. It was like a game fighting the wind and the strong surface current.

The sleek boat passed safely through the passage. Salama, our captain, sang out, "*Sheraaa*, raise sail!"

We sprang to the rope that raised the heavy yard, which was forty-six feet long, made from one tree, thick at the bow end (front or heel of the yard), very thin and flexible at the stem end. From this flexible yard, a huge lateen sail unfurled. This sail was not a perfect triangle. All three sides were fair curves. It was a beautiful sail when full of wind and most efficient when sailing against or with the wind blowing from one side. It took a thousand years of experience to achieve this design, always eliminating the unnecessary and finding elegant and clever solutions for problems while avoiding complicated parts.

The way this boat was ballasted was ingenious: the crew kept themselves to windward, but they also had a number of smooth, heavy stones, which they moved from side to side. When tacking, these stones served as moving ballast and extra anchors when needed. They were stored in a special compartment high on each side of the boat. Boatbuilders understood that the inside hull of the boat had to be kept clear of stones and ballast so wind and sun would dry it and leaks could be quickly located and repaired.

We turned and sailed south, running before the north wind. I felt all my cares dissolving. It was good to be on a fast boat again. There was no thrill in sailing the large lumbering boats we had in Alexandria. These small fast boats were the best. A third of the vessel was covered by the foredeck. Three men could sleep comfortably beneath it. Under the stem deck was ample storage space for ropes, nets, fishing gear, and carpenter tools. In the middle of this boat, a huge watertight box with a heavy cover was secured to the boat's ribs. Four grown men could sit comfortably inside it. In here, the crew stored everything that had to be kept dry: blankets, clothes, firewood, and food, especially sun-dried fish.

I sat near Salama as he carefully steered his boat, trying to minimize the rolling motion. I asked our captain, "Can you teach my son how to steer in a rough sea?"

"Call him. I will show him how to handle this fast boat."

I called Ari. "Come on, join us."

He walked easily on the moving boat like a seaman should, his strong legs absorbing the rolling motion, and stood on the stem deck, his hands grasping the *gafla*, a wooden beam erected about five feet high to support the sail boom when it was down and to afford a restful grip for sailors standing on the stem deck.

"Ari, do you wish to steer?" He nodded his head, and I told him to watch Salama for a while to see how he kept the following wind at an angle, never running straight before the wind. If you let your boat run straight before the wind in a rough sea, sudden gusts will make the bow dive deep into the water. You should always watch the waves following you. If a big one lifts your boat, you have to come down the face of the wave at an angle, never straight down, or else you will lose control of your boat. When more than half the rudder is in the air and out of the sea, the boat might broach and slide sideways down into the trough and may ship seawater over the side.

My son took the tiller. He watched the wind and the sail, the sea and the waves. He had extensive previous experience sailing small boats. However, this was his first time in such a rough sea. He was a tall young man, with strong limbs, soft black curly hair, brown eyes alight with curiosity, and a ready smile that showed perfect white teeth. He was only eighteen years old, and already his chest was covered with hair. He wore a white turban to protect his eyes and face from the strong glare of the sun reflected by the sea, a linen loincloth around his waist, and his dagger in his belt. He stood barefoot. His body was tanned a light golden brown like a Greek god who had come down from Olympus to join the Red Sea sailors in their uninhabited, lonely land.

Ari was a thinker, always questioning, always eager to learn about the world around him. I told him, "The gulf of the Red Sea[29] is narrow, about thirty miles across. You can see the mountains of Sinai. The mountains on the African coast are higher and nearer to the edge of the sea. All their peaks are sharp and weathered, like the rusting teeth of a giant saw. The sailors align these peaks and use them as beacons to know where they are. Here is the famous mountain with a spear, *Abu-Harba*.[30] A huge monolith on its peak points straight up to the sky. And this one is *Abu-Shaar*, the mountain with hair, because of white cirrus clouds like hair surrounding its peak. And this one is named *Al-Shayib*, the old man with white hair, because of all the white rock on the sides of this high peak.

"Both the western and eastern sides of the gulf possess a chain of high mountains," I explained. "Between them, the steady north wind is funneled, squeezed, and pushed out howling into the Red Sea. This is the windiest place in Egypt, and the surface current is very strong, bringing nourishment for the reef-building corals that flourish here. Many barrier reefs rise out of the deep water like a wall. Some of them have small coral islands sitting on top, and a few high islands are called 'mountains' by the local sailors because they look like mountains in the sea."

We were inside the strait, long barrier reefs on both sides, the waves getting bigger and steeper all the time. Salama was steering, enjoying the excitement and the challenge of controlling his boat.

---

[29] Gulf of the Red Sea here means the Gulf of Suez.

[30] *Abu* means "father." It also means "he that has," so the mountain named *Abu-Harba* means "the mountain with a spear."

There was motion all around us. Whitecapped waves rising out of the dark and deep blue sea crashed on the stem of our boat. Strong gusts of wind blew the salty spray over us, the sunlight making the droplets shine with the colors of a rainbow. It was a thrilling scene. All good sailors get excited in rough weather, and Salama was no exception.

There he was on the stem deck, steering and singing, no lifeline around his waist. Then it happened in two heartbeats. He felt the boat being lifted under his feet. A mountain of water rose up behind him, and he looked upward at the great wave, his hands holding the steering tiller. He did not utter a sound, neither a shriek nor a groan. In two seconds, the rough wave curled, crashed, and washed him off the deck into the turbulent sea. The boat broached and slid sideways down the face of the wave, the sea coming in over the side. No doubt it would have filled the boat if we had not had the big watertight box securely fastened to the ribs.

The two brothers, Heysha and Maui, exploded into action. With a loud roar, they grabbed the oars and tried to stop the boat. I went to the stern, grabbed the steering tiller, and turned the boat into the oncoming seas. The sail was torn to shreds. Galen, with Marcus helping him, lowered the yard. Ari and Adoo were at the oars. I shouted at the top of my voice, "Pull hard! Now! Pull hard!"

Heysha and Maui started their hypnotic chant, "Pull, Brother Heysha. Pull, Brother Maui." The sound of their own voices made them forget the pain in their forearms. All the time, I kept my eyes on the man in the sea. He was swimming toward us, the strong current helping him, but the boat moved away from him, pushed by the same current. I could see the veins standing out on the rowers' necks. They fought the current and won. Salama reached the boat and pulled himself on board. I let the boat turn around and drift with the stream. Ari and Adoo were bailing water out with the two available buckets.

Heysha and Maui knew exactly what had to be done. Without saying a word, they lifted the lid of that great box and pulled out a long woolen blanket. Quickly they made an emergency sail. It worked like a square sail and took us safely to the lee of a small island. The anchorage was well sheltered from the north wind with a half-moon beach of white coral sand. We dropped anchor and bailed out all the water from inside the boat.

I now noticed Justin, sitting with one arm around the mast, his face very pale. I went over to his side. "Justin, are you seasick?"

"No. I fell down when the boat broached. I think I broke my leg."

"Why didn't you call for help?"

"I did not want to distract you when you were trying to save the boat."

"Galen will take care of your broken bone. Is it very painful?"

"Not too bad."

I kissed Justin on his head. I admired his courage and self-control. Once again I thanked the gods that Galen was with us on this voyage.

Every boat carries at least one dugout canoe, about fifteen feet long. We placed Justin into this canoe and lowered it down gently into the sea. Ari and Adoo jumped in, paddled to the beach, and laid Justin comfortably on the sand. Then Adoo paddled back to the boat and loaded the canoe with food and blankets, and we paddled back to the fine-sand beach.

As soon as we landed, Salama, the captain, grabbed my left hand and kissed it. Before I could pull it away from him, he said, "Please don't tell my father what happened."

"Don't worry, captain," I promised. "The story of your misadventure will not leave this boat."

Then Galen said to us in a firm voice, "I want you to build a big fire here on the beach."

There was no wood on the island. It was made entirely of coral, which was once a living reef. Most probably a great earthquake had elevated this reef above sea level. The waves ground the corals into fine white sand and created the marvelous half-moon beach. But the island was dry, with no trees of any kind. However, the fishing eagles[31] had built six nests here from twigs, sand branches they carried from afar. Each generation of ospreys kept adding wood to the same nest for a hundred years. Now these nests were huge, almost four feet

---

[31] Osprey (large sea eagle: *Pandion haliaetus*): It catches fish in the shallow water on the coral reefs, mostly triggerfish and parrotfish, and builds large nests on uninhabited islands.

high and as wide as one's outstretched arms. We took some dry branches from each nest, taking care not to destroy their shape.

Once we had the fire blazing, Galen ordered us to heat some large stones. Then he pulled the canoe up on the beach, leveled it on the sand, and said, "I want this canoe half full of water." We obeyed quickly and filled the canoe with seawater. "Now put the hot stones in the canoe to heat the water," instructed Galen. We kept adding more hot stones to the water until it was hot enough to satisfy him. He tested it with his hand and ordered us to lay Justin inside this canoe.

Galen sat down near the boy and told him, "You must relax, even if you feel pain. Don't tense your leg muscles."

Adoo grabbed Justin under his arms, and I took hold of his ankle. I looked at the boy's face; he was very pale. Galen kept running his fingers up and down the broken shinbone. He found the fractured ends and said, "Now, pull steady as hard as you can." I pulled the ankle, and Adoo held Justin from under his armpits. Fortunately, it did not take long. Galen had the broken ends of the bone fitted together. Then he put wooden splints around the leg, tied them with cloth bandages, and told us to lift the boy out of the warm water and to keep him dry and comfortable.

Galen smiled at Justin. "This bone will heal well. You will have to walk with crutches for a month. Take care not to put your weight on this leg, and always call for help when you want to move."

While everyone was busy preparing the meal and a place to sleep, I sat down near Justin to keep him company. I asked, "Do you feel much pain in your leg?"

"No. I will be well soon. When that great wave rolled over us, salt spray hit my eyes, and I tripped and fell down near the mast. I knew my leg was broken."

I was silently proud of my son, a young man of sixteen years, tall and thin with the personality of an explorer. He had found in Marcus a good companion who appreciated his humor. His blue eyes and fair hair were not common in Alexandria, catching the attention of the young ladies there. I feared he might admire himself to distraction like Narcissus, but fortunately, he appeared unmindful of his own good looks.

We gathered around Justin and talked far into the night. The excitement of our misadventure kept us awake. I was the last to fall into a deep and restful sleep.

CHAPTER 9: Myos Hormos

At sunrise I looked at the western horizon and watched a phenomenon fairly common in Egypt. Shafts of light, red-orange and purple, radiated up into the sky like spokes of a giant wheel while the sun was rising in the east as a fiery red disk out of the deep blue sea. There were marvelous colors in the east and the same on the western horizon.

The first hour after sunrise was the hardest to bear. The surface of the sea was like a silver mirror reflecting the glare into our eyes.[32] We sat down at the edge of the sea, our backs to the rising sun, and we let the heat warm our stiff and cramped muscles. The three brothers, Salama, Heysha, and Maui, were busy with needles and string, sewing three blankets together to make a square sail. While they were busy making this emergency sail, I watched the sea eagles hunting (I should say "fishing") for their first meal. Salama told us they do this twice a day, every day. It was a marvelous sight, ten or more sea eagles circling above the coral reef observing schools of parrotfish and triggerfish feeding in the shallow pools. It was easy to recognize the parrotfish, their colorful dorsal fins and tails waving in the water. One by one, the birds of prey would glide down, fly low over the reef, and snatch a small fish in their talons.

One of these eagles came down and could not rise up into the air again. He flapped his wings mightily but to no avail—his talons were locked into the back of a large parrotfish, and he could not lift the heavy fish into the air. The fish dragged the sea eagle into deeper water, and both hunter and hunted drowned together. I asked Salama, the fisherman, "Have you ever seen this before?"

He said, "Yes, we have. The osprey cannot release the fish because his talons are locked. Only when he sets the fish down in his nest or on a rock will his talons relax their grip."

---

[32] Fishermen in the Red Sea call this blinding glare *Al-Sorum*.

As soon as the sail was ready, we jumped into the boat, heading for the harbor of Myos Hormos. Justin was comfortable on the foredeck in the shade of the sail. Ari and Adoo sat next to him. They would stay close to Justin until his leg healed. Che and Marcus were in the center of the boat, sitting near Maui and Heysha, who were controlling the square sail. Salama was steering, and I stood next to him with Galen by my side.

I looked at Galen, his white turban pulled down to protect his eyes from the glare, and I said, "This will be a pleasant sail. You can see several islands and coral reefs sheltering us from the north wind. They will keep the waves small. However, the wind will be as strong as yesterday, and we will sail at a good speed. We should reach harbor in four hours."

Galen turned his handsome face toward me. There was a flicker of amusement in his eyes, and he said, "Whether it takes four or six hours, I am enjoying the ride."

Salama called to his brother. "Maui, we are hungry. Try to catch a fish." There was a coral reef ahead of us, a young reef, straight and without a lagoon, awash at low tide. The fishermen call this kind of coral reef *shabroor*. Salama steered toward it and said, "We will find breakfast there on the deep side of this shabroor." We sailed closer to the reef. The water was crystal clear, and the color changed from dark blue to light blue.

As we trolled our fishing lines at the edge of the reef, a group of seven hunting fish called *girm*[33] by the Red Sea fishermen chased our lures. We could see them clearly. Two fish were hooked, and the lines were pulled in as fast as possible, wrapped around a wooden cleat to take the pressure off the fisherman's hand, but we were not fast enough. A couple of sharks that were following the girm dashed in and took great big chunks of them. Maui shouted, "Look at the sharks!"

Salama said, "Sharks always follow the girm because he is a good hunter and they eat his leftovers, but if one day he gets hooked, they attack him without mercy, just as the jackals follow the lions."

---

[33] The *girm* of the Red Sea can reach ninety pounds in weight and is a powerful hunter. It is likely a member of the jack family.

Our boys were enjoying the fishing. Their excitement increased when a group of dolphins rushed to our boat, jumping playfully. Salama exclaimed, "Look at our friends! Here they are! When they play, we are never bored. If there are many dolphins, that means fish are plentiful, for them and for us."

Maui, laughing, shouted at his brother Salama, "Your father was not here yesterday to save you!" He was obviously very pleased with his joke. Maui was playing with words. The dolphin in the Red Sea is known as *Abu-Salama*, which means "Salama's father," but it also means "he guarantees safety." The fishermen tell many tales about dolphins helping drowning men, and they describe how the dolphins will attack any large shark by ramming his soft belly.

Suddenly, the dolphins left us and went after a group of garfish.[34] The garfish made a mighty effort to escape, flying above the surface of the sea, only their tails in the water, propelling them at top speed, the dolphins right behind them. As soon as the garfish got tired, they fell back into the sea and into the dolphins' mouths.

Salama told us, "There is a large male dolphin that plays in the harbor. He lets the swimmers touch him. The fishermen give him fish and squid, but I don't think he stays to eat. The sea is full of food."

I asked, "Why do you think he stays in the harbor?"

Salama said, "I sense he was once a chief in his tribe, but he lost a fight and was driven out. He misses his own kind but takes whatever comfort he can from people."

Early afternoon, we were inside the harbor. I gave Salama a small pouch filled with silver and told him, "Go tell your father we need this boat for one week, and buy two new sails, a small one for rough weather and a larger sail for fair weather."

I walked with Galen on the beach toward the small fort[35] at the northern end of the bay. This beach was covered with thousands of

---

[34] The garfish (*Belone bellone*) in the Red Sea are as thick as a wrist and long as an arm. They are known locally as *Khirm Toory*.

[35] This fort was built by the King Ptolemy II. It is called Ptolemy Philadelphus (brother/sister loving) because he married his full sister, Queen Arsinoe. After her death, she was worshipped as a goddess in Alexandria. In the year 24 BC, the Roman general Aellus Galluis returned to this fort after defeat in Arabia. The desert and the

empty seashells.[36] Galen said softly, "Now I understand why they call this place Mussel Harbor [Myos Hormos], but of course there is no sea room for a hundred ships."

I told him, "The only reason this fort was built here is the availability of fresh water. There is a well about four miles inland, and the water travels in clay pipes to the fort and to the fishermen's village. There is a better natural harbor nine miles to the south, sheltered from every wind. But with no fresh water, that harbor is used only in the winter to build and repair ships. Come summer and the fleet sails to India, and this harbor remains deserted till fall. The name of this place is Gardaka because it is surrounded by *garqad* bushes."[37]

Walking on the beach toward the small rectangular fort at the end of the bay, we could see to our left a dry, uninhabited coastal plain, sloping gently upward to where the mountains of red granite rose in the distance. I told Galen, "This high mountain is Gebel Kattar [*Gebel* means 'mountain,' and *Kattar* means 'dripping with water']. High on Kattar, there are many rock pools, each overflowing into the pool beneath it. One good storm will fill these pools with rainwater for a whole year. The water dripping over maidenhair moss gives this great mountain its name. Next to Kattar is another high mountain, Dokhan [Mount of Smoke]. Carved into the natural beauty of these mountains are the hard-featured stone quarries for imperial porphyry, where miserable criminals are condemned to cut stone for the rest of their brief lives. One of the few duties of the governor of this port is to supervise the work in these quarries. His other duties are to ensure that the trading fleet is kept in good condition. New boats are being constructed all the time, and when the fleet returns from India, he collects taxes for the king and, of course, enriches himself at the same time."

---

sea saved the Arabs from the Roman yoke, so they remained free while the whole Mediterranean world submitted to Rome.

[36] These are *tridacna* shells. The muscle that closes the shell is thick as a cucumber, white in color, and very sweet. People eat it raw, and the remainder of the animal is used for bait.

[37] *Nitraria retusa*. Camels and goats love this plant.

The governor of this fort was Heraclitus, a valiant officer and a good friend who had lost an eye in battle. He was rewarded with this post. Every governor of this trading port returned to Alexandria a rich man, if he could stand a few years of boredom.

Two young officers conducted Galen and me to a large room overlooking the sea with many open windows to let in the cool north wind. The governor, Heraclitus, was sitting at his table eating and drinking. I was shocked by his appearance. He had grown so huge and fat in the last four years, there was no trace left of the fine officer I had known so well.

Galen stood back. I approached Heraclitus to greet him. The moment I looked at his puffed face and saw the blank expression in his good eye, just as vacant as his glass eye, I realized he was drunk, beyond recognizing his old friend. I said a few words to him, but there was no answer; he just stared at me, uncomprehending.

One of the young officers took my arm and said, "The governor needs to sleep it off . . . for quite a while. Come with me, please. You will be our guest tonight."

We sat at a faraway table, near an open window to stay cool. They served us a fine meal with strong wine made from fermented sweet dates. Galen tasted the wine and winced. "No wonder this wine made him drunk! I am surprised it did not crack his glass eye." He diluted his wine with spring water, and we followed his example.

I asked one of the officers, "How did the governor change so much in four years?"

The officer replied, "His wife was bored here right from the start. She complains incessantly about wanting to return to Alexandria. The governor, after about a year, also became bored, so his hobbies went from hunting and fishing to eating and drinking. You can see the result for yourself."

The second officer said with gracious manners, "You are welcome to stay here. Have a hot bath and a restful sleep. You will be able to talk to the governor tomorrow when he wakes up."

We finished our meal in the company of these two cheerful young men. However, every time I looked at Heraclitus, there was no sign of recognition. He put away vast amounts of food and drank bottle after bottle of the strong wine.

At first light I walked out of the house with Galen to have an early morning stroll and swim before breakfast. As we walked, I saw Ari running on the beach toward us. I immediately realized that he was not running for exercise. The boy wanted to reach us urgently, and when he did, he was so excited and out of breath he could not talk coherently. We sat him down on the sand.

After regaining his breath, Ari said, "Last night, after midnight, two officers arrested Che and Marcus and took them away. We could not save them. Adoo said it is wiser not to move."

Galen put his arm around Ari's shoulders and said in a reassuring voice, "Calm down. We will find them as soon as the governor wakes up."

I said, "Ari, tell us the whole story. Every detail. What happened last night?"

Ari told us, "After midnight, three men walked onto the stone pier. They sat down at the end of the pier, their legs swinging in the air, their feet almost touching the water. One of them was huge and appeared drunk. The other two helped him when he swayed from side to side. Marcus decided to give them a good scare. You know how much he loves practical jokes. He took off all his clothes, lowered himself into the sea, and swam slowly toward the pier without splashing. No one could see him except us. We watched his head from the boat. Marcus filled his lungs with air and swam underwater until he found the stone pier. Then he gave a mighty push with his feet on the bottom of the harbor, and he shot out of the water, right under the men's feet, roaring like a great white monster! We saw the three men kick their feet up in the air and run as fast as they could all the way to the end of the pier. The fat man stumbled and fell down. The other two did not have the courage to stop until they heard Marcus laughing. He walked out of the sea stark naked and stood there laughing loudly, his whole body shaking."

Galen interrupted, "A fat man? I hope you don't mean the governor."

Ari quickly said, "Yes, it was the governor. The officers helped him up, and I heard them say, 'Are you hurt, Governor?'

"And then he said, 'My glass eye is broken. Get that boy.' Marcus was still laughing when they grabbed him."

I asked Ari, "And then what happened to Che?"

Ari told us, "There is a lone palm tree next to the pier. They forced Marcus to hug that tree, his arms around the trunk, each wrist held by one of the officers, and the governor whipped him on his bare back and legs without mercy. Che could not stand the screams of his friend, so he ran to help him. Adoo tried to hold Che back, but he was enraged. The officers grabbed Che and whipped him, too, just as they did to Marcus." Ari kept repeating over and over, "It was terrible, it was terrible."

Galen asked, "Where are the boys now?"

Ari told us, "They were dragged away in the night, their wrists bound with strips of cloth and a cloth rope choking their necks."

The three of us, Galen, Ari, and I, walked back to the boat. I told Ari, "Stay here with Justin and Adoo." Then I picked up six small bags filled with gold coins. We returned to the governor's house. He was still asleep, and all we could do was wait for Heraclitus to wake up.

Galen was observing two oceanic terns. These beautiful white birds of the sea were performing marvelous aerial aerobatics. Fishing was easy for them. They dove into the sea and rose up again with small silvery fish in their beaks. The blackbirds with a forked tail immediately attacked the terns. These piratical birds (*skuas*) found it much easier to steal from the terns than to fish for themselves. If the tern caught a small fish, it would swallow it in flight, but if the catch was a larger fish, usually a *zoragana* (a fish called a halfbeak), the skuas would force the tern to drop it, and these blackbirds would snatch it in midair.

Galen remarked, "Hiro, do you think the terns are enjoying this competition? The fishing is so easy, I think the tern would get bored if they did not have these skuas to provide some excitement. It is like a game between these two birds, and the skuas never hurt the tern that does the work of fishing."

I replied, "I think you are right. The birds have a healthy, exciting life while they catch their food, unlike most humans, who have a boring life that slowly erodes their health."

Galen said, "You were thinking just now of Heraclitus, no doubt!"

I smiled. "Yes, a sedentary life is a sin against the gods."

"On the other hand," Galen noted, "I hope our young man Marcus is learning that there are worse things in life than an occasional boring night. These skuas here are wise enough to taunt terns, not governors."

Late in the afternoon, Heraclitus, the governor, walked onto the terrace. Smiling, he advanced toward us and said, "Hiro, my friend, forgive me. I did not recognize you last night." He extended his hand to Galen and greeted him with great courtesy. Then he turned around and hugged me like a long-lost brother. "Please, come and join me at my table."

We walked with Heraclitus, who was wearing a cloth patch on his eye. He led the way to his private table in the shade of an old grapevine. His wife joined us. She was eager to talk about Alexandria. Galen entertained her with stories about the ruling class. He seemed to have an endless supply. It became increasingly obvious that she was homesick for the Great City.

Heraclitus asked me, "What are your plans, Hiro?"

I said, "I need two fast ships. I am going to India with the fleet."

Heraclitus replied, "The fleet has already sailed. You are late, Hiro, and you will probably miss the good sailing weather and hit some rough storms."

I said, "Yes, you are right, of course, but I was detained in Alexandria by business dealings."

Heraclitus was astonished. "Are you a trader now, Hiro?"

I assured him, "Yes, I am a merchant, and you should think about it, too. If you set yourself up in Alexandria, you will easily make a fortune."

Heraclitus laughed out loud, and I noticed greed plainly written over his wife's features. This was the right moment to show her the gold. I put two bags filled with coins on the table between Heraclitus and his wife. I gently pushed one of the bags toward the governor and the second bag toward his wife. He opened the bag, smiled, and said, "Hiro, what on earth is all this?"

I said, matter-of-factly, "Payment for two fast ships."

He said, "You don't have to pay, my friend."

I replied, "All the traders pay. I will, too."

Heraclitus's wife looked at Galen. "Is it easy to make a fortune in Alexandria?"

Galen reassured her. "All you need are the connections and the money to charter the ships and pay for the goods." I looked at the lady. Her features softened. I am sure she had visions of the aristocratic life she so obviously craved. This was another good moment, so I slowly put two more bags of gold on the table, one near her hand and the other near her husband's hand. She opened the bag, looked at the golden coins, and gave me a beautiful smile.

Heraclitus questioned me seriously about the proper way to start a business. I was sure he had a small fortune safely stashed away in the fort. When the conversation lagged, I produced two more bags of gold coins and put them on the table. Heraclitus and his wife opened them and looked at me with astonishment and wonder, respect and love written all over their faces.

Heraclitus said, "Hiro, my friend, what can I do to repay so much generosity?"

I said, "There is something you can do that will make me happier than I am right now."

Before the governor could answer, his wife said, expansively, "Anything, anything you want." Her husband smiled and nodded his approval.

I said, "My two servants were sent to the quarries yesterday. Kindly forgive them."

All thoughts of vengeance and punishment had vanished from the mind of Heraclitus by the magic elixir of gold. Dreams of future wealth and happiness pushed all other desires aside. Heraclitus stood up and said, "Follow me."

He moved with unusual speed for a man his size. Near the gate, he seized a whip and swaggered out of the house. He called two young officers, and they rushed to obey. His orders were brief and clear like a naval captain's, and he had the habit of command. He ordered, "Go to the quarries and release the two prisoners I sent yesterday." And to the second officer, "Ride to Gardaka, find Mobareek and tell him his friend Hiro needs the best two ships." Mobareek was the master of the shipbuilders in the harbor of Gardaka, nine miles to the south.

I thanked the governor and told him, "I would like to show Galen the stone quarries because he has never seen them."

"Well," Heraclitus said, "I will provide you with horses, food, and water. Please spend the night at my house, and you can leave tomorrow at first light."

We walked with Heraclitus back to his house. Galen asked him, "Where did you find this unusual whip?"

The governor said, "A fisherman gave it to me. This is the tail of a huge stingray, a spotted one called a leopard ray."

We started for the quarries before sunrise on horseback with a young officer accompanying us. Galen asked him how far the stone quarries were, and the officer replied, "About ten miles from here, all uphill."

The hot, sunburnt coastal plain sloped upward, and soon we were inside a canyon called Wadi Beli. Our horses were stepping in pink sand brought down by mountain torrents from the red granite mountains. There were endless small pebbles of porphyry smoothed by the flash floods, translucent, and more beautiful than the huge columns of the same stone smoothed by the hands of miserable men. To our left rose Gebel Kohla. This small mountain of bare rocks without a bush or a tree was named *Kohla* because of the strata of blue and black rock, like lines of kohl, the blue or black eyeliner Egyptian women paint on their eyelids to emphasize the beauty of their eyes.

As we came closer to this small mountain, blue and black rocks were mixed into the pink sand. Amidst all this natural beauty, there was so much human misery. Ahead of us, on the sides of Gebel Dokhan (Mountain of Smoke), were the stone quarries at an elevation of about four thousand feet. The air here was cooler than the coastal plain.

I was surprised at the intense activity in the quarries. Small gangs of prisoners were working the stone while blacksmiths with hot fires were busy forging, hardening, and sharpening the chisels and wedges the prisoners had to use. Galen said, "Now I understand why they named this the Mountain of Smoke. These prisoners are engulfed in fire and smoke and sweat, deprived of everything that makes a man's life worth living."

The young officer accompanying us found the supervisor and showed him the orders to release the boys. All prisoners slept in caves that they dug out themselves. The officer led the way to a small cave, where we found Che and Marcus on the ground in a frightful condition. They were suffering from exhaustion, hunger, and thirst, their backs and legs covered with dried blood mixed with dust. They had refused to work and had been severely flogged.

We did not try to clean their wounds but made them drink as much water as they could. Then we went back down the mountain. Marcus rode behind Galen, and Che was behind me. He managed to smile and said, "I was sure you would come." I smiled at him. "And I was sure you would survive." Marcus was leaning on Galen's broad back, sobbing.

After about two hours, we stopped for a much-needed rest in the shade of a big boulder. Galen sat beside me and observed the boys for a while. Then he said, "They are young and strong, and will recover quickly. This ordeal will make Che a better leader of men, more compassionate toward the soldiers who may risk their lives for him someday."

I replied, "Now Che has seen the evil side of this world. He was disguised as your servant, but his noble nature compelled him to try to save his friend."

As soon as we reached the boat, Che and Marcus went into the sea. Then we cleaned their wounds with fresh water and let them dry in the sun. Galen covered their wounds with balm, which made an excellent dressing. The boys ate a hot meal and went to sleep. The next morning we sailed south to Gardaka Harbor. This was the shipbuilding site with two sandy beaches sloping suddenly into deep water. Five paces from the beach was water fifteen feet deep. That was perfect for launching and beaching heavy sailing boats.

Land sheltered this harbor from the north and west winds. Two islands and a long coral reef protected it from the south and east winds, and there was sea room for at least a hundred ships. Only those engaged in shipbuilding lived here in small houses built of sticky clay and palm fronds. The houses were round and oval. There wasn't a straight line in the whole village. All fresh water came on camelback in waterskins from Myos Hormos.

The people in Myos Hormos filled the waterskins, then let the hungry camels go to Gardaka[38] on their own. They had a well-trodden path at the edge of the sea, and they knew they would find *gardok* bushes there to eat. The people in Gardaka would unload the camels and turn them loose. The animals would feed for three days and then thirst would drive them back to Myos Hormos to the well of fresh water to drink. The animals were so used to this routine, they did not need anyone to guide them.

As soon as we anchored, I went looking for my friend Mobareek. He was the chief in charge of boatbuilding. We were the same age, forty-four years. As I walked in the harbor, my steps quickened when I saw him from afar. He was working on a new boat.

Mobareek was the only surviving son of a black slave woman from Sudan. His father was an Arabian navigator and a free man. A giant with a huge chest and a big muscular waist, he made a majestic figure with his mane of grey hair falling back from his lofty brow. I have never seen bigger hands on a man. His thick fingers and huge arms bespoke a lifetime of shipbuilding. He was also a blacksmith who made his own tools—heavy axes and adzes that no one but he could handle.

People rarely spoke of his ability as a shipbuilder. His fame was spreading because he was a great navigator. Stories were told and retold about how he ran his ship aground at night on a coral reef and then sat down, calmly playing music, waiting for the high tide before attempting to refloat his ship. And yet this masterful man spoke softly,

---

[38] Today this harbor is a tourist resort for divers. The Arabic name *Al- Gardaka* has been corrupted to *Hurgada*, and another tourist resort has been built on the site of Mussel Harbor (Myos Hormos) north of Hurgada.

for he was a stutterer. Only when singing did his words come out loud and clear.

Mobareek saw me approaching. He stopped work, put down his great axe, and gave me a powerful hug that almost crushed my ribs. "Hiro, my friend, you are back."

We sat down and exchanged all our news. I looked at my friend, strength and kindness shining on his face, and wondered, not for the first time, *How does the soul form the body? How does courage and goodness show on one man's face and evil betray itself in another?*

This is a mystery without a clue.

CHAPTER 10: The Sorceress and the Sword

Every morning we walked over to the beach to the shipbuilding site and watched Mobareek and his carpenters finishing our new sailing ships. Mobareek was trying to teach his son, Atiya, the art of shipbuilding. However, Atiya, a young man about eighteen years old, slim and black as ebony, had a deep-seated aversion to work of any kind. I watched him resisting his father's efforts with clever stratagems. Today his performance was of a higher caliber than usual and really worth watching.

Atiya was carrying a heavy beam of wood balanced on his shoulder. He walked a few unsteady paces toward the ship, groaning all the way. Then he dropped the heavy beam and leaned against the side of the new ship, rubbing his lower back and making loud noises intended to convey agony and pain. At the same time, he gave an extraordinary display of facial grimaces—he twisted his red lips, rolled his eyes, and managed to move his scalp and wiggle his ears, all the time moaning, "Ah, oh, ah!" His father remained calm and unrelenting. The noises became louder and more extravagant. The carpenters stopped work and gathered around the boy. Maybe this time he was really hurt. Now Atiya used his most effective ploy, a long, drawn-out "Aaah," rising up the scale and building increasing tension in the audience. Then he gave a loud piercing scream and fell to the ground. Mobareek relented. He picked up his son and sat him down in the shade without saying a word, turned around, and went back to his work, slowly shaking his head from side to side·.

I sat down next to the boy. His dark eyes gleamed, and his large, red lips split into a delighted grin. He had a homely, good-natured face, and I liked him immediately. Atiya's laughter was infectious.

I asked Atiya, "You clearly hate shipbuilding and woodwork. What do you like?"

He looked at me and smiled. "Everybody knows that I like to play music."

"How about fishing?"

"I enjoy playing in the sea, but what I really like is playing my *simsimiyya*[39] and singing songs. I love to improvise. I never tire of that."

I thought for a moment. A musician would be a valuable addition to our crew. The only entertainment at night on-board ship was music and songs. I said to this born musician, "Atiya, will you sail with us to India? Your only work will be making musical instruments and playing your simsimiyya."

"Yes, yes, I would like this very much if you can get my father to give permission."

"I am sure I can get it if you can go and do a bit of sanding work with the crew. This will please your father before I ask him a favor."

Atiya rose to his feet, picked up a piece of round coral, and joined the crew sanding the new ships. They worked carefully, rubbing the hull beneath the waterline to make it perfectly smooth. They used clean white pieces of dead coral, and they worked to the beat of a small drum.

The inside of the ship was left rough to minimize the danger of slipping and falling. As soon as Atiya joined the other boys at work, there was much merriment and hilarity. The crew joined him in songs that made work easier, and time flew by. I was glad Atiya would sail on my ship and happier still when his father agreed to command the second ship. Mobareek was a great navigator, and his son, Atiya, was a talented musician—the best possible companions any mariner could wish for on a long cruise.

Three days later, Mobareek was standing like a giant colossus, leaning on his great axe, admiring the two sailing ships he had just completed. I walked up to him, and he greeted me with pride in his voice. "These two ships are ready. This one will be named *Al- Sahira* [the *Sorceress*], and that one will be *Sayf-Al-Bahr* [*Sword of the Sea*]."

I noted the very sharp prow and the long, curved stem, and I said, "This boat will cut the waves like a sword, and the *Sorceress* will perform some magic for you on the waves."

---

[39] *Simsimiyya*: A musical instrument with five strings.

Mobareek laughed. "You craft words the way I craft wood!"

"Shall we put your craft to the test? We will race your ships against each other."

There was pride and contentment in my friend's voice. "Yes, we shall have a grand race."

Mobareek loved racing, and every ship he built had some small variation. He was always experimenting, trying to improve his boats. He wanted his ships to be safe, fast, and elegant. There was no decoration on the hulls, no wood carvings, and no names. What good would it do? Only a handful of people here could read. However, every ship had different colors, and every seaman here could tell one ship from another with ease, just as a shepherd knows each of his sheep. To an outsider, the ships looked alike, but to us, every one was different in color and shape. Below the waterline, all sailing ships in the Red Sea fleet were painted white, a mixture of shark liver oil and caustic lye, which stops the growth of seaweed and barnacles for three months.

In this archipelago, sharks are easy to find and easy to catch. At sunset they abound near the coral reefs, and smaller ones are plentiful inside the lagoons. About twenty small sharks were caught in one night on hook and line, including a large tiger shark, so named because of the dark stripes on its skin. The tiger shark, over twelve feet long, was too heavy to haul inside a boat, so the fishermen tied him alongside. He was weakened after struggling all night on hook and chain, but he was not dead. As the crew sailed into the harbor, they came close to our boat to show it to Justin. Several remoras[40] were attached to the shark's fins and body, and when the fishermen hauled it onto the beach, a remora more than a foot long left it and swam over to our sailboat. Justin saw the fish and threw small pieces of bait into the sea. The remora ate them and attached itself to our boat.

Justin's broken leg was healing well, and whenever he wanted to exercise, he would lower himself into the sea and swim around the boat. The remora entertained him for days and sometimes would attach

---

[40] The *remora* is a fish (*Echeneidae* family) with a suction disk on top of its head. It often attaches itself to sharks and manta rays to get a free ride and tidbits of food.

itself to his thigh or back as he swam in the sea. The fishermen call this strange fish the "shark's tick" (*Gamla-Al- Girsh*) because it sticks to the shark like a tick clings to a camel.

The men were lighting many small fires on the beach and chopping shark livers in iron pots. Because of so many small fires on this beach, it was named Charcoal Beach (*Gad-Al-Fahm*). The liver oil was left in the pot to simmer on a small fire for several hours. The end result was sticky oil, perfect for painting ships' bottoms.

Sword of the Sea and the *Sorceress* lay careened on their sides in the hot sun, ready for painting with a white mixture of caustic lye and shark liver oil. The wood was hot, dry, and very smooth. It absorbed the oil quickly, and soon the ships stood gleaming in the sun. Four coats of this white mixture were applied beneath the waterline. The inside of the ship was painted with a brown resin, collected from injured trees, and when dissolved in boiling linseed oil, it made the inside of the ship waterproof. Had they painted the inside with shark liver oil, the odor would have been unbearable. The painting work was done, and we had to wait five days to be sure the ships were perfectly dry before launching them into the sea.

These were fine days. The steady north wind coming from the desert was dry and invigorating, and it seemed to urge us on to launch our new ships and sail away. The young crew, whom Mobareek picked, was adventurous and eager to go to Serendib. For most of them, this would be their first cruise in the Indian Ocean.

Atiya entertained us while we waited for the ships to dry. He played his simsimiyya and sang many hilarious songs. The crew loved it. It was interesting to watch Atiya and to see how he captivated the audience with his music. He would start loud, and his voice in the silence could be heard all over the beach. Then he would lower his voice gradually until it became a whisper and the words were barely heard. Soon the boys sitting next to Atiya would raise their voices and sing while he would concentrate on playing endless variations of the original melody. The expression on his face would change as he concentrated on inventing new musical variations. To me, Atiya looked like a man in a trance.

Marcus was subdued. I noticed he was not playing practical jokes as he used to. What he had suffered in the stone quarries had affected him deeply. I didn't know if he would ever recover his cheerful character. Che seemed to be his normal self, at least outwardly, despite his ordeal in the stone quarry. It had probably made him a stronger man.

Ship launchings were festive occasions for the people who lived in this small village. It seemed that everyone came to Charcoal Beach[41] to watch us launch two new ships—men and women, old and young, in clean and colorful clothes, their children and grandchildren running all over the sandy beach. The young men were barefoot and wore loincloths and turbans. They were ready to wade into the sea and help us float the ships. A few of the older men wore golden-colored turbans on their heads. At their advanced age, they had earned the right to wear this special headdress. It was a badge of distinction because they were experienced pilots who knew every reef, every pass, every rock, and evert hidden danger in the sea.

Lying beneath each of the careened ships were four long masts, smooth and slippery, greased with animal fat. These served as launching rails. The men would pull and push the ships on these slippery masts and slide them into the sea. Long, stout ropes were tied to the ships, and all able-bodied men gathered around, waiting for the signal to launch. The *Sorceress* would go first, followed by *Sword of the Sea*, when the tide reached the high-water mark.

The drums started beating a slow rhythm. The men grabbed the ropes, and suddenly there was total silence. A tall man with a powerful voice raised his arm to silence the drums, and then he shouted, "*Hey! Hawal! Halamboo!!! Hob!*" When he said the word "*Hob!*" every man pulled as hard as he could, but nothing happened. The ship did not move. The man with the stentorian voice shouted, "More hands! Everybody to the ropes!" At this command, we stepped into the shallow water and grabbed the ropes. The drums started beating again. The man in charge raised his arm, and the drums were silent. Then he

---

[41] Today there is a hotel on Charcoal Beach. The fishermen still use the old name (*Gad-Al-Fahm*).

shouted, "*Hey! Hawal!! Halamboo!!! Hob!*" This time the ship moved a little, and the drums began to beat again, a rumbling, slow beat.

I noticed Ari and Che next to me pulling as hard as they could, sweat dripping from their foreheads, but they were pulling at the wrong moment. I told them, "Wait until you hear the word *Hob!* When the drums beat, take a rest. When you hear, *'Hey! Hawal! Halamboo!!'* get ready. And at the command, *'Hob!!'* you pull with all your might."

The secret was timing. If every man pulled at the same instant, the ship would move, and move she did, and when she slid into the sea, up went a great cheer on the beach. The children were clapping and laughing, the women were singing and ululating, and the older men were beaming with pleasure. There was excitement in the air and a certain pleasure that went along with moving this big, heavy ship on muscle power alone. The young men felt proud to be part of the group of men who were capable of this miracle. They felt themselves to be members of a victorious team.

Now we had to launch *Sword of the Sea.* The second launching was easier than the first, and when the ship floated, a great cheer went up on the beach. We felt the same pride I am sure the ancients felt when they raised their great obelisks of stone.

The two ships were tied together with ropes for extra stability. The men on the beach formed a human chain and passed the smooth ballast stones, baskets full of supplies, and waterskins from one man to his neighbor, up to the crew on board, who stowed everything in its proper place. The work continued into the early evening, and then we provided a feast on the beach for everyone. Tomorrow morning, we would sail out with the cool offshore breeze.

I was surprised that Heraclitus, the military governor, did not attend the launching. However, early the next day, I saw him on horseback riding toward us. He dismounted and walked up to me and said, "Hiro, if I were younger and healthier, I would sail with you. I want to learn more about this trade with India."

I greeted him, and we walked together toward the new ships. I thanked the governor for riding to Charcoal Beach to say goodbye, and he said, "Have you heard, Hiro? The queen and Mark Antony are both dead. Octavian is in Alexandria. I have received orders to welcome my replacement and to arrest the queen's son, Caesarion." He was silent for a moment; then he said, "All the *parasitos* in the Nile Valley are looking for the son of Caesar, tempted by the great reward."

Then Heraclitus walked to Che. "What is your name, young man?"

"I am Che, the servant of Galen."

"You are a Nubian."

"Yes, Governor."

Che had smiled a bit too much when he replied. The governor smiled back. I felt a need to speak. "This young servant is very proud of his homeland, but he is excited by having his first taste of salt water."

Heraclitus put both his hands on Caesarion's shoulders and looked deep into his eyes. Then he closed his one good eye and said in a solemn voice, "For your safety and happiness, I will give a special offering to the gods." Then he turned toward me, laughing. "Oh, by the way, Hiro, when you return, if you return, will you remember to bring back some pearls and rubies on my account? I will sell them and pay you back."

I took the governor's hand and assured him, "I promise you, I will select the best pearls and rubies for you, and we shall meet in Alexandria."

It was time for us to board the ships and sail. The men and women on the beach kept a respectful distance from the governor, who was waving his arms and saluting us. I waved back at Heraclitus.

Che approached me and whispered, "Do you think he recognized me as Caesarion?"

"Yes, I am sure he did. He has never shown so much interest in a servant who wasn't female. And I'm afraid you were a bit too pleased when he called you a Nubian. I had to make it sound like you took pride in your heritage, not your deception. But my old friend is still as sharp as ever when he needs to be."

I looked at Galen. He was smiling and nodding his head in approval. All was well.

As the ships drifted away from the beach, the men and women on land sang a beautiful traditional song:

Sail out, sail far on the deep blue sea, Under the starry night sky, And pray for wind that stirs your soul, And makes your sailboat fly.
Return safely, O Sorceress!!
Return safely, Sword of the Sea!!

There was a warm, dry wind blowing offshore, filled with music and joyous sound from the people on the beach. We raised our square sail, and the wind pushed us out to the deep blue water, away from the dangerous coral reefs. Mobareek had ordered the sailmakers to cut pieces of cloth into the shape of reef fishes and to paint them faithfully, copying the bright colors of live fish. This they did and sewed them to the square sail. It was a huge and beautiful sail, filled out to a perfect shape without any need for a boom to spread out the lower corners. A massive sixty-foot yard held up this sail, and this same yard would hold our great lateen sail when we used it.

Soon we were miles away. We could no longer see the beach or the people, but, strange to say, we could hear their music and singing. Galen, standing beside me, touched my shoulder and said, "Can you hear the music?"

I answered, "Yes. All our crew can hear it."

Smiling, Galen called Ari and Che to his side and told them to listen to the songs. The huge sail was capturing the sound and reflecting it back on deck. Here Galen said in a low voice, "Many fantastic stories are believed by our sailors, such as the myth of the Sirens of the sea, beautiful magical maidens with voices so enchanting their singing drives lonely sailors out of their minds, and they dive into the sea looking for the Sirens and drown."

Che said, "I remember that. Odysseus tied himself with a rope to the mast so he could resist the song of the Sirens. Now I know the kernel of truth in this tale."

Ari added, "I never liked that story. It doesn't make sense that men would lose all of their good sense and be lured by women to their certain destruction!"

"Well," Galen said, smiling, "You are obviously still very young."

I laughed with my friend as the two boys just stared at us.

Our destination was Gebal Elba, a high mountain between Egypt and the land of Sudan. This is the wettest place in Egypt, and flash floods come down that mountain and flow across the dry coastal plain, replenishing the wells with fresh water. The wells of *Shalatein* are near the coast. Sailing ships stop here to get fresh meat and sweet drinking water. Ships going north wait here patiently for the south wind instead of beating against the strong north wind. This south wind—*Azyab*, they call it—will not last more than four days. However, that would be enough to take a fast ship from Shalatein to Gardaka. We, too, could easily reach Gebal Elba and the Bir (well) of Shalatein in three or four days if we sailed day and night without stopping with the north wind behind us. However, I agreed with Mobareek that we should not do that. Our young crew would need more time to get used to the ships before entering the Indian Ocean.

The best way to avoid boredom and to give the crew the experience they needed was to race the two ships in a long zigzag course and stop every night for a rest. Natural harbors and safe anchorages abound on the coast of the Red Sea. This proved to be a sound plan. The crew suffered many bruises and minor injuries the first few days, but after that first week, they were used to the ship, and we had almost no injuries among our crew. Soon they would be able to maneuver their ships at night under starlight or moonlight without any trouble. We did not have to teach this young crew anything about sailing. They had grown up in their fathers' fishing boats. They just needed time to get used to the large ships. However, they had to be taught how to use weapons to defend the ship and save themselves should the need arise.

At noon I gathered the crew, and Mobareek did the same on the *Sorceress*. We had agreed that we would race against each other every day for twelve days, and now I explained the rules of this race to the eager, young crew. I told them, "There is no starting line. Both ships will lower their sails and ghost along, drifting with the current. Then the *Sorceress* will take off using any sail she wishes. *Sword of the Sea* will raise sail and pursue her. There is no set course. Mobareek will take his ship anywhere he wants—upwind, downwind, any course he chooses in the wide open sea—and we will give chase. The object is to catch the other ship and overtake her, just like a game of 'catch me if you can,' and before sunset, we will end the race on the coast, the leading boat choosing the anchorage. There are many natural harbors and safe anchorages on the coast of the Red Sea, almost all uninhabited because they lack fresh drinking water."

The *Sorceress* lowered her square sail, and we came alongside and lowered our sail. The rule of the game was that I had to wait till the crew on the *Sorceress* raised her sail. Would Mobareek use a square sail and run before the wind, or would he use his giant lateen sail and escape on a broad reach with the wind on his side? Our young crewmen prepared their muscles for sudden exertion by clapping their hands and stomping their feet on the deck forcefully and rhythmically, accompanied by a slow and rumbling sound from the drums: *Trrmm-tom tom, ta-rum, ta-rum; Trrmm-tom tom, ta-rum, ta-rum.* The men on the *Sorceress* were doing the same, warming up for a great effort. The noise and the din were unbelievable, but the boys loved it. The excitement in the air was palpable, and it affected each and every one of us.

Suddenly, we heard the powerful voice of Mobareek. "Sheraaa!! Raise sail!" His crew gave their all, straining against the halyards, pulling the heavy yard upward, thirty young voices answering in unison, "*Rawaga! Rawaga! Rawaga!*"[42] We had to wait for a moment until we saw their great lateen sail unfurling. I did not have to give any order. The crew jumped at the sixty-foot yard and with fierce concentration tied our lateen sail to it. It took three hundred laces of short cord to attach our sail to the wood of the yard.

The drummers were possessed by the devil, beating a wild rhythm when the long streamer was tied to the very tip of the yard. I let them hear what they wanted to hear: "Sheraaa!" It sounded like a battle cry. Up went our sail. *Sword of the Sea* was cutting the waves, and there was a swooshing sound under the hull, but the *Sorceress* was flying away on a broad reach with the speed of the wind, heading southeast, out to the open sea.

---

[42] *Rawaga* is the name of the halyard because of the sound this rope makes when moving over the wood roller in the truck at the top of the mast. The ship has two halyards attached to the yard (the beam of wood that lifts the sail upward).

Again and again Mobareek would slow down, and just as we smelled victory in the salty air, he would run before the wind, jibe, and move his sail to the other side of his mast, then run to the southeast. Every time we came close to the *Sorceress,* her drummers beat their drums and her crew jeered at us. As we struggled to turn around and catch up with her, we could hear their taunts and laughter.

We lost all hope. Then Mobareek tried to change his sail. His crew did not waste much time, but I decided not to change sail. Instead I kept our lateen sail full, and *Sword of the Sea* passed the *Sorceress.* Now it was our turn to laugh. Our drummers came to life, and the crew chanted with mighty voices, "*SayF-Al-Bahr! I SayF-Al-Bahr! I SayF-Al-Bahr!!*" Now I was sure the *Sorceress* would never catch us.

We ran to the southwest on a broad reach. I was aiming at a famous mountain that was a beacon for a safe anchorage on the coast, and we entered well before sunset. Mobareek tied the *Sorceress* alongside. He was happy; I could see it on his face. After being cooped up on land too long, he was now racing his boats on the open sea. He came aboard and walked toward me, saying, "Ah, you cut my heart out, *Sword of the Sea.*" Our young crew looked up at him with great admiration and respect.

That same night, Mobareek taught the boys a new song he had improvised during the day. He picked up his simsimiyya, played the melody several times, and then sang:

You pierced my heart,
Oh, Sword of the Sea!
I built you and I shaped you, and I cut down the tree!!
And now, you beat me and defeat me,
Oh, Sword of the Sea!!

The chorus for the crew was:

SayF-Al-Bahr, Wal, Saahira
Sword of the Sea and the Sorceress!!
Gatat, Galby, ya, SayF-Al-Bahr
You cut my heart out,
Sword of the Sea!!·

Atiya repeated this song over and over until the boys learned it to perfection. They would never forget this day or this song. I asked my friend, "When did you compose this song?"

Smiling, he said, "Today, when you passed me, my *Jinn* took charge. Whenever I hear the Whisperer, I have to drift and obey."

CHAPTER 11: Cape Berenice

The high peaks of the coastal mountains were touched by the first rays of the rising sun. The grey and red granite rock changed colors as the sun rose higher. Certainly the best hours of the day are sunrise and sunset. The horizon was clear, a dark blue line separating sea from sky. No clouds and no haze. A marvelous day.

The crewmen were awake and silent, sitting wrapped in their camel-hair blankets. Some were praying on their knees, looking at the bright splendor of the sun, and who can blame them for worshipping the sun god Ra, giver of life, warmth, and light? It seemed like the most natural thing to do. When your cup overflows with joy, do you thank your stars? Better to face your great god and offer your thanks for another marvelous day.

All the crewmen, those who prayed and those who didn't, were spellbound by the great red fireball rising out of the dark blue sea. As the sun rose higher, it changed color from bright red to a beautiful orange, then golden yellow, and finally dazzling white, so bright we could not look at it anymore. Only in a sea surrounded by dry desert land can you witness such a glorious sunrise.

Calmly and carefully, I lowered myself into the sea and swam to the most inviting beach I had ever seen, a perfect, clean-washed white-sand beach without a human footprint, untouched and unspoiled. For lack of fresh water, humans did not settle here. The seabirds and sand crabs would have this place to themselves till the end of time.

I walked to the far end of this beach and sat down in the shade of a large bush on a mound of soft, windblown sand. Day after day, the wind swirling through the branches of this bush deposited fine sand under the bush over its roots. This windblown sand under the plant absorbed the morning dewdrops like a sponge. As a result, the bush spread its roots into the pile of sand and grew bigger, capturing yet more sand from the passing wind, and so it got more moisture and survived in this dry land without rain. The fair wind gave it life. No wonder the fishermen call the wind by the same word that means *life*, *Al-Haya.*

Looking toward the end of the bay, I could see our beautiful fast ships, *Sword of the Sea* and the *Sorceress.* They, too, came alive because of the wind. If we were to smash them on a coral reef at night, we would be lost. There would be no other ship to save us. It was a wise decision to sail by day and rest at night. When sailing in a convoy with the fleet, if the leading ship runs aground on a reef, the following ships will save her crew. However, two fast ships sailing at night in a coral sea with a strong following wind will be in great danger of breaking up on a reef.

Walking back slowly toward the anchored ships, enjoying the silence and the marvelous natural beauty of this place, I promised myself that I would return here someday. Whenever we anchored, I would explore and walk by myself for an hour or two, enjoying the solitude; take a swim in the warm sea; and return to the ship refreshed, hungry, and ready for another day of sailing.

This early morning walk was just what I needed. Back on our ships, I found the crew doing military exercises. The possibility of being attacked by pirates was remote; however, we had to teach our crew, these sons of fishermen, how to use weapons to defend themselves and our ships. I felt a quick stab of pride when I saw Ari instructing the crew of the *Sorceress* in the proper use of sword and spear. On board our ship, *Sword of the Sea,* the instructor was Adoo. He pushed the crew hard for two hours every morning; however, after the exercises, he allowed them time to rest, swim, and other comforts that he denied himself. They loved him like an older brother. Nobody thought of Adoo as Galen's servant. He was our friend and brother.

The crewmen on both ships were rubbing their limbs with olive oil to get the stiffness out of their tired muscles. Then they all went into the sea for a swim. Some of the boys had fishing spears, and they returned with a large catch of fresh fish, mostly large groupers, which are easy to spear.

I was glad to see Galen and Mobareek enjoying a morning swim. Justin, too, was in the water. His leg was not completely healed, but he was beginning to walk normally again.

Before noon, masses of hot air rising from the desert forced the northwest wind to veer to the northeast. We raised sails and went out for another day of racing. Today it was our turn to take the lead, and Mobareek in the *Sorceress* would try to catch us.

Galen stood close to me on the afterdeck and said, "Hiro, try to keep the ships close to each other. You cannot appreciate the beauty of your sailing ship standing as you are on her deck. But when you are on another ship nearby, then you will see how beautiful and graceful she is."

Galen was right, of course, and I kept the two sailing ships close to each other. Mobareek noticed that I slowed down to let him come closer with the *Sorceress,* and whenever he passed us, he would slow down and *Sword of the Sea* would catch up with him. We sailed so close to each other that the crews could exchange jokes. It was a fine day with strong, steady wind, and we enjoyed ourselves immensely.

Che wanted to learn how to steer a large, fast sailing ship. I showed him how to tie a thin rope to the tiller and wrap it once around a stanchion on the weather side of the ship. With this twiddler line in his hand, the steersman can exert tremendous pressure on the tiller, which controls the huge rudder. Without this twiddler rope, it would be impossible to steer a fast ship in heavy weather. On the *Sorceress,* Mobareek was showing Ari how to steer, and when the ships came close, the boys Ari and Che would look at each other and laugh, a young and hearty laugh, which meant, "Look! See what I can do."

At the end of this exciting day, we entered another safe harbor on the coast. Every day we were a little closer to our destination, the great mountain known as Mount Elba. On the eleventh day we sighted Cape Berenice, named after a famous Egyptian queen. A square room built with white limestone and topped by a white dome was visible at the end of this cape on the windward side. Many long poles with flags of all colors stood near this room, planted in holes in the rock by mariners who wanted to warn ships running before the north wind to stay away from this dangerous cape. If a sailing ship was wrecked on the windward side of this peninsula, it would be easy for her crew to reach this dome. Inside the small room, they would find everything a shipwrecked sailor needs to survive—blankets of camel hair; drinking water, boiled and kept in glass bottles sealed with beeswax; fishing hooks and fishing lines; and an adze and knives. The food in such a cache would be grain and dried dates. A man could live here until rescued by a passing ship or until his drinking water ran out.

Every island has a cache on the windward side similar to this one but without the stone-built room. Instead you will find a windbreak built of large pieces of coral rock, fitted together without cement and shaped like a circle, with one opening facing the warm south wind. Ten men can sleep here, sheltered from the cold north wind. Any man who uses anything from such a cache has an obligation to replenish it the next time he stops there. The children are raised with a strong taboo, which keeps even the most mischievous from stealing anything from these emergency shelters.

We rounded Cape Berenice and dropped anchor in the calm water. That evening the crew gathered around Galen, and he told them the story of Queen Berenice and her golden hair. Many of these young men had never heard the story before.

Queen Berenice II was married to Ptolemy III.[43] To honor the return of her husband from war, Berenice cut her incomparable amber tresses and placed them on the altar in the temple of Aphrodite, goddess of beauty and love. Thus, Berenice gave the most beautiful thing she owned to Aphrodite and prayed for protection from all evil.

One day the king and queen found out that the tresses of hair had been stolen from the temple. On a clear night, an astronomer went to the king and queen, showed them a cluster of stars twinkling in the sky, convinced them that the goddess Aphrodite had taken the tresses for herself, and pointed up in the sky. Thus the astronomer calmed their anger. The Arabic name for this cluster of stars is *Al-Hizma* (the Sheaf of Grain), but now the whole world knows it as *Coma Berenices* (Berenice's Hair). The traveling bards and the storytellers spread the fame of the queen of Egypt and her golden tresses all over the civilized world. Mobareek said, "If you want to see the tresses of Berenice, choose a clear moonless night from the end of spring to the end of

---

[43] There is a good harbor on the Red Sea coast sheltered by *Ras-Banas*, known to this day as Port Berenice.

summer and look for the bright star named *Denebol-Assad* [Tail of the Lion]. Berenice's Hair is near it, to the north and a little to the east of this star."[44]

Everyone slept on deck, looking at the constellations moving slowly from east to west. The ships Mobareek built were much more comfortable than the ships in Alexandria. The decks were clean and open, unlike the cambered and cluttered decks of other ships. We had flat decks, sloping forward. Every man slept wrapped in his blanket with his feet toward the ship's prow, and because the deck was inclined, our feet were always lower than our heads, even when the ship pitched a little. Every sailor had a linen bag filled with his clean clothes. This was his pillow. The men of Yemen taught us to sprinkle perfume on our pillows to remind us of loved ones and to ensure pleasant dreams.

The next morning, I asked Galen and Adoo, "We should check the emergency cache. It might need replenishing with food and water."

Galen replied, "Ari and Che should also go with us to see what the place looks like."

We jumped into two long canoes and paddled to shore. The land was old coral rock, wrinkled and sharp like spearpoints (*haraba*). It was impossible for a man to walk barefoot here between these sharp points of coral and shallow pools filled with sea urchins. We paddled along till we found a small pebble beach and pulled our canoes up there. The higher ground was also made of ancient coral rock; however, the wind, blowing grains of sand, had smoothed it out. Here it was easy for us to walk with sandals on our feet.

The small room with the white dome was on the windward side a short distance away. When we reached it, we could see the remains of a once-proud ship at the fringe of the coral reef. Huge beams of wood that used to be the ribs of this lost ship were high and dry out of the water. Obviously, they had been pushed there by waves in a big storm. It was easy to imagine the fear and panic of her crew. If any lives were

---

[44] *Denebol-Assad is the* Arabic name for the bright star that marks the Tail of the Lion in the constellation Leo *(Denebol = tail of Assad = lion)*. On star charts, the name of this star is corrupted to simply *Denebola*. The constellation *Coma Berenices* is near Denebola.

saved, it was because of this shelter under the dome stocked with food and water.[45]

We entered the small room. We tasted the dried dates and the water. They were still good. Galen turned toward me and said, "Hiro, how long ago did the mariners in the Red Sea establish caches of food on all these islands?"

I replied, "Since the time of the pharaohs and their sailing fleets to the land of Pont."

Galen said, "I am amazed that a tradition can be maintained for so many centuries uninterrupted."

I said, "It is possible to keep traditions alive for a thousand years. Look at the religion of the Jews and the cult of Isis. The fishermen believe that the gods of the sea will punish any mariner who neglects to replenish these holy places of refuge. A religious taboo will be passed on from generation to generation."

We walked out of the small room, and Galen said to Ari and Che, "For the mariners, these stories about the gods of the sea are *true*; for the philosophers, they are *fanciful*; for the generals and the magistrates, they are *useful*. That is why we honor our gods."

---

[45] Many of the emergency shelters were well maintained until about 1960. Motorboats and radios ended the need for this useful tradition.

CHAPTER 12: Gebal Elba

We had been at sea twelve days. Before sunset, *Sword of the Sea* and the *Sorceress* would be safe inside the harbor of Shelateen, in full view of Gebal Elba, out of the land of Egypt in a place beyond the reach of the arms of Rome.

We anchored in the bay of Shelateen. We were in a land held and defended by fierce warriors, the *Bisharees.* Six of these wild men came aboard our ships to be certain that we were not enemies. Mobareek was well known to these warriors. He had stopped there for fresh water many times when voyaging in the Red Sea. The wells of Shelateen were not far from this anchorage. When the warriors saw Mobareek, their fierce expressions softened, and they gathered around him, greeting him warmly. He invited them to join us for our evening meal. They accepted, but two of them insisted they must go up into the hills to report to their tribal leaders that we were friends. These people were always vigilant. It was impossible to approach their mountain by sea or through the desert without being seen by their scouts. No enemy could surprise them, and they had kept their freedom through the ages. The pharaohs of Egypt could not enslave them, the Romans and Greeks failed to conquer them, and slave traders did not dare attack them.[46]

The next morning we followed four warriors up into the steep hills to visit their chief. Justin and Marcus stayed behind with the crew. We were a small group: Mobareek, Galen, Adoo, Ari, Che, and I. The warriors were walking at a fast pace, and only Adoo could keep up with them.

Soon they noticed that we lagged behind, and they slowed down and waited for us to catch up. Adoo, being a great tracker, noticed that their feet were shorter and had a higher arch than most people's. Galen

---

[46] The bravery of the Bisharin in fighting against the British was saluted by Rudyard Kipling in his poem "Fuzzy-Wuzzy," a name the British gave these warriors because of their hair.

remarked on their tall, well-muscled bodies and their black, fuzzy hair, which formed a large ball over their heads, effectively keeping them cool in the hot sun. Their dark brown backs glistened with oil. Each man had a long, straight Greek sword slung over his shoulder. They preferred these weapons to the curved swords of India. They each held in their hands two spears—a short one, not meant for throwing, and a longer spear.

As we walked uphill, Mobareek told us that he knew these people well because he had spent some time among them when he was a young man. "Their warriors," he said, "are not trained to fight like soldiers. They are hunters who know every cave and every water hole in their mountain and the hills around it. When attacked by a foreign army, they melt away into the gorges and canyons; then they return to attack their enemies at night."

Our guides were listening to Mobareek as he told us about their courage and prowess in war. When he finished, one of them, as if to reinforce the impression we had, sang a war song for us. His style was not really singing but more like declamatory recitation:

I will build my fires in a cave at night.
You will not see the smoke or the light.
My voice will join the lion's roar,
And you will lose your sleep and your might.

We followed our guides uphill for three hours. At last we reached their chief's tent and found it surrounded by a large circular *zariba* (a hedge made of dead thorny bushes to keep the animals out). I followed Mobareek into the tent, Galen by my side and Adoo behind us. It was a large tent supported by many poles. Some weapons were hanging on these poles—spears with polished, shining points; Greek straight swords; and whips of hippopotamus hide. Carpets and animal skins covered the floor. The atmosphere was one of masculine comfort.

Their chief rose to greet Mobareek, his old friend. He was a tall, lean, muscular man, over sixty years old. He looked like a born leader of men and radiated massive dignity. He wore nothing but a clean, white shirt and sandals made of leopard skin on his feet. He had no flowing robes, no gold chain, and he needed none.

The chief welcomed Mobareek formally according to their time-honored traditions; then he relaxed and sat down. Now it was Mobareek's turn to speak. He introduced us to the chief. The man looked at Galen as if to take his measure; then he said, "Hakeem [physician], I have a sick child, my granddaughter. Will you try to cure her?"

Galen, nodding his head, replied, "Bring her here to me."

The chief said, "Follow me. Women and children are not allowed in this tent." He took Galen by the arm, and we followed them outside into the sunlight.

The chief called for his daughter and her child. Someone ran to the women's tents to bring the girl. The daughter came walking toward her father. She was a beautiful woman, not yet twenty years old. A green transparent veil covered her head and also covered the little girl cradled in her arms. The daughter sat down, and I saw silent tears wetting her cheeks. The young mother showed her child to Galen, pointing at her ears. The little girl looked very vulnerable. She had had no food or sleep for two days, her voice was gone, and she was too tired to cry. We all felt for the young mother. Her little girl was sinking fast out of the realm of the living.

Galen ordered in his commanding voice, "Get me a mirror, quick!"

Mobareek said, "There are no mirrors here."

Galen turned to Adoo. "Get me a shining spearhead."

Adoo ran into the tent and returned with a broad new spearhead. The child was lying in her mother's lap. Galen made the mother hold her girl's earlobe. Then with his left hand, he pulled the ear open. In his right hand, he held the shining spearhead and used it to reflect a ray of sunlight deep into the ear. Then he told Adoo, "Get two sharp thorns." Adoo walked to the zariba and returned with the sharp thorns. He handed them to Galen.

Out of the little girl's ear Galen pulled a maggot[47] impaled on a thorn and gave it to the young mother. I saw hope shine suddenly in her sad, doe-like eyes. With the second thorn, Galen pulled out another

---

[47] These live maggots are from the eggs of the *Oesterus ovis* fly.

live maggot and gave it to the chief. The old man, relieved, raised his hand and caressed his daughter's head with a gesture that said much. A gentle smile lit up the young mother's face. It was one of the most marvelous and satisfying cures that Galen had ever achieved, a sudden magical change from despair and pain to hope and life.

The chief, his weathered features radiating benevolence, took Galen by the arm and led us back inside his tent. Then he said, "The gods send good men to our land." That was his way of saying thanks.

Galen told the chief, "If you see these maggots in a child's ear, try to pull them out. If you fail, boil some water and dissolve as much salt as you can into it. When it cools down, fill the child's ear with this salty water. It will kill the worms."

I walked out of the tent. Several old women were gathered around the chief's daughter. She smiled at me, and I could see how she loved her child with a strong, protective passion. Her beautiful young face was now alight with pride and affection as her little girl slept in her arms.

Adoo walked back into the tent and told the chief, "Your granddaughter stopped crying, and she is in deep sleep. When she wakes up, she will eat, and her health will be restored." After a moment of silence, he asked, "Is this little girl your favorite?"

The chief smiled and replied, "My favorite is the sick child until she is healed, the absent child until he returns, and the youngest until he grows."

The following day, we walked to the coast. The chief came with us halfway down the mountain. I was surprised at the large number of gazelles, ostriches, ibex, and other wildlife. I asked the chief, "Why is wildlife so abundant here?"

He said, "All these herds of gazelles and ibex are our food reserves. We hunt only in times of severe drought. If we have three years without rain, we sell our herds of camels in the Nile Valley. The gazelles are hardy, and they can survive on the leaves and flowers of the seyal trees, which have very deep roots and can survive three years of drought."

Mobareek remarked, "The people here never cut the trees to make charcoal. They depend on dry camel dung and dead bushes for their fires. See how dense the old trees are in the wadi?"

The chief told us, "We teach our children to despise three kinds of men: *Kata-Al-Shagar*, the man who cuts trees to make charcoal; *Baya-Al-Ba_shar*, the man who sells humans as slaves; and *Nahat-Al-Hagar*, the man who cuts and shapes rock."

I asked Mobareek, "Why shun the hewer of stone?"

He said, "These warriors saw the prisoners in the stone quarries of Egypt, and they despise them for accepting a life worse than death."

On our way to the sea, we passed by many small villages, encampments really, because there were no huts or stone structures, only large tents. The women's tents were pitched close to each other in a large circle surrounded by a hedge of thornbushes to keep the children in and the goats out. The men's tents were at a small distance away from their wives. Every man chose the campsite he liked best. The camp would be moved in the rainy season when thunderstorms fill the wadis with flash floods.

When we approached the sea, the chief stopped, put his hands on Galen's shoulders, and thanked him with great dignity. Then he held Mobareek's hands and told him, "I know you love the sea, but I want to live in the hills. When you are an old man, come back and live with us." Then he turned around, followed by his warrior, and walked back up the mountain.[48]

At night, sitting on the deck of the *Sorceress* and listening to Atiya playing his marvelous music, I noticed some high clouds gathering and the wind veering to the south. I told Mobareek, "The wind is changing."

He replied, "Yes, I expect a few days of calm. We will be stranded here until the north wind returns." Before going to sleep, he said, "Tomorrow I will show you the village where the divers collect the

---

[48] "Who hath desired the Sea? . . . His Sea that his being fulfils? So, and no otherwise—hillmen desire their hills."— "The Sea and the Hills," by Rudyard Kipling.

money shells. They trade the seashells with the tribes in the African interior for ivory and then sell the ivory in Egypt to buy weapons."[49]

The divers' village was about three miles down the coast, built on a small inlet and surrounded by numerous coral heads and coral reefs in shallow water. Since the sea was calm, we visited the village with three large canoes, five men in each. We reached this small village in less than a half hour. Young men who chose to be divers lived here three months every year with their young wives and children. In the fall, after the excessive heat of summer, they came down from the heights of their cool mountain. They found the seawater very warm, for the sun beat down on it all summer, and the air temperature was tolerably cool.

We hauled our canoes up on a sandy beach. Mobareek gathered the young men around him and ordered them not to stare at the women when walking through this village. That would be extremely bad manners and offensive to their husbands. We saw many beautiful girls in this village. They were allowed to stare at us. The women had nut-brown skin with blue tattoos on their lips and hands. They wore transparent veils, which they drew over their mouths and noses, but left their curious, luminous eyes visible. These veils protected their soft skin from sun and wind, and they also used them to protect their babies' eyes from flies.

One of the local young divers greeted Mobareek, then guided us to a large man-made pool about thirty paces across, built in the sea with coral rocks fitted on top of each other without cement. The sea flowed through into the shallow pool. The bottom was of clean sand. Twenty children or more were playing and splashing inside this pool. Their source of delight was a huge but harmless shark, a nine-foot *frinka*[50] with a broad head and very long tail fin, whitish stripes on his dark back. The children were riding on the shark's back, screaming with delight, while this huge fish swam leisurely around the pool.

Our guide explained, "We keep the very young children out of the sea because venomous fish and stingrays roam the shallow water. We

---

[49] The cowrie shells were used in some parts of the ancient world as money.

[50] *Frinka* is the local name for the harmless nurse shark, which is common in the Red Sea.

built this pool for them to play in. Here they learn how to swim, and they get used to the big shark. When they start diving in the sea, the dangerous sharks will not cause them to panic."

Late in the afternoon, we witnessed an amazing dance. All of the children were sitting in a large circle on the clean sandy beach. The adults sat behind them, and in the center of the circle there was a large venomous stonefish, dead, sun-dried, and filled with sand. Four stingrays, also sun-dried, surrounded the stonefish. The fishermen call the stingray *SayFan*, which means two daggers, because it had two barbs at the base of the tail covered with venomous mucus, which could inflict very painful wounds.

Suddenly, a young man jumped over the heads of the spectators into the ring. He sang a song warning the children of the evil stonefish and bad stingrays. The dancer in the ring carefully avoided the stingrays, stepping around them, pretending he was wading in the sea. Then, as if by mistake, he stepped on the stonefish! His cries of pain and his screams of terror were truly frightening. He rolled on the sand, writhing with imaginary pain. I am sure this left an indelible impression on the children. The songs and the dance entertained and educated them at the same time, and that is as it should be.

CHAPTER 13: Korna, Korna

The next morning, Mobareek taught our crew how to make a stable raft from three canoes. The canoes were held together by the strong arms of the crewmen. Those sitting in the middle canoe grabbed with two hands the outside canoes and held the three boats fast, touching each other. The men in the outside canoes grabbed the central canoe by the gunnels and pulled hard to keep the three boats touching. This way, they made a stable raft for divers to jump in and out of the sea without capsizing the canoes. As soon as we learned this maneuver, we followed the divers to the reefs and lagoons, where they collected the money cowries and the pearl shells.

It was their established custom to dive in the shallow lagoons in the mornings and go to deeper water in the afternoon to prepare their lungs and hearts slowly for the exertion of deep diving. Another reason was their firm belief that large, dangerous sharks go down to colder, deeper water to rest at midday. One diver told me, "Midday, when the sun is high in the sky, you can go to the most dangerous reef and you will not see any sharks, I mean the big ones that can eat you alive. But go there at sunset and they will be all around you as soon as you spear one fish."

The canoes, about thirty of them, were drifting, caused by a weak surface current, and in every canoe, one man kept his eyes peeled for danger and with a paddle held his canoe as near the divers as he could. Every now and then, the divers would come back to him and throw their valuable shells into the canoe. There was nothing in these canoes except fishing spears, drinking water, and some sweet dried dates. We joined the young divers in the water, enjoying the endless variations of shapes and colors around the coral reefs.

The older men stayed in their canoes, the younger boys were collecting seashells, and the best divers were spearing large fish for food.Every man wore goggles made of hardwood carved to fit his eyes, and the glass was the finest available from Alexandria. Their spears were about the height of a man with a sharp point, barbed to keep the fish from slipping away. In every canoe there were a few stones. When the hunter saw a large fish near the bottom, he would take a stone from his canoe and hold it in his left hand; then he would fill his lungs to capacity and let the stone pull him down. Before hitting the bottom, he would let go of the stone and aim his spear at the large *taween* (grouper), always trying to hit the brain and immobilize the big, powerful fish. If he missed the brain, the experienced hunter would quickly grab the fish by its eyes, pressing as hard as he could with his thumb and middle finger. The pressure would immediately stop the movement of the fish. These people knew from long experience that if a large fish is allowed to struggle on the spear, the vibrations it sends through the water will attract big sharks, and the shark dashing in to take the fish sometimes hits the man by mistake.

I noticed Atiya trying his luck with a fishing spear, but he did not have the experience and training of the local divers. He was surrounded by many canoes, and I thought he was safe. I swam back to our canoe and urged the crew to get closer to Atiya and stay near him.

A young man stood up in his canoe, shaded his eyes with his hands, and looked intently at something in the sea, something the rest of us could not see. Then I was surprised to hear him shouting at the top of his voice, "*Korna, korna, korna!*"[51]

The other men in their canoes repeated the alarm, "*Korna, korna!*" Most of the divers in the sea heard it, and they swam back to their canoes with deliberate fluid strokes, without hurry. They knew that splashing might attract the big shark. While swimming back to safety, these men kept their faces down in the water and made a loud rumbling noise from their chests, which sounded like *home, home, home*. The sound traveled fast underwater and warned all the divers of danger at sea. The men heaved themselves into their canoes as silently as they could, and I saw every three canoes forming a raft held tightly together by the strength of the men inside them. Our crew did the

---

[51] *Korna* or *gorna* is the large, solitary hammerhead shark *(Sphyrna mokarran)*. *Mokarran* in Arabic means "with horns." *Garn* or *karn* means "horn." The small hammerhead sharks, which swim in schools, are harmless. However, the large, solitary karna, found in the Red Sea, is very dangerous.

same. We sat in a stable raft, watching the great hammerhead shark swimming near the surface.

There was no fear and no panic. All our eyes were on Atiya. He was swimming fast to safety, kicking hard and splashing with his arms, unable to control his fear.

Mobareek, Atiya's father, was shouting, "Slow down, Atiya! Calm down!"

Two young men stood up with spears in their hands, ready to strike the shark, but it was useless. Atiya grabbed the canoe with his two hands, and his father took both his sons' wrists in his powerful grip. As he pulled the boy out of the water, the korna struck. The shark had the boy's leg in his belly and the teeth closed above the knee. The korna was jerking its head from side to side, and the giant Mobareek could not hold against the weight and pull off the monstrous shark.

Without hesitation, Mobareek let himself be pulled into the sea with his son. Father and son were underwater, the shark pulling them both down. On the surface, a circle of blood enlarged itself rapidly. Through this red circle, Mobareek rose up holding his son by his hair, lifting his head high in the air. With his free arm, he grabbed the canoe. Adoo leaned over and took hold of Atiya under his armpits, and with one powerful heave, he pulled the boy into the canoe. He was alive and breathing, but he had lost one leg, cut above the knee. The crew held the three boats stable like a raft, and Mobareek heaved his great body out of the sea, then stood up behind me, his hands on my shoulders to steady himself. I held tightly to the gunnels. Mobareek looked around for the shark; then he said, "Korna will not return." True enough, the huge shark did not come back for a second attack. I wonder what went on in its small brain. Did the korna think Mobareek was another predator trying to share his prey?

Adoo stopped the bleeding with a tourniquet around the leg. We headed straight back to our ships, and in less than a half hour we were on board the *Sorceress*. Galen did his best to ease Atiya's pain. His father showed his outward sadness, but how much greater was his inner grief.

As I write the story of Atiya fifteen years after he lost his leg, he is a famous musician in Alexandria. Surrounded by many friends who love him, he can make them rise and dance with his happy music, and he can make them pensive and tearful with his sad songs. And if he so chooses, he can soothe them and put them to sleep with his simsimiyya. After the shark took Atiya's leg, he spent more time with his musical instruments. He devoted all the energy of his soul to perfecting new songs and melodies. Had he remained whole, I doubt he would be so great a musician today.

Early the next morning, some divers came to our ships to inquire about Atiya. They presented him with a gift, a sackful of cowrie shells. They were generous and kind people, and I could see they were happy that Atiya was alive. The young men sat around him in a circle and told him how they planned to catch the big shark.

"We will kill this korna that took your leg even if it takes a whole month," said one of them. Another young man sitting next to Atiya looked at him intently and said in a loud voice so all of the crew could hear, "This shark's teeth and brute strength will be no match for our cleverness. We shall have a long, stout rope stretched between two coral heads in the same spot where the korna attacked you. Many canoes will be securely tied to this rope, and under every canoe we will dangle a chain with a large iron hook, and every day I will bait these hooks myself." He looked up to the sky and raised both hands high. "This I promise before everyone here: I will put big fish and large eels on these hooks, and small sharks too." The man stood up and shook his spear, all his muscles tightening with his mounting excitement. He looked into Atiya's eyes and said, "I can see your soul thirsting for revenge. One day soon the korna will be caught on a hook, and before he can break loose, I myself, and no other man, will jump into the sea with this spear in my hand. I will thrust it into his gills on one side and out the other side, like this! Like this!! Like this!!!" He made violent thrusting motions with his spear. His voice hoarse with excitement, he then said, "Atiya, you shall have your revenge. You will find it sweeter than honey."

Atiya smiled for the first time since the shark had taken his leg. His big grin returned to his face, his funny, ugly, lovable face. We all felt better, knowing and hoping that this monstrous korna would not live to attack another boy.

CHAPTER 14: Bab-El-Mandeb

Mobareek increased our sailing time to fourteen hours a day, but we anchored every night. There were too many reefs and islets—too many dangers—for night sailing. We were headed for the famous strait, or gate, that connects the Red Sea with the Ocean of India, a narrow strait about fifteen miles wide, known to mariners as *Bab-el-Mandeb*,[52] or the Straits of Tears and Lamentations. Here, the Horn of Africa and Arabia Felix are only fifteen miles apart. In this narrow body of water, large sailing dhows bring young African boys and girls to be sold as slaves in Yemen. The winter caravans take them north to be sold all over the east and in the Roman Empire. In the straits lies a small island near the coast of Yemen called Mayoon.

Galen urged Mobareek to reach Mayoon as fast as he could. He hoped to find there a trader who supplied all Africa with opium, which Galen was near to running out of in his medicine chest. We drove the *Sorceress* and *Sword of the Sea* as fast as they could go, and we all prayed for a stronger north wind. Mobareek gave a demonstration of superb sailing and reached Mayoon in three days.

We landed in a fine natural anchorage and walked over to a large stone house. There were no black boys or girls to be seen anywhere. I asked Mobareek, who knew this island from previous visits, "Where are the slaves?"

He replied, "They are free to roam the island all day long unrestrained. At sunset, hunger brings them back here, where they are fed the only meal of the day. The opium business has been good. This trader always has an abundance of ivory and slaves."

Galen, walking with us, asked, "Is it true that this trader has three hundred and sixty-five concubines, one for every night of the year?"

---

[52] *Bab* means "gate"; *Mandeb* means "lamentations." This passage is known as the Mandeb Strait.

Mobareek laughed. "No, but I am sure he is the one who started that rumor. As you see, there is only one stone house on the island. The young slaves sleep on the beach in the open air and bathe in the sea. They are deliberately kept naked and hungry."

We were ushered into the stone house by the guards, and the trader walked into the room. I was repulsed by his appearance: short and shriveled, with a nose like a monkey-eating eagle. He sold Galen all of the opium that the physician needed, and I watched the trader's ugly face as he counted the gold coins. The idea of a smile ever moving over his lips was unthinkable.

Late in the afternoon, from the deck of our ship, we could see the slave boys and girls coming slowly toward the stone house. They sat in the shade of palm fronds, hunger eating at their insides and sorrow gnawing at their young souls. Their numbers grew as time went by. They sat patiently waiting for food.

A large, beautiful dhow sailed into the anchorage, and a couple of sailors went to the stone house to alert the trader. Mobareek looked at this scene and said, "Hiro, come down on the beach and watch what will happen next. I am sure you have never seen anything like this."

I went down to the beach with Che, Ari, and Justin strolling by my side. We walked slowly toward the Arabian dhow. It was a wide, stable ship, built for carrying cargo. On deck I could see her captain, a dignified Arabian sheikh, wearing a white cloak with gold thread all around the edges and a dagger with a golden handle in his belt. His headgear was of the finest Chinese silk, with gold braided rope holding it in place. He just stood there surveying the scene. The slaves were gathering around huge pots of steaming hot food, and the men serving them forced them to sit in one long line on the sandy beach while they ate their meal, which was quickly finished.

The ugly trader came out of his house and walked toward the sailing dhow. His helpers forced all the black boys and girls to their knees, and they remained kneeling. The Arabian chief came down from the bow, flanked by two gigantic black bodyguards. He walked slowly toward the slave trader. There was complete silence. All eyes were on him. The slave trader fell down to his knees, and the Arabian sheikh slapped him across his ugly face once. Then he inspected the slaves. Whenever he saw a boy or girl in good health, he gently rubbed his or her head with his left hand and looked into the child's eyes to judge his or her intelligence. The sheikh's two bodyguards would gently raise the child to his or her feet and make him or her follow them. Soon they had a long line of black boys and a few girls walking behind them, and they slowly led them aboard the sailing dhow.

Mobareek shook his head and said, "Did you see that, Hiro? Now the slaves will be given the sweetest dates of Arabia and clean spring water to drink. They will be clothed in clean shirts and taught how to wear a headcloth to protect their eyes from the sun." He paused awhile, then said, "To us, this was acting—a transparent charade, all pretense but to the young Africans. This great sheikh was their deliverer, and they will be loyal to him. Like his own sons, they will fight for him and defend his herds of camels and his valuable horses, and they will guard him and his wealth from all enemies."

Between the island of Mayoon and the coast of Africa, the distance is less than fifteen miles. Early morning before sunrise, we left this island, and after two hours we entered a natural anchorage on the African coast with the sun behind us, which made it easy to avoid the many coral heads blocking the entrance to this harbor. The natives called it *Argeego*. The only reason we were stopping there before entering the Ocean of India was to buy long spars for our ships. From this harbor, the land rises to a high, cool, green plateau. A black tribe lives there, and they never come down to the coast, but if we took the trouble to climb all the way up to their land, they would gladly sell us any spars or booms we wanted, and they are happy to take money cowries in exchange for the fine wood.

It was a long, hard climb to the high plateau four thousand feet above the sea. I had with me Adoo and fifteen crewmen armed with swords. Sixteen men could easily carry two fifty-foot long spars down the hills back to our ships. We needed these in case we broke one or two in a storm. Before sunset, we found ourselves on the high, flat plateau. This was the land of the black *Ethiopes*. I was struck by the appearance of this tribe. They were tall, handsome people, well proportioned with fine straight noses, good teeth, and remarkably large eyes. I had never seen this tribe before today, but of course, I had seen paintings. I had always believed their extraordinarily large eyes were an exaggeration by the artist. Not so. They really are handsome people. Some of their men look like Greek gods made of ebony.

None of us could speak their language, but when we offered them money cowries, they understood that we wanted something in exchange. Adoo took one of them by the hand and led him to a tall, straight tree. Adoo touched the tree, then gave the Ethiopian a sackful of cowrie shells. The man exclaimed in a loud voice, *"Saroo, saroo,"* and led us to a large shed where hundreds of tree trunks were stacked to dry. I realized that it would take many hours to select two fine spars without defects.

That same night, we slept in the wood storage shed. The next day, after we found two perfect trees as thick as a man's leg at the base and tapering to a thickness of a boy's wrist at the end, flexible and strong, we gave the Ethiopes another sack of cowries. They were surprised and obviously pleased. They offered us food and with gestures made us understand that we should sleep another night here to see wrestling contests and a tribal dance. The young unwed women would choose their mates from the crowd of young men, who would wrestle each other tonight.

A whole month had passed since we had left Alexandria. This was the night of the full moon, a magical African night with a clear sky and cool air scented with smoke from many small fires burning in a large ring. The smoke kept all bloodthirsty biting insects away. Inside this ring of light, young wrestlers sat down in a circle, their naked bodies covered with grey ash and their faces decorated with colorful designs. Each man improvised his own pattern; no two were alike. We joined the spectators inside this ring of fires. The Ethiopes offered us a warm, strong wine. I ordered the crew not to drink, and they obeyed. Adoo, however, drank this fruity wine and liked it and, every time he was offered more, he accepted until the wine flowed richly in his veins.

The wrestling was a good show. The young men would try to intimidate their opponent before the fight with roaring sounds like angry African lions, and when they clashed, whoever fell to the ground first was defeated and had to return to his place.

117

I watched Adoo standing with his feet wide apart, shifting his body weight from one leg to the other. He was watching the wrestlers with fierce concentration. I thought, *He will join, and there is no harm in that.* The wrestling matches were a friendly competition to test a young man's speed and strength. Wrestling was popular in Egypt since the time of the pyramid builders. There are many wrestling scenes decorating the ancient tombs and temples.

After many exciting bouts, the winner stood proudly in the center of the ring. Adoo was well trained in the Greco-Roman style of wrestling, which he had learned in Alexandria. He leaped over the heads of the spectators and challenged the young man with gestures to a friendly match, all the time flashing his boyish, happy smile.

When they gripped each other, Adoo's superior speed and strength gave him an easy victory. The young wrestler was surprised and astonished. Every time he fell down, Adoo would raise him up to his feet, never pressing him to the ground; he was careful not to humiliate the Ethiopian champion. All he wanted was a good wrestling bout, and the young wrestlers cheered him, laughing out loud and clapping their hands in a good-natured, friendly way.

After the wrestling, a dozen drummers walked into the ring of light with a variety of drums of different sizes and shapes. They started playing an insistent, hypnotic rhythm, complicated but unvarying. The wrestlers began swaying from side to side and chanting softly. We could not understand a word. Adoo, however, sat among them and joined them, singing and vocalizing, "*Ho, ho, ho, haaa.*"

After some time, a few men were in a trance-like condition, and they would jump up and dance, reveling in unlimited energy, and one by one they approached the musicians and threaten`led them with clenched fists and loud, angry shouts. They wanted madder music and stronger wine. Some men foamed at the mouth. They were affected more than the others, and they continued their mad dancing until one by one they fell to the ground with their arms and legs outstretched and rigid like wood. Immediately, one of the dancer's friends would sit on his chest to pin him to the ground, and others would forcefully bend his arms at the elbows and by force bend his legs at the knee. When these dancers came out of their trance, they would sit near the drummers, some crying uncontrollably, their tears flowing like children.

I had never seen anything like this before, and I am not ashamed to admit that I felt the effects of this mad music. A feeling of great energy and tension started low in my leg muscles and moved higher up to the larger muscles above my knees. I surrendered to this tension and jumped up and danced with the men, luxuriating in a feeling of great energy. Finally exhaustion set in, and all the wrestlers were back in their places. The sweat that flowed down their lithe, muscular bodies washed away the ashes that covered them before the dance. Now they were like statues of shining black ebony.

These young men watched in silence as forty or more young girls entered the ring of light and performed a graceful athletic dance. Each girl held in her hands a long, thin, flexible cane. The drummers beat a faster rhythm. Faster and faster they danced, and to banish fatigue, the dancing girls struck each other with their canes on their bare skin. The girls were dancing nearly nude, their only covering a layer of reddish-colored oil and a belt of large fertility cowries. They also wore wrist and ankle bracelets of small seashells and on their heads a crown of sweet-scented flowers.

This dance went on at an impossible pace, the girls striking each other with their canes and screaming with feigned pain, "*Hayee, hayee, hayee!*" Writhing and whirling in the moonlight, they were magical creatures from another world. Their cries of pain were like cries of sexual ecstasy, and the effect this mad dance produced on the men was palpable amid mounting excitement.

Suddenly the music stopped and the girls sat down to rest, forming a ring around the drummers, swaying from side to side with a new and slower rhythm. One by one the girls rose to their feet and danced alone, a slow and sinuous dance. The wrestlers clapped their hands and chanted the dancer's name. Near the end of her dance, each girl picked one of the men and approached him slowly. When she was so close to him he could touch her, she lifted her right leg and let her thigh rest on his left shoulder. This was a signal to her tribe that she had found her mate. Her chosen man lifted her in his arms and walked slowly into the darkness toward the huts.

One by one the girls danced their slow, sensuous dance, and every single girl found a young man eager to pick her up and walk away with his prize. The last girl to dance was the prettiest of all. She had a smile of rare sweetness in a beautiful young face not more than sixteen years old. The men chanted her name, "*Seenara, Seenara, Seenara,*" and all our crew joined in, carried away by their excitement. They called her name over and over again, "*Seenara, Seenara!*" The beautiful young woman danced in the moonlight, adding magic to this African night.

Adoo rose to his full height and looked up at the moon. He put his hands on his ears and sang out, "Oh, Seenara, ah, Seenara, this night is thine, and tonight you will be mine."

The girl could not understand his words, but his voice was enough. Her sinuous dance brought her closer and closer to Adoo. When she was near him, he sat down, drinking her beauty through his eyes. She bent her torso backward, her head almost touching the ground, her young, firm breasts pointing at the full moon. Then she stood up in front of Adoo, her oiled skin shining, her eyes brilliant, and without shame rested her thigh on Adoo's shoulder. The wine was flowing richly in his veins. The full moon and the maddening dance loosened his reins. Seenara was in his powerful arms. He carried her through the ring of small fires, and she showed him the way to her hut.

They say the gods will pair like with like. Does the full moon have anything to do with this, I wonder?

I drifted into restful sleep, wrapped in a mantle of unreality, the pretty faces of the dancing girls surrounding me in my dreams.

Before long, loud screams jerked me brutally out of my sleep. The young men of our crew were on their feet, every man with a sword in hand and grim determination on his face. Every hut in the village was on fire. This must be an attack by enemies or slavers. These cursed devils chose the right time, when the men were drunk and tired. I ordered the crew, "Stay together. Check every hut. We must find Adoo." We ran the short distance to the village, yelling out loud for Adoo, but we never found him. If he was still here in these burning huts, he would have heard us and come to us.

After checking every hut, we walked slowly through this unhappy village. The sobbing and wailing of the old women told us an eloquent story of pain and suffering. This must have happened before, the slavers attacking the village at night and kidnapping the children. We never got a glimpse of those devils. They must have done their work quickly and disappeared into the jungle.

A great wave of anger and shame crashed over me. How could I have been so careless? How could I let Adoo go to the village drunk and unguarded? In my heart I knew there was no way of stopping him. We searched till the sun was up over the horizon, then ran down the hills back to the coast, our valuable spears forgotten, our lungs burning because of the smoke and the exertion of the run. I kept telling myself, *We have to get to the ships as fast as we can. Mobareek and Galen will know what to do.*

When Mobareek heard my story, the lines on his face hardened, and there were flashes of anger in his dark eyes. He did not say a word. Galen listened to me with an expression on his face that I had seen many times, intense concentration and fast thinking. He said, "We cannot go to every slave market, but we can intercept the ships crossing the straits from Africa to Arabia."

Mobareek gave the orders to sail. His whole demeanor bespoke calm power. The crew was excited and agitated, and they sprang to their tasks. Mobareek looked at me and said with assurance in his voice, "Hiro, keep *Sword of the Sea* close to the *Sorceress.* If we see a sail crossing from Africa to Arabia, chase her. If she is carrying slaves, signal to me and I will follow you with the *Sorceress.*"

We patrolled the Strait of Bab-el-Mandab all day long. I kept a man at the masthead scanning the African coastline. Every hour he came down and another man climbed up to relieve him. Only six ships—slow, large dhows—left the African coast. This day we stopped and inspected every one of them.They were carrying wood, charcoal, skins, and live sheep—no slaves. At night we drifted in the straits, and the full moon was so bright, it would have been easy for us to see a sail if any ship tried a night crossing. However, we knew that none of the traders would cross at night for fear of the coral reefs and rocks near the Arabian coast. But we still kept the lookouts at the mastheads.

All night I was beset by fears; not irrational fears, but the sickening thought that tomorrow at sunrise, many ships might depart the African coast, and we could fail to catch and inspect every one of them. What if we saw five or six sailing dhows headed for Arabia at the same time? I knew they could make the crossing in four hours. Our ships were twice as fast, but could we stop every one? I didn't think so, slow as they might be. For us to run from one end of the straits to the other would take time, and some of the slave traders would slip through.

At sunrise my worst fears were realized. The lookout at the masthead sang out, "Six sails—two to the south, four to the north." I saw the *Sorceress* rushing at top speed to the south. I had no doubt that Mobareek would catch these two traders and inspect them.

As we rushed to the north, chasing after the four sails, I kept telling myself, *There must be a way to stop them. There must be some trick that will make them stop.* Then the idea came to me in a blinding flash. Instead of chasing after the ships, I sailed for the Arabian coast to position *Sword of the Sea* between the traders and land. In less than two hours, we were sailing fast between these four ships and the land of Arabia. Now was the time to try to stop them.

I ordered the crew to start a fire on deck. Soon we had a big fire blazing in a huge pot full of sand. The wind spilling out of our sail fanned the flames. I shouted to the crew, "Boys, bring all your old clothes, soak them in oil, and throw them on the flames! Now, down with the sail!" The sail came down, and at the same time a huge column of black smoke rose to the sky. Every mariner would come to the rescue of a ship on fire without hesitation. Without asking your name or religion, they would be at your side. More cloth soaked in oil was thrown on the fire, and the black smoke was like a cloud hanging over our ship. The crew saw the four sailing ships coming toward us, and a great triumphant shout filled the air. The boys were so excited, they were jumping up and down on deck, clapping their hands. I shouted so they could hear me above the din. "Get your swords, bring the grappling hooks, and pretend you are scared! I want to hear some wailing!"

The four trading ships were close to us, coming to the rescue. We doused our fire and raised sail. *Sword of the Sea* raced toward them.

Galen was smiling, and he said, "Can you imagine what is going through their heads now?!"

We passed close to the first ship. She was loaded with lumber. Her astonished crew was shouting at us. We paid no attention and raced to the second ship. She was loaded with sacks, probably full of salt. The third ship was very close to us, and when we came alongside, we looked down into her. She was crowded with slaves.

Every man on deck was shouting Adoo's name. A thundering roar came from the slave ship, and there was Adoo on his feet, shouting at the top of his voice. Our crew swiftly brought the slave ship alongside with grappling hooks. Adoo burst through the crowd, and with one great leap, he was on deck. He rushed toward me and said, "Your knife, Hiro! Your sharp knife!" He extended his two hands toward me, and I cut the rope that bound them at the wrists. Galen stepped forward and hugged Adoo like a long-lost son.

Adoo jumped back into the slave ship and lifted up Seenara. Both Che and Ari reached down and held her by her forearms, then gently pulled her onto our ship. The poor girl was frightened. From one ship to another, surrounded by all these men with swords in their hands, everything that she saw was strange. She sat down on deck, tears streaming down her face. Adoo knelt down by Seenara and took her head in his hands. He kissed her forehead; then he spoke softly. Did she understand his words? I don't think so, but she understood the sweetness and kindness in his voice. She looked around her at all the smiling faces of the crew, and she calmed down.

Adoo walked over to me and said, "Hiro, can we take all these boys and girls back to Africa?"

I said, "To please Seenara, we will take them back. Here comes *Sword of the Sea*. Mobareek will be happy to see you, and we can carry all of these children in our two ships."

Mobareek came alongside and shouted, "What was all that smoke?" The crew explained our trick to Mobareek, all of them talking at the same time. He threw his head back and gave a great and hearty laugh. Then he sang out, "Adoo, who is this fine young beauty next to you?"

Adoo put his arm around her shoulders and said, "She is my wife, Mobareek. I found her in Ethiopia."

We embarked the black boys and girls onto our ships. The captain and crew of the slave ship were unarmed and shaking with fear. They were sure death was near. Galen, because of his innate kindness, went down into their ship and told the captain, "Do not fear us. We will not hurt you." Galen surprised everyone by giving the frightened man a few pieces of gold. The slave ship drifted away from us, and we headed for the African coast, carrying all of the slaves with us.

Che asked Galen, "Why did you give them coins?"

Galen replied, "They are poor people. To their simple minds, they were not doing anything evil. They transport salt or slaves, any cargo they can find. They will have a hard time explaining how they lost this cargo to pirates. Fortunately for them, three other ships witnessed the fire on our ship."

Che said, "I grew up surrounded by servants and slaves. I never thought about it until today when I looked down into their ship and saw our dear friend Adoo tied up. It hit me like a blow in the face. It could happen to any of us. One lost battle, and we would become the slave ship's cargo."

Galen put his hand on the young man's shoulder and said calmly and deliberately, "Now you understand why every honorable person hates slavery and torture—because it can happen to us, to those we love, to our children. The only way to be sure that it will not happen to your children is to remain strong. And the only way to be sure that it will not happen to your grandchildren is to abolish slavery from the face of the earth."

Che was silent and pensive before he asked, "How can slavery be abolished when people like me feel normal growing up with it?"

Galen replied, "Perhaps slavery and torture will always remain with the human race in one form or another. Any time you look for this evil, you will find it somewhere, someplace, even in an innocent young prince's face."

We landed the black boys and girls on the African coast. Our crew gave them food and water, and twenty armed men accompanied them to the green foothills leading up to their highlands. Adoo stood beside

Seenara, holding her hand. She looked up at him with childlike trust and waved goodbye to her friends as they walked away. She stared at her green hills for a long time. I looked at Adoo. He had a boyish, invincible grin on his face. I reflected on what thoughts went had gone through his mind these past two days. I am sure he felt fear for his freedom and for Seenara. He must have suffered the kind of worry that comes from not knowing what evil awaits around the next corner.

Back on board, Seenara followed Adoo around the ship like his shadow. As the days passed, I developed a deep admiration for her indomitable spirit. She was always smiling and was always near Adoo. She had strength and dignity, and she adapted quickly to life aboard a sailing ship.

The *Sorceress* and *Sword of the Sea* sailed out of Bab-el-Mandab, this aptly named Strait of Tears, into the wide-open Indian Ocean. There were no dangers here, and we sailed continuously, day and night, for three days, the green mountains of Arabia Felix visible on the horizon. In the afternoon we sighted the town of Al-Mokalla. Almost all ships going to India or returning from Serendib stopped here to resupply and rest their crews. Our boys were happy and excited. Like all sailors before them, they knew where they could have a good time. Atiya was no exception. He produced his simsimiyya and played the melody of a funny song. The crew gathered around him and joined him in his singing. Every one of them knew the words by heart:

Oh, the sweet girls of Mokalla!
I will rest in their garden and sip wine from their olla!
Dreams, I say, dreams!
You are nothing but a poor Sailor Wallah!
Do you have pearls for the girls, and gold, and a silken Hilla?
Poor Sailor Wallah, you poor Sailor Wallah![53]

---

[53] *Hillah:* Arabic word meaning "dress." *Al-Mokalla*: A good harbor on the southern coast of Yemen, famous for the beauty of its women.

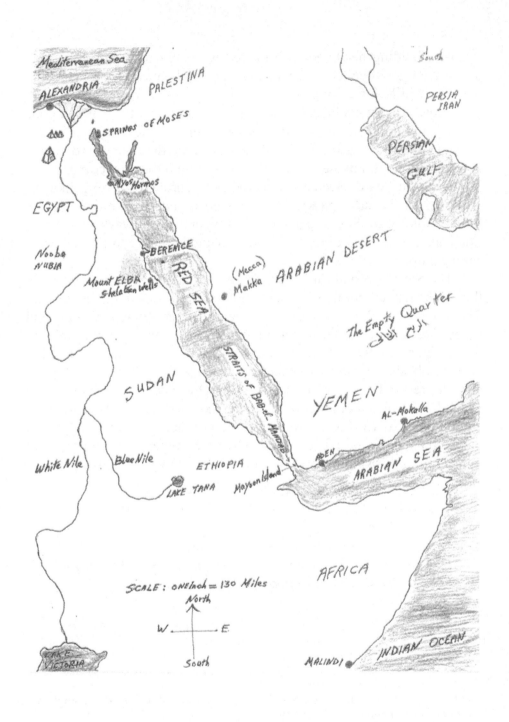

CHAPTER 15: Al-Mokalla

Sword of the Sea and the *Sorceress* approached the town of Mokalla, a fine, safe harbor on the southern coast of Yemen. Our crew stood gazing at the green mountains behind the town. I could see signs of excitement in their movements and could hear it in their voices. As we passed through the entrance to the harbor, we saw a light tower on our left-hand side and a breakwater on our right-hand side. The breakwater was a wall built of stones and boulders to break the force of the waves and protect the ships anchored inside. Every big wave crashing against these rocks created a waterspout that rose high into the air, and the receding water flowing rapidly through the rocks made a loud hissing sound like the breathing of a whale. The children of Mokalla, and quite a few superstitious adults, believed that the ghost of a dead whale had found a home in the entrance to their harbor. Several years previously, a dying whale had been pushed ashore by a violent storm. The people still talk about the amazing quantity of ambergris[54] found inside the body of this gigantic whale, and so the myth of the ghost whale lives on.

I had marvelous memories of previous visits to Mokalla. This time I was surprised to see both the light tower and the high wall around the harbor painted red. At the base of the light tower was a vast room with one side totally open to the sea, giving everyone in the room an unobstructed view of the whole harbor. This was the meeting place for shipowners, traders, captains, and navigators. Here they conducted their business as they watched the shipping traffic in the harbor. I was eager to get to this meeting room to see old friends, especially Taleb Ali Zol, the old navigator who had taught me so much about the Arabian Sea and the Indian Ocean.

---

[54] *Ambergris* is a valuable waxy substance used as a fixative in perfumes and found on the beach in tropical seas. People believe it originates in the intestines of sperm whales.

We anchored the *Sorceress* and *Sword of the Sea* with their bows touching a beach of pure, white sand. Here the ships would he hauled out and careened, and their fouled bottoms cleaned. Mobareek and I walked at a fast pace toward the light tower. He knew many of the navigators in town and wanted to find his friend Taleb Ali, the most famous of them all. On our way, I asked him, "Did you ever see a harbor surrounded by a red wall and light tower also painted bright red?"

Mobareek laughed and said, "Knowing merchants the way I do, the red paint was probably on sale." We walked on and he said, "There is great wealth in this town. The merchants trade with India and Africa, and they sell frankincense to the Romans. It is collected from trees that grow wild in their mountains."

We walked into the meeting room, and Mobareek was instantly recognized and greeted by old friends. We sat down with them and asked for news. The best news was that no ship from Egypt had inquired about us, and from Rome and Alexandria we learned that Octavian had made himself master of Rome. The Senate had given him the title "Augustus." Now the Roman senators had outdone themselves. Flattering their ruler, they had voted to give Octavian another title, "Divi Filius," or "Son of God" Octavian forbade all Roman senators from traveling to Egypt. He did not want to see one of them making himself king of Egypt and stopping the grain shipments to Rome. Egypt after Cleopatra had become a province of the Roman Empire and was no longer an independent ally.

Mobareek inquired about our friend Taleb Ali. "Is he at sea, or did he coil his ropes on land?"

We were told that the famous captain spent his evenings in the tavern at the far end of the beach. "From sunset to midnight, you will find him there."

We walked back across the beach to the tavern. We stopped by the ships and invited Galen, Che, and Ari to come with us. I knew that they were eager to meet the famous navigator. The sun was setting, and we walked barefoot on the wet sand toward the tavern with tiny wavelets lapping at our feet.

When we entered the tavern, Mobareek smiled broadly and said, "There he is! I want to surprise him. It will be good to see the expression on his face. Many years have passed since we sailed together."

We sat at a table to one side and watched Taleb Ali, a dignified old man, surrounded by a group of young sailors, obviously spellbound by the stories he was telling them. Men both young and old were listening as he regaled them with tales of adventure. Whenever he stopped, they would offer him wine to drink and delicacies to eat.

I whispered to Mobareek, "Your friend, Taleb, seems to have found the same occupation as my friend the governor . . . drinking wine and spinning tales!"

Taleb Ali turned toward us, but there was no sign of recognition on his face. Then he launched into his next story, his powerful voice vibrating with emotion. "I was the only navigator leading a fleet of six ships across the ocean to India. No man on board knew the secrets of the high stars that guide you at night, no one but me and the devil. We were sailing fast, day and night, with a fair wind behind us. Finding our way between hundreds of small islands and coral reefs was not easy, and when I judged that we had passed these dangers, I put my arm in the sea every night until the devil of the depths held my hand and I knew land was near."

Taleb Ali stopped his story, had a drink, then looked toward us, but he still did not recognize his friends. He continued, raising his voice gradually for effect. "The wind blew stronger and our ships gathered more speed, and that same night, with a full moon above, the leading ship, my ship, crashed into a hidden reef! What could this be? Were the sea gods angry because I did not say the right prayers? I ran to the bow and looked down into the dark waters."

Here Taleb raised both his hands up high, as in prayer to heaven. He took a deep breath and said, "Great gods of the sea, my ship was grounded on the back of a huge whale! My ship sprang many leaks because she was going at a great speed when she struck the heavy beast. Soon she was listing to one side with the gigantic creature still under her keel. Was this whale dead or dying?

"Every man worked hard all night bailing buckets of water out of the ship. Daybreak found the carpenters busy repairing and stopping all of the leaks. At sunrise I stood on the bow, looking down at the great whale. He was still breathing, still alive. Thirty or more sharks were circling around him, but none dared take a bite." Taleb stopped for effect, took a sip of wine, then continued. "I watched the sharks for a long time. How did they sense that the whale was near death? And why did they wait till he was dead before striking? What goes on inside their small brains? We shall never know. In the afternoon, the whale stopped breathing. One of the largest tiger sharks I had ever seen attacked from below, taking a large chunk of blubber. This served as a signal to the others. They went mad, dashing in from all directions, twisting and writhing, trying to pull the flesh away. In their mad frenzy, more than one shark grabbed our ship's rudder and left a few teeth in the wood."

Here Taleb Ali stopped the story. His audience was silent, spellbound. The old navigator was shaking his head from side to side. He reached deep into his pocket and pulled out a few sharks' teeth. He stretched his hand toward the listeners and said, "Here, look, and feel these. Did any of you ever see bigger sharks' teeth? I pulled them myself out of the wood, out of the rudder. The serrated teeth are from the *nimr*,[55] and the long, evil-looking fangs are from the *deeba*."[56]

Mobareek rose to his full height, stretched leisurely, and, smiling at me, he said, "Now let us surprise him. It will be fun to see the expression on his face." He walked slowly through the crowd, and I followed. He came very close to his friend, Taleb, and he stood there motionless and speechless.

At first I thought the man possessed a glass eye like my friend the governor. But then I realized that both of his eyes saw nothing. "Mobareek," I whispered, "your friend is completely blind!"

The old navigator, the bold captain of countless voyages, had been reduced to telling stories in a tavern for food and drink. Mobareek put

---

[55] *Nimr* means tiger shark *(Galeocerdo cuvier),* named because of dark stripes on its skin.
[56] *Deeba* means wolf shark because of its long teeth, like wolf's fangs.

both of his hands on his friend's shoulders and repeated his name. "Taleb Ali Zol, Taleb Ali, Taleb!!"

The old navigator stood up, an expression of wonder and surprise illuminating his wrinkled face. "I know this voice," he said. "Is it you, Mobareek?"

Mobareek took his old friend in his arms and hugged him repeatedly, then led him slowly to our table. The old navigator sat down between us, and we drank the best wine available there while Mobareek told his friend as much as he could about our voyage without revealing the identity of Che, Cleopatra's son.

Finally I asked Taleb, "Tell me, what happened to you since we last sailed together?" He held my hand and recited the words of a famous poet in a soft, singsong voice:

See, my friend, what time has done to me!
Wrinkled my face, blinded my eyes, weakened my knee,
But inside this old body there will always be
A soul, forever young, forever bold, always free!

It was almost midnight. Taleb's grandson walked into the tavern. He held the old man's arm, looked at us, and said, "I am here to take my grandfather home."

Galen took the boy's hand and pressed a golden coin into his palm. "Tomorrow morning you must bring your grandfather to me."

The old man heard Galen's words and said, "Tomorrow I will come to your grand ship, the *Sorceress*, and then you must come and rest in my fort. I have enough room for all your crew." He put his hand on his grandson's shoulder and let the young boy lead him home.

After Taleb left us, we sat down in silence for a little while. Then Galen turned his handsome face toward Mobareek and said, "Tomorrow, when Taleb comes to us, please try to convince him to submit to my care. I will try to restore his eyesight. It will be painless. However, success is not sure."

Che said, "That sounds like magic."

Galen replied, "There is no magic here. It is a simple operation well known to the ancient Egyptians. Have you seen how clear egg white becomes opaque when heated? When the lens of the eye is exposed to heat or strong sunlight, the passage of time causes the lens to become clouded. If Taleb lets me, I will pierce the lenses of his eyes. A very small hole will let the light in, and if he is lucky, he will see again."

We spent some time in the tavern eating and talking. Ari and Che had been amazed at the tales they had heard from the old navigator. Che asked me, "What did he mean when he said he put his arm into the sea and the devil held his hand?"

Ari asked, "Why does he say no one knows the secrets of the high stars except him and the devil?"

Mobareek was smiling. I told the young men, "All navigators keep their knowledge a closely guarded secret, not to be revealed except to their sons and members of their clan. This knowledge brings them honors and riches, and they want the common sailors to keep believing that there is something magical about their talent. When a navigator puts his hand in the sea, the 'devil' he seeks is simply a warm current. These currents run steadily all year round. If the current is going his way, he joins it, and the devil will carry his ship along at a good speed.

"As for the secrets of the high stars that Taleb and the devil keep to themselves, these are zenith stars that rise in the east and then pass overhead before setting in the west. These high stars will guide us to a safe passage through the Indian Ocean, through hundreds of low islands and coral reefs, maybe a thousand islets or more. The navigators found a safe passage through these islands. They keep the names of the guiding stars to themselves. When we are at sea, I will show you these stars, and I will share with you their names. You will learn, and you will never forget."[57]

---

[57] Vasco da Gama, the Portuguese navigator who opened the sea route between Europe and India, had two Arabic-speaking interpreters on his ship. After rounding the Cape of Good Hope in South Africa, he sailed north along the African coast to the port of Malindi, now in Kenya. Here he took on board an Arabian navigator who showed him the way to India. They crossed the Indian Ocean in twenty-three days, safely avoiding more than a thousand islets and coral reefs, the Maldive and the Laccadive Islands.

Early the next day, the blind navigator came to the *Sorceress*, his grandson guiding him by the hand. We greeted him, and he said, "Even a blind man could find the *Sorceress*. Everyone in the harbor is talking about her." He meant this as a compliment to Mobareek, the shipbuilder.

Mobareek and Galen sat next to Taleb in the shade. Gripping Taleb's arm, Mobareek said, "I am glad you came. Now, listen carefully. I swear by all the gods that I have never met nor heard of a physician wiser than Galen. He is the queen's own physician, and he is sitting right next to you." Taleb extended his hand, and Galen silently held it in his two hands. Mobareek continued, "Taleb, let Galen try to give you back your eyesight."

He replied, "Giving me back my eyes would be a miracle . . . like bringing a dead man back to life! You can do anything you want. I shall remain perfectly still, Hakeem."

Galen gave me two pieces of clean cloth and told me to cover the eyes when he finished the operation. He held the eyeball between the forefinger and thumb of his left hand. In his right hand he had a very sharp needle made of gold. With this needle he pierced a small hole in the clouded eye lens, and I covered the eye with a clean cloth. Galen repeated the painless operation on the other eye, and we immediately moved Taleb into a dark tent to protect him from strong sunlight.

Inside the tent, Galen removed the cloth covering Taleb's eyes. We were watching the old navigator's face. There was surprise written all over his features. He looked at Mobareek. "I can see you, Mobareek! I see you, my friend, and the whole world again!" Then he looked at Galen. He took Galen's small hands in his big, powerful hands and kissed them repeatedly in a gesture of gratitude familiar to all humans everywhere.

Taleb spoke, his voice loaded with emotion. "I'm afraid all the jewels of India would not be enough to repay you. I can only pray that someday, somehow, I will be useful to you." Taleb took his grandson into his arms and kissed him. "Now, lead me home. Take my hand for the last time." Then he covered his eyes with the clean cloth and said, "Please come to my fort and be my guests. I have room in the house for all of you. Come, follow me. All your crew are welcome. Follow me, all of you!"

We followed Taleb and his grandson into the town, passing through massive doors in that red wall surrounding the harbor. We noticed shriveled human hands nailed to the doors. Thieves here lose their hands, and pirates lose their heads. Punishment is swift and severe, so the harbor is safe for trade.

Our young crew was amazed at the sights of this town. All the buildings were at least three stories high, and some were six stories high, decorated with fantastic geometrical designs. The construction was done with sun-dried mud bricks made from a mixture of clay and ash, which gets stronger with the passage of time. The high walls leaned inward, so the top stories were smaller than the ground floor for stability during earthquakes. Every house had a large garden surrounded by a high wall. Taleb's house was three stories high, and the wall around his garden was as high as the house. This high wall shaded the house and garden all year round.

We entered through a heavy wooden door. Now I understood why Taleb called his home "my fort." The top floor of the house was for the women and children. The middle floor was for men. The ground floor was for guests and storage rooms. We made ourselves comfortable in the guest rooms. The floor was covered with wool rugs. Many large pillows were strewn near the walls. The windows provided cross-ventilation and views of the garden. Signs of former wealth were evident in this large house.

We heard joyous ululating cheers and praise for the gods all throughout the house. The old navigator's family had just discovered that his eyesight had been restored by a miracle they could not understand. Large wooden trays filled with steaming hot food came down from the women's quarters. Rice, mutton, and fish were followed by a variety of fruits.

After this delicious meal, I was resting and reclining on the pillows, Galen and Mobareek nearby, when the young crewmen who were here in Taleb's house gathered around us and politely asked for half their pay. This is a well-established custom in the Red Sea and the Arabian Sea: sailors can ask for and receive half their pay at any time.

The second half is paid at the end of the cruise. Some men choose to leave a portion of the money with their families; some will buy trade goods, which they can sell later; and many young men will use this money to marry a second wife. In Mokalla, the man would have to pay a sum of money to the bride's family. Powerful families will not allow the husband to take his wife with him. She has to live close to her clan, where she and her children will be protected and cared for if the husband dies or is lost at sea.

I paid the young crewmen in gold and silver coins. Mobareek, chuckling softly, was watching every one of them counting his riches. He laughed and said, "Watch these boys. They will spend it all in two days in Paradise."

CHAPTER 16: Paradesios

And now it is time to tell you the story of Paradise, a beautiful, fantastic garden of delights where only a few men are allowed to enter. The Greeks call it Paradesios, which means a garden surrounded by a high wall. Many years ago, as a young man, I visited this garden, situated north of town on the green slopes of the mountain at an elevation of about four thousand feet. Here the air was always cool, and biting insects did not exist.

To reach the garden, we rented mules. It was a cheerful group of young men going up the mountain, clean-shaven and suntanned, wearing their finest clothes. Every man must have heard a few stories about the beautiful girls of Mokalla, the *houris* in Paradesios, but they had never seen them. I was the only one who had been inside the walls of Paradise, and that had been a long time ago. For Che, Ari, Justin, and all the rest of the crew, it would be a complete surprise. Adoo, Seenara, and Mobareek stayed behind. A small number of sailors remained with Mobareek to do necessary maintenance work.

As the mules climbed higher up the hills, the view looking down was marvelous, and the red harbor of Mokalla was like a ruby on a finger of the endless blue sea. At this altitude, the hills were greener and the air cooler than at the coast. Finally we reached the wall of Paradesios. It was about thirty feet high, decorated entirely with colorful geometric designs. The higher part of this wall was perforated with holes to let the breeze flow through. Wild doves and pigeons nested in these holes. A peregrine falcon was circling in the sky, a reminder that amid all of this joyful life, sudden death is always near.

The guardians of Paradesios charged an exorbitant sum of money. They let us in through a small door, one man at a time. The sun was low on the horizon, and the birds were coming home to their trees. The sounds of their chirping and chattering rose to a noise so loud that we could not have a conversation, but when the sun set, all was calm and quiet again. Many torches were lit, throwing a reddish light over the whole place. After a month at sea, our sense of smell was sharper than ever, and we were overwhelmed by the powerful perfume in the garden. We sat on large silk pillows under trellises covered with Arabian jasmine.

The young men were hoping and praying that the beautiful girls, the houris, would make their entrance soon. They did not have to wait long. First, five older men walked in, each carrying a stringed *kithara*.[58] They sat around a large fountain built with thin, translucent marble inlaid with colored stones and fed by a cold mountain spring. Their musical instruments were made of the finest woods and decorated with mother-of-pearl shell. The music they played made us turn away from the food and delicacies we were eating. Many of us had never heard such marvelous melodies before. This was heavenly music, the kind that stops your mind from thinking and can soothe all worries away from your soul.

Every young man was waiting for the young women to appear, hoping and praying that one would dance close enough for him to touch her. Every sailor held in his hand a thorn, taken from a bright red fish called a *kahaya*.[59] The local myth these boys were told says if you catch a red kahaya on a moonless dark night and you take its sharp thorn and scratch any girl's skin with it, and if you draw blood, she will love you forever.

The music never stopped. The women walked into the garden, swaying gently, wearing transparent veils made of silk with threads of gold woven into the fabric. Only their eyes could be seen, large and liquid, their eyelids painted with kohl, which made them seem even bigger. The whites of their eyes were of purest white, and the dark parts as dark can be, brilliant and bewitching in the light of a hundred fire torches. They danced a slow, graceful dance, giggling and singing at the same time:

---

[58] *Kithara:* Ancient Greek musical instrument similar to but larger than the lyre.
[59] *Kahaya:* A red fish with a large thorn on its gill cover, of the *Holocentridae* family.

Do you know what is in the heart of a pretty girl?
Can you guess?
All she wants is to be loved.
She wants to be loved by the man she loves!

As the girls danced, we could hear tinkling sounds coming from tiny silver bells on their ankles. I looked at their feet. Their toenails were painted red, and their sandals had strings of small pearls. The movements of their hands were expressive. Gradually and slowly, the girls approached the men, and with a sudden, graceful motion, they lifted their silk veils and twirled them round and round. Then every girl chose a young man and covered his face and hair with her veil. The boys grabbed the silk veils with no intention of giving them back, and the girls, giggling and laughing, playfully rubbed the men's faces and hair with their small, delicate hands. In the palm of each hand was a heavy, powerful perfume like a paste, and it stayed in the men's hair and on their faces. The young men were taken by surprise and missed their chance to scratch the girls with their thorns taken from a kahaya on a moonless night.

All except Che; he was the only one who kept his wits about him. When a beautiful girl with a blue-green tattoo threw her veil over his head, he reached down to her leg and scratched her with the magical thorn. The girl shrieked, more from surprise than pain. Then she came back at him like a young tigress and slapped him, hard, across his face. I couldn't help but wonder whether the local myth was only in the minds of men.

The music changed, and now the dance was not a gentle, happy dance anymore. It became a sensual belly dance, and the eyes of the spectators caressed the women with looks of admiration and desire. Only one young woman had a blue and green tattoo near her navel in the shape of a human eye to protect her from the harmful looks of envious people. She was the one Che had scratched. At midnight, the women retreated into the shadows and quietly left the garden. The sailors sat down patiently, listening to the music and waiting for the dancing women to appear once again, but they never returned.

Galen looked happy. He was smiling when he looked at me and said, "Hiro, I want to thank you for bringing me here to this

Paradesios." He waved his hand in a gesture that means, *Look at all this*, and said, "To see so much beauty in one place is a miracle—these young girls, this garden, and the music. What is more, tonight I found the answer to a question that I have been pondering for a long time."

I said, "Let me guess. Is it something about beautiful women?"

Galen laughed. "Always!"

The waiters in the garden served us milk sweetened with honey. It was laced with a drug that they obtain from the leaves of a bush growing in their green hills. Every last one of us fell into deep sleep, and we were awakened as if from a marvelous dream by the rays of the rising sun. All the young men dipped their arms and heads into the cold running water of the marble fountain. Now we had to get back on the mules and ride down the hills to Taleb's fort in the town of Mokalla.

Taleb Ali was waiting for us, all smiles. We sat down to join him in his large guest room, where he had prepared a feast for us. Che sat silently next to the old navigator. He was pensive and barely touched the food. Taleb looked at him and said, "My boy, you must eat. Some fat on your body will save your life if we are caught in a big storm." Che looked at the old man, not comprehending, and Taleb explained, "People think you cannot die of cold in a warm sea, but I have seen thin men die while big men survive. When the wind and rain and the sea spray keep you wet and chilled, and the howling storm deprives you of sleep, your body gives up, and the mind does not care whether you live or die. Some call this serenity in the face of death. I call it surrender. Now, eat. We have ten days of rest here before we sail. The winds of the *mawsim*[60] have stopped. It is time to go to sea."

I was surprised and turned to Taleb. "We have a dangerous journey? Do you plan to sail with us?"

Taleb laughed out loud. He was animated. "Now that I can see again, do you think I will sit on my coiled ropes? True, my sight is far from perfect, but my experience and judgment should earn me my keep!"

---

[60] *Mawsim* means "season" in Arabic, and from this comes the English term "monsoon winds."

139

Our whole crew feasted daily in Taleb's guest rooms, and Galen managed to send a bag of gold coins upstairs to the ladies who did the cooking. He made Taleb's grandson swear he would not say a word about that, then gave him the golden coins to take discreetly to his grandmother.

Mobareek was doing minor repairs to the ships. I was watching him, and Taleb was sitting next to me in the shade of some palm trees. He looked with admiration at Mobareek. He said, "Captains who know nothing about shipbuilding are the ones who are lost in big storms. Some of them cannot tell if their ship is seaworthy or not. When the seawater starts leaking in . . . " His voice trailed away as if he were remembering some adventure in the past he would rather have forgotten.

A few days remained before sailing, and I remarked to Mobareek that I didn't see most of our young crew. Where were they? What were they doing?

Mobareek roared with laughter. "Don't you know, Hiro? They used all their money to get married. Not to the beautiful dancers in the garden, of course, but to poor, plain-looking girls. A sailor gives his money to a girl's family, and the sailor has a bride. When he sails away, her family and her clan will take care of her and her children until he returns. Many of these young sailors have two wives, one at home in Egypt and a second wife in Mokalla. You did not know that?"

Che spoke up. "I wish I could marry the girl with the tattoo on her belly."

Taleb looked at Che and said, "You have seen Sondosa, and the flashes from her eyes are like the sheen of a sharp dagger. When they strike a man's heart, he never recovers."

Che looked at Galen. "All these sailors around me are getting married. We have enough gold and silver to please her family!"

Galen was silent. However, Taleb spoke up forcefully. "Her family wants more than money. They want a man who has proved himself worthy of honor, a great captain or warrior, a famous navigator or shipowner, and when accepted, he will not be allowed to take his young wife away. The gold he presents will be used to build her a house near her family home. If the husband dies in battle or is lost at sea, her large clan will take care of her. Only weak, poor families allow a husband to take their daughters away."

Galen looked at me. Smiling, he said, "It is time our young prince learns that he cannot have everything he wants."

All that remained for us to do here at Mokalla was to buy supplies. Mobareek needed spars to replace those we had lost in Ethiopia. However, here you cannot buy spars with seashells; you must pay in gold and silver coins. After you select the spar you want, you lay down your coins on the wood, one piece of silver next to the other, until you cover the whole length of the wooden spar. For provisions, we would buy fresh fruits, dried dates, and large quantities of a sun-dried fish called *sigan*. This is a small, delicious fish, cleaned and dried in the strong sun without any salt.

I walked with Galen and Mobareek to a warehouse inside the harbor walls. Wood of all sorts was sold here for shipbuilding. We walked in and asked the owner for the finest spars without knots, cracks, or checks. The man surprised us by saying, "Please buy what you need from my Jewish neighbor. He hasn't sold anything for a month, and his wood is just as good as my stock."

I looked at Galen and Mobareek. They were pleasantly surprised that this trader would think of the merchant next door, and we gladly walked over to the next warehouse. After buying the spars, the Jewish merchant thanked us and said, "Are you the physician who restored Taleb's eyesight?"

Mobareek answered, "Yes, Galen is the great man."

The merchant approached us, touched our arms, and said, "Please stand still. Allow me to bless you." The man recited a long prayer blessing the three of us. Then he said, "Repeat after me. Amen." Strange to say, we felt grateful for the blessing even though none of us understood the merchant's faith.

Mobareek was eager to sail. After a few days, Taleb Ali joined us, and he came aboard my ship, *Sword of the Sea*. Galen, Adoo, and Atiya were with me. The young men Che, Ari, Justin, and Marcus were aboard the *Sorceress* with Mobareek.

Out of Mokalla we sailed with a strong, cold land breeze coming from the mountains, and the rays of the rising sun made our white sails golden against the clear horizon. I looked around me at the happy faces of the crew, every one of them lost in his own private thoughts. For me they were the memories of Paradise; the feel of the clean, cool wind rubbing against my face and whispering in my ears; and the kindly motion of the ship invigorating the body and soothing the soul, washing away all cares and worries.

CHAPTER 17: The Storm

After we had sailed a few days in a southeasterly direction with a fair wind, the wind stopped about midnight, and I knew the next day would bring intense heat. Before sunrise we lowered two canoes into the sea and towed *Sword of the Sea* close to the *Sorceress*. We tied both ships together to keep them from drifting apart in the currents. The crew used all our sails to make a shade covering the entire ship, and the huge rudder was lashed so it would stop its creaking noises. We sat in this shade, watching the sun rising out of the oily sea, not a ripple between us and the horizon. We had a good supply of melons; they last more than two weeks when stored in the shade because of their thick rind.

Everyone was eating sliced melons for breakfast, and some of the younger boys jumped into the ocean for a morning swim. The rest of our crew aimed and threw melon rinds at the swimmers' heads with great force but not much accuracy. In a short while the sea around us was covered with floating melon rinds. Adoo was the best, and with every throw he hit a swimmer.

Suddenly he shouted at the crew, "*Girsh dahyadahya*, big shark, big shark!" The boys scrambled out of the sea, and we saw a gigantic shark swimming slowly just under the surface. He came close to our ship, and I estimated his length at twenty feet or more. The huge fish went about eating the melon rinds one by one. Adoo threw a whole melon at the shark just in front of it. The shark swallowed it, showing us the inside of its mouth filled with very small teeth.

Taleb said in a loud voice that everyone could hear, "This is a harmless shark. See the long slits of his gills covered with loose, flapping skin?"

I asked Taleb, "Do you know this kind of shark?"

He answered, "Yes, I saw them in the open ocean many times swimming near the surface, feeding on huge jellyfish [*Hamathamat*] and other creatures drifting in the water."[61]

Adoo, laughing, shouted at the crew, "That shark is harmless unless you are a melon! Taleb says it is safe for you to go back into the sea."

The first to jump in was Che, followed by Marcus, his faithful friend, who would do anything Che did without a second thought. The shark stayed near the ships awhile, gobbling the melon rinds that the crewmen were happily throwing at it.

As the sun rose higher in the sky, the heat became intolerable, and the crew begged Atiya for some music. He played his simsimiyya and sang many songs; then he stopped, exhausted. In the afternoon, the entire crew stretched out to try to sleep, but sleep would not come in the heat of the day. In the total silence, their breathing seemed like a loud, irritating sound. At night we did not remove the sails shading our ships because with the heat and humidity, there would be heavy morning dew.

The second day of dead calm brought more heat, and swimming was not refreshing anymore. There was a layer of hot water on the surface about two feet deep, and with each stroke my hand reached down to cold water. To refresh myself, I dove down about five feet and swam underwater for as long as I could hold my breath. The crew was watching, and soon everyone was in the sea diving down to the cooler water. When the boys came up to breathe, they stayed very close to the ship to keep their heads in the shade.

The second night of dead calm was worse than the first. Atiya was too hot and tired to play his music, and we sat or stretched on deck, bored and tired. Our minds stopped thinking, and there was a hushed silence without conversation or songs.

Galen asked Taleb Ali, "When did you first notice that you were losing your eyesight?"

---

[61] This harmless shark is called the "basking shark" (*Cetorhinus maximus*) because it is always basking in the sunlight near the surface of the sea. It grows to thirty feet.

Taleb told him, "It happened so slowly. I cannot even remember the year when I first noticed my eyes getting weak. On my last voyage, I crashed a ship into a deep reef. There was a substantial quantity of silver on the ship to pay for goods from India. Most of it belonged to merchants in Mokalla, and the rest was my own wealth. We were sailing on the windward side of a reef. When you are on the moving deck of your ship, it is difficult to determine whether your zenith star is exactly overhead or not. I made a small mistake in judging the ship's course, a small mistake that grew larger with every mile. Had my eyes been good, I could have seen the white breakers on the reef even at night. When I finally saw them, it was too late. I lost the ship and her silver. The second ship saved my crew. After this, no merchant would trust me."

Taleb stopped his story, drank some water, looked at Galen, and said, "I could still see but not clearly, and back in Mokalla I was not my true self. I was walking and acting like a blind man, looking this way and that way, straining to see. And as my eyes got weaker, I tried to hear better, moving my head from side to side. Everyone knew that I was almost blind. I often thought of ending my life the old navigator's way."

Galen interrupted him. "The old navigator's way?"

Taleb continued in a soft voice, but every man could hear him in the total silence of the night. "All navigators teach their sons that death in the sea is a sweet death, and the old blind navigator will formally visit all his friends. Then he would take a small boat and sail out to sea and never return."

Galen asked, "Do old navigators still do this to end their lives?"

Taleb nodded. "Many do. I remained on land and alive, not because of fear but for the love of my grandchildren. I could not see them, but I could hug them, listen to them, and tell them stories. I did not want pity from other people, so I held my head high and walked like a whole man with my hand on my grandson's shoulder. Now I can see the moonrise and the sunset, and every night I look at the sky to drink in the majesty of the stars, as if it is the end of my last day. I am grateful, truly grateful."

The third day of heat was upon us—not a breath of wind, not a ripple in the sea. Each of us bore a changed expression on his our face. Fatigue and lack of sleep changed our features, and no one had any appetite for food. The crew poured buckets of water on the awnings and deck to no avail. We dove down into the sea to reach the cold water under the hot surface, but we got tired of this after a while. That same night after midnight, there was a show of lightning on the horizon, too far for us to hear any thunder.

Mobareek told the boys, "Come, pray for wind!" The lightning increased and became a sheet of light like a curtain between the clouds and the sea, continuously moving, but always there on the western horizon. We watched fascinated for a long time, and now the moon was setting, slowly, very slowly, going down into the ocean behind this curtain of light.

At sunrise, dark clouds covered the western horizon, and the wind arose, blowing from the west. Mobareek said, "A storm is coming our way. A big one. We have time to prepare."

I asked Taleb, "What do you make of these dark clouds?"

He said, "Mobareek is right. Six hours at the most and these clouds will be on top of us."

Mobareek stepped onto the deck of his *Sorceress*, saying, "If we get separated, give me a smoke signal after the storm." He untied with his own hands the two lines holding the *Sorceress* close to *Sword of the Sea* and calmly gave orders to the crew to prepare for rough weather.

As the wind picked up speed, energy was restored to our bodies and wakefulness to our minds. We could see high clouds all over the sky, white like long strands of hair, blown by a high and powerful wind. The low black clouds were moving toward us, but we still had time to finish our preparations without rushing. There was no fear among the crew, but they were tense and excited. They knew that in the open sea, where there are no rocks or coral reefs to smash your ship or break your keel, all you have to do is to run before the storm. If your ship is well built, she will not sink. You will suffer fatigue and exhaustion, aches and pains. You will be bruised and cut. But the ship will survive.

Everything below deck was tied down in its place. The deck hatches were closed tight. No one stayed below; even the strongest would have been thrown about like salt in a shaker.

Four thick ropes were coiled near the steersman. When the seas got too big and boisterous, he would order the crew to pay out the ropes. They would trail behind the ship and help her to run steadily before the great waves. The men passed strong lines through holes in the heavy rudder. These ropes would to hold it amidships when steering became too difficult. The mast, thick, heavy, and very strong, normally had only one moving stay. This rope was secured to the bows. Attached to it we had a small, tough, triangular storm sail, stretched tight and flat amidships. When running before the wind, if she turned to the right or left, wind would fill this small, tough sail and push her bows back on course, straight before the wind, always keeping her running before the waves and the wind. The mast was also secured with four extra stays (ropes).

Every man on board had a piece of sheepskin tied around his waist and wore a safety line like a belt. Without the sheepskin, this line would have cut into his flesh. While the safety lines would inhibit the crew's movements, still the men would not be washed overboard. We enjoyed a big, hot meal, knowing that for two or three days, there would be no hot food, only sigan and dried dates.

The wind was picking up speed. Taleb ordered a small square sail to be raised. The crew jumped to obey him. His tremendous self-confidence encouraged them. The young men were aware of the impending danger. There was nervous anticipation in their voices, but they were still eager to watch this grand spectacle of nature.[62]

The storm clouds were now close to us. We could hear their thunder and see lightning bolts. Dark clouds were racing toward our small ship. Taleb shouted, "Tie your safety lines! Here comes the wind that you love, bringing terror from high above!" Taleb looked at Galen, then reached over to check the knot in the physician's safety

---

[62] "To face the elements is, to be sure, no light matter, but when the sea is in its grandest mood, you must then know the sea, and know that you know it, and not forget, that it was made to be sailed over." –Joshua Slocum, the first navigator to sail alone around the world

line. Laughing, Taleb said, "Now the gods will play with us like young boys with hooked fish."

I watched the storm clouds coming toward us, low and menacing. They were in two separate layers. The top clouds, more grey than black, flew before the west wind. The lower clouds, more black than grey, swirling and rising, were driven by gusts of unseen wind from different directions. The sound of thunder was like the chariots of the gods racing in the sky. The lightning bolts cracked like whips over their horses.

The swirling wind hit us with unexpected violence. The square sail was torn away. The crewmen barely had time to secure the rudder amidships. But our tough storm sail on the forestay held. From the low black clouds, thunderbolts came down to the sea, and flashes of lightning went up to the grey clouds.

Turbulent winds were hitting us from every direction, the salty spray stinging our eyes. We tasted salt on our lips until the rain came flying straight into our faces, warm and welcome. We were enveloped in low black clouds, and I could not see the *Sorceress* anymore. Naturally, I worried about Mobareek and his young crew, Ari, Justin, Marcus, and Che. This was an irrational, unfounded fear. Mobareek was a great captain, and his *Sorceress* was a perfect ship, built with great care. But would the lightning spare her? Would it miss our ship?

After about six hours of this rough treatment, the gods relaxed their grip. There was a strange, menacing calm, with clouds forming a high wall around us. The crew took advantage of this and made a hot stew of dried fish, dried vegetables, and olive oil. They rested their aching bodies on deck, and most of them fell into deep sleep. The air was warm and loaded with moisture. I was resting on the stern deck with Galen, Taleb, and Adoo nearby. Adoo grabbed me by the shoulder and shouted, "Our mast!"

A ball of fire, real fire, grew on top of the mast. Sparks were darting up and down the whole length of it. The stays holding our mast were sparkling with dancing lights. Adoo's powerful voice woke up the crewmen. They were hushed and quiet, but on many faces you could see fear.

The ball of fire came down, slowly swirling around the mast, and when it touched the deck, it rolled slowly toward the stem, getting bigger and bigger. We could not escape it, and the ball of fire rolled over our feet. There was no heat, no burning, and no pain. I looked at my friends. Galen had a halo of light above his head, and Adoo had both arms outstretched, his hands glowing with light. Suddenly, this ball of magical fire faded away, but the stays and the mast kept sparkling, and there was a hissing sound heard all over the ship coming from this fire of the gods.

I asked my companions, "Have you ever seen anything like this?"

Taleb said, "Yes, I have, and this fire that does not burn signals very rough weather ahead."

I looked at Galen, and he said, "I never saw this phenomenon before, but I read about it in the story of Moses. He approached a dry bush burning with a fire that did not consume it, and he heard a hissing noise that sounded like his name. Who can blame him for being frightened while his God circled above the mountain, hurling thunderbolts to the earth?"[63]

The calm center of the storm moved away from us, and the wind hit us from the west with sudden unexpected violence. The wind by itself had no sound, but when it hit the mast and rigging it made a sound, and when it blew against our ears it made a sound. Now the wind was flaying the crests of the waves, turning them into whitecaps and picking up the spray. The noise was loud and not unpleasant.

---

[63] KJV Bible, Exodus 3:2, 4: "And the angel of the Lord appeared unto him in a flame of fire, out of the midst of a bush: and he looked, and, behold, the bush burned with fire, and the bush was not consumed. . . . And when the Lord saw that he turned aside to see, God called unto him out of the midst of the bush, and said, 'Moses, Moses.' And he said, 'Here am I.'"
The electrical display described in this passage of Exodus is probably the natural phenomenon known as Saint Elmo's fire.

"Last night I saw St. Elmo's Stars,
With their glittering lanterns all at play,
On the tops of the masts, and the tips of the spars,
And I knew we should have foul weather today."—from The Golden Legend, Henry Wadsworth Longfellow

Taleb Ali had four coils of thick rope near at hand. He paid out the ropes behind our ship to steady her before the seas. We were driven before this storm for a full day and a night, when finally the wind slackened and it was possible to steer. Taleb released the rudder, which was bound amidships, by cutting the ropes with his sharp knife. We took turns steering *Sword of the Sea* over the crests of the waves. Fatigue and lack of sleep prevented us from admiring the grand spectacle all around us—the ocean showing its might and Taleb expertly guiding the ship from the high crests of the waves down into the troughs. This was a display of endurance and expertise that few mariners possess.

Now that the worst was over, the crewmen slept on deck, their bodies exposed to the elements with only their heads and shoulders covered with sheepskins. They huddled together, steadying themselves against the motion of the ship, their hands on their safety lines, even in this fitful sleep.

It was my turn to steer. Everyone was trying to get some rest. The wind was gradually getting weaker, and our deck was almost dry. The waves were still huge, and even after the wind calmed down, they would remain as big swells in the ocean for a few days. When two or three of these waves joined and merged into one big wave, it looked as if the whole surface of the sea was rising up and coming at you. And this is what happened to us. A huge green sea rose up and came at the ship from the side like a never-ending wall of water. From where I stood at the stem, I could see nothing but the mast. The deck and every man on it were underwater for a brief moment that seemed too long.

When there is sudden danger, the mind works faster and time seems to slow down. After a long moment of fear, the ship came out from under the great wave and shook herself free. It was then that I saw Galen entangled in his safety rope, his body twisted in a very unnatural position. I felt a knot in my stomach and shouted at the top of my lungs, "Adoo! Adoo!" I could not leave the steering tiller, but Adoo was at Galen's side in a flash. He cut the rope with his knife and freed Galen from the tangles and compression of the safety line.

Adoo lifted Galen and dragged him to the high stem. I could see pain clearly on Galen's face, but he never uttered a groan as Adoo tried to make him comfortable. "Are you injured?" I asked.

"I think I broke a few ribs." He winced. "Or cracked them at least. When the wave came over the side, I didn't hit the deck fast enough."

Taleb Ali asked, "Is there anything we can do?"

Galen said, "I will be all right. My ribs will heal. It will take time, but they will heal."

From this moment on, Adoo was never far from Galen until we entered the harbor of Serendib.

After one more day of our extreme fatigue, the wind lost much of its force. Our deck was dry, and I wrapped myself in a blanket and fell into a deep sleep. A vivid, powerful dream came to me. I saw a man standing near the tiller, smiling at me. I asked him, "Who are you?"

He said, "Don't you know me, Hiro? We have the same name! I am Nearchus, the pilot of Alexander the Great. Go back to sleep. I will take care of your ship."

The dream was so real, I stood up on my feet and walked toward the stem. The phantom pilot was still there, smiling at me. I said, "Thanks for your help. I never thought I would meet you." I wanted to hug him and to shake his hand, but he vanished before I could touch him. I went back to sleep, and the next morning I told Galen, Adoo, and Taleb about this marvelous dream.

Adoo said, "That was the ghost of Nearchus. He came to help us." I never suspected that Adoo had this streak of superstition in him.

Galen laughed. "It was just a vivid dream, induced by your extreme exhaustion. Let your living crew sail the ship, not a noble ghost. Go back to sleep and have a good rest."

The next day, the wind was calm. A smoke signal would go straight up in the sky and not be blown away. Once again we got a big fire going and added some oil-soaked cloth to the flames. A black plume of smoke rose high above our ship, and we kept the fire going all morning. Some of the younger boys danced around the fire, shouting, "Mobareek, Mobareek, where are you?" They were in high spirits. The storm was over, and they needed to release the tension. Mobareek and his crew would certainly see this smoke signal, even if they were as far away as the horizon. Sure enough, in the afternoon, the *Sorceress* was sailing toward us. I admit that I had been worried about her because my sons, Ari and Justin, were on board.

The sight of the *Sorceress* flying toward us sent a great wave of joy all over the ship. Many among our crew fell to their knees and pressed their foreheads to the deck, gratefully thanking the gods of the sea for the safety of their brothers and friends.

I thought the *Sorceress* more beautiful than ever, her sail bleached as white as could be and her graceful curves outlined against the dark blue sea. She came alongside. We raised our sail and moved close to her, and both ships sailed together, their crews exchanging smiles and small talk. Ari shouted that he wanted to come aboard *Sword of the Sea*. A long rope was thrown to us and kept slack, almost touching the water. Ari came over on this line, pulling himself hand over hand with a strong, sure grip, his head and shoulders in the air and his body in the sea. When Ari stood on deck, I hugged him. Galen and Adoo did the same.

The crew gathered around us, wanting to hear from Ari about what had happened to the *Sorceress*. Ari said, "The first hour was an exciting show! Did you notice the two large clouds? The grey cloud floated higher up, and the black cloud swirled nearer to the sea. They exchanged angry lightning bolts up and down at each other."

Several voices answered him. "Yes, yes!" "We saw those dark clouds!" "We also saw the fire of the gods!"

Ari continued, "This huge, black cloud passed right over us. Lightning bolts hit the ship, and one hit the mast. One side of our mast is blackened and charred. The heavy rain and the ocean spray kept the ship wet, and there was no fire. As long as this cloud was overhead, there was fear in our hearts. But everyone remained calm because of the example of Mobareek. He was on his feet steering for a full day and night. When the wind slackened, he finally let me and Che steer the ship." I detected a note of pride in his voice.

Galen asked, "Is anyone injured or sick on the *Sorceress*?"

Ari answered, "No. They are all covered with cuts and bruises, but they are happy to be alive."

Che was steering the *Sorceress*, Justin standing beside him. They were waving their arms and smiling at us. Mobareek was resting on deck, his legs braced against the bulwark.[64] Our ships were so close to each other that we could hear his voice clearly. "Hiro, you can be proud of these boys. They did well." Mobareek was a man of few words, but these came from his heart.

---

[64] A ship's bulwark is a solid railing that prevents objects from rolling into the sea.

CHAPTER 18: Altair

All around us was the vast expanse of the Indian Ocean, above our head the azure dome of the sky—no islands, no mountains, nothing to give us any bearings except the sun, twice a day at sunrise and sunset, and the bright stars at night.

Mobareek on the *Sorceress* and Taleb Ali on *Sword of the Sea* were steering by the deep, constant swells of the open ocean. I reflected upon how fortunate I was to have these two great navigators with us, for I had never mastered the art of steering by the swells. Every now and then Taleb would tell the steersman, "I am going to sleep. Keep your sail full of wind and follow the *Sorceress*." And whenever the *Sorceress* followed us, I knew that Mobareek must be sleeping.

I was happy to see both Ari and Adoo eager to learn from the old navigator. Taleb, who instructed them, said, "I am holding the ship on her correct course. Now it is your turn to steer. Choose a star low on the horizon and straight ahead of us, and aim at it. Never forget—this star serves you for two hours only! As it rises higher above the horizon, the star moves away from the point that you are aiming at, so you must choose another star lower down on the horizon and straight ahead. Don't worry about the name of the star. But you must remember, when that guide star moves up and to one side, select another."

Ari asked, "What do we do if the horizon is clouded?"

Taleb said, "Then we go back to steering by the swells."

The following night, two hours after sunset, Taleb called to Adoo and Ari. "Come and learn the secret of the high stars. They will show you the way to India." The old navigator ordered the young men to lie down on their backs and make themselves comfortable because they would watch the stars for many hours. Taleb Ali smiled at me; then he looked at Adoo and Ari.

"Be patient," began Taleb. "You must get to know the shape of the constellations when they are rising in the east and when they are setting in the west. The stars will look different to your eyes, like a man rising out of the sea, his head high, and the same man diving into the sea, his head down and his feet up." The old navigator was silent for a long time. Then he said, "Do you see the Milky Way? That river of light in the sky?" Taleb pointed at three stars in a line. The star in the middle was very bright. "These three are called the Flying Eagle [*Nesr-Altair*]. The bright one in the middle is the eagle's body, and the other two are his wings."[65] Then he said, "Always look for Altair inside the Milky Way."

Ari asked Taleb, "I see many bright stars in the sky. How can I be sure that I am looking at Altair?"

Taleb told him, "It is not enough to know the shape of the Flying Eagle. You must also know the constellations nearest to Altair."

Adoo said, "You have to know all the features of a man's face—his eyes, his nose, his mouth—so that you can recognize him anytime, even with half of his face masked."

Taleb repeated in a solemn voice, "Never forget—Altair is in the Milky Way, three stars in line, the eagle and his wings, and nearby the dolphin, always pointing toward the eagle. Here are the four stars that will remind you of a graceful dolphin arching out of the sea, and a fifth star, a very faint one, on his nose. Your young eyes can see it. Just keep looking and be patient."

Ari, the thinker with a quick and curious mind, sat up and said in a respectful voice, "Amir-Al-Bahr,[66] what if the dolphin is also covered by clouds?"

The answer was, "You must know more than one group of stars near Altair. Move your gaze slowly to the north. You will see the

---

[65] Today, on all star charts, this star is named *Altair*, "the Flyer" in Arabic, or "the Flying Eagle," *Al-Nesr Al-tair*. It is the brightest star in the constellation *Aquilae* (Latin for "eagle").

[66] *Amir* in Arabic means "prince" or "commander." *Amir-Al-Bahr* is "Commander of the Navy" or "Prince of the Sea." It is the origin of the English word a*dmiral*.

Flying Swan,[67] two very bright stars—*Deneb*, the tail, and *Sadr*, the breast. And just like the eagle, two stars for the wings, *Geinah*, and a long neck and a faint star for the beak." Taleb pounded the deck with his fist five times to give the shape of the swan like a huge cross in the sky.

The next day before sunset, Taleb called Ari and Adoo and ordered them to take their sharp knives and scratch on our deck the shapes of the constellations. He looked pleased when they remembered three stars in line for the eagle, four stars like a diamond for the dolphin, and five stars like a huge cross for the flying swan. "Now," he said, "watch Altair moving slowly across the sky going to the west. Will the eagle pass over our heads tonight, or will he pass a little to the south? If Altair passes exactly overhead [*Samt-Al-Ras*], then you can be sure you are in a safe channel, avoiding a thousand small islands on your way to India."[68]

Ari asked, "*Amir-Al-Bahr*, how did the navigators discover that Altair keeps us in a safe channel if the ship is right under the star at its zenith?"

Taleb told him, "When a navigator discovers a safe channel or an island, he will wait for a bright and well-known star to pass over his head. He will divulge the name of this overhead star only to his clan and his sons. Remember, the overhead star for summer is not the overhead star for winter. The good navigator will wait until the safe sailing season before he selects his overhead star."

The old navigator stood beside me smiling. I told him, "Taleb Ali, you will make great navigators of these young men. You taught them so much in two nights."

---

[67] The constellation Cygnus, the Swan, features the pattern of stars known as the Northern Cross. The Arabic-derived names for some of the stars in this constellation are *Deneb* (tail), *Sadr* (breast), and *Geinah* (wing).

[68] The Minicoy Channel lies near the Maldives, and it is also known on admiralty charts as the Eight Degree Channel (because it lies eight degrees latitude north of the equator). The star Altair has a celestial altitude of approximately eight degrees north of the equator.

He said, "Hiro, I just taught them the easy part. The rest will take years and years of experience at sea, and there are some secrets they must discover for themselves, secrets no one can explain."

The third night after the storm, Altair passed overhead, and at the same moment the *Sorceress* and *Sword of the Sea* changed course and headed eastward. With every change of the wind, Taleb ordered a change in the trim of our sail. He steered all night. At sunrise we were in a wide, safe channel between a thousand reefs and islets. Adoo and Ari wanted to steer the ship. I told them, "It is not an easy matter to keep a sure course in the daytime. However, if we drift out of the safe channel in the daylight, we will see the islands in time to avoid them."

After four days of sailing between the low-lying islands, we could see the coastal mountains of India clearly. Both ships changed course, and now we were sailing due south, the land of India on our left side. If the wind from the west held strong and steady, we would reach the island of Serendib in two days. The crew was relaxed and happy that the end of the voyage was near.

On the foredeck in the shade of our sail, Galen was observing the dolphins playing around the bows of the ships. I joined him, and he said, "Hiro, my admiration for Taleb Ali grows every day. It seems as if I have known the old man for years."

I replied, "Mobareek was his good friend for many years, and I sailed with him over twenty years ago. I have a great admiration for his knowledge of both the Indian Ocean and the Arabian Sea."

Galen asked, "And his honesty?"

"The merchants trust him with their ships and their wealth," I said. "He is an honorable man."

Galen turned away from the playful dolphins and faced me. "Please ask him to join us. I want to tell him the purpose of our voyage."

I shouted, "Taleb Ali, Amir-Al-Bahr!" He heard me, and I waved at him. "Come, join us in the shade."

Galen took Taleb into his confidence and told him the whole story of Che, the son of Julius Caesar. "I promised Queen Cleopatra that I would take her son to Serendib and leave him with the governor of the port, a good friend of Julius Caesar."

There was an expression of disbelief on Taleb's face. "That would be taking a great risk, Hakeem." He gripped Galen's forearm. "Pay attention. There is so much evil in this world, and so much of it is hidden in the hearts of men."

"What would you do if you were in my place?" asked Galen in a soft voice. "Pray tell me, what would you do to ensure the boy's safety?"

Taleb Ali did not hesitate. He spoke like a man accustomed to command. "I have been many times to the port of Serendib, and I have seen military governors come and go. Their only goal is to get rich quickly and then retire to Alexandria. Trusting a man we don't know with the secret of the true name of this young prince would be a fatal mistake!"

Galen was a man who could not hide his emotions. He turned his noble head toward me, concern written all over his face. "Hiro, I have been worrying about Che for many nights. Taleb is right. I asked him because he is a man of the world. I needed his advice." Galen shook my shoulder with his hand and said, "And now I need yours. What do you think we should do?"

I replied, "We did our best to hide Che's identity. I keep asking myself the same question over and over again: how can we be sure this military man in Serendib will protect Che and treat him well when he can gain so much by sending the boy in chains to Rome?"

Galen looked at Taleb and said, "We will achieve the queen's purpose by disobeying her orders. We will find a place where Che will be safe. Maybe you can help. You know all the ports of India."

Taleb Ali stood up and stretched luxuriously. Then he said, "Let me steer for a while. Then you, Hiro, can take over till sunrise. I will think about a home for Che tonight."

Steering at night, I found that my thinking was clear. No one disturbs the steersman, and most of the crew were asleep. I asked myself, *How can we leave Che alone in Serendib? Who will teach him everything a man should know? Who will guide the boy and watch him grow?* My conviction grew more powerful and insistent with the passage of every hour of the night. *We must never reveal Che's identity, and we will never leave him alone without friends.* Taleb was right: steering at night is conducive to clear thinking.

At first light, it was my turn to rest and sleep. The mind does not stop searching for a solution. Many times during the day when I came out of deep sleep to find a more restful position, I found my mind thinking about Cleopatra's son. Where will he be safe? Who will take care of him?

At sunset I sat down with my friends and watched the changing colors over the western horizon. The sunlight playing with the golden cloud formations gave me a feeling of calm contentment, and I told Galen and Taleb, "Here is the question that cries for an answer: where and how will Che live?"

Galen did not take his gaze away from the beautiful sunset, and Taleb smiled. He said, "We came here as traders, and we will behave like traders. I know all the important merchants of Serendib. Your ships will be filled with the most valuable goods, the finest rubies, the most perfect pearls, rare silks from China, ivory from India, everything of high value and low weight. When we return to Mokalla, this wealth will be multiplied many times. Your prince will become a trader. He will learn navigation and shipbuilding, and every sailing season he will return to India. I will introduce him to all the big merchants, and every year he will multiply his wealth." Taleb grinned. "Who knows? It may someday even rival the wealth of a prince!" He looked at us to judge our reaction. In Taleb's eyes I saw total confidence, not a shadow of doubt. Then he turned his gaze back to the setting sun and said, "Time flies by. After a few years, when Che's hair is streaked with white, he will be an accomplished navigator guiding his own fleet. I can see the desire to learn in his eyes. He will live with me, and I will look after him as if he were my own son."

We were silent for a long time. Then I touched Taleb on his shoulder. He turned and looked at me, a broad smile on his face, and I asked him, "Do you think Che will accept this plan and go back with you to Al-Mokalla?"

Taleb roared with laughter. It was so infectious that Galen was smiling and laughing, too.

"Hiro, I want you to watch the boy's face when I tell him he is going to marry Sondosa, the girl with the blue-green tattoo in the Garden of Paradise! You will see for yourself the meaning of joy!"

Galen looked at Taleb. "How fortunate we are to have found you!"

Taleb took a step forward and hugged Galen. "I am the one who is truly fortunate. Who would believe that my eyesight would be returned to me? Hakeem, you gave me a new life and another son to look after. You can sail back to Mokalla anytime you want to see him. He will be a great man. That is his *Kismet*. Whatever is written on a man's brow shall come true, and my Kismet is to go back to the sea and take care of your young prince."[69]

---

[69] The moving finger writes; and, having writ,
Moves on: nor all your Piety nor Wit
Shall lure it back to cancel half a Line
Nor all your Tears wash out a Word of it.
    —Omar Al-Khayyam (as translated by Edward Fitzgerald in Rubaiyat of Omar Khayyam, fifth edition [1889])

CHAPTER 19: Serendib

We reached the Fortunate Island, Serendib, watered with a hundred small rivers and adorned with a hundred sparkling waterfalls. Fruits and flowers were everywhere we looked. No wonder the early Arabian navigators called it the Fortunate Island. Their eyes were accustomed to islands of sand, coral, and rock. When they saw this green mountain rising out of the ocean, they thought they had found paradise! It was an island of dreams that delighted the eyes and gladdened the heart, surrounded by a sea full of life with whales, dolphins, fish, and seabirds. But when they stepped ashore, the reality was very different from their dream. Mud, sticky mud was everywhere, and hordes of buzzing, biting insects. The early explorers encountered many nameless diseases and unbearable humidity. They thought, *We can be healthy only where our horses and camels are healthy.* So they sailed back to their dry, windy, clean desert and returned to Serendib every winter after the monsoon rains. They came back for the riches of this island: rubies, sapphires, ivory, colorful bird feathers, and a plentiful supply of pearls from the atolls in the Ocean of India. They paid with Greek and Roman silver coins for beautiful luxuries desired and valued for their shape, texture, and color but not really necessary for a happy life.

Sword of the Sea and the *Sorceress* sailed into the harbor, passing near an ancient barrier reef protecting a huge, shallow bay. Big winter swells were crashing with a booming sound on the ancient reef, raising sea spray high in the air, offering many small rainbows to delight our eyes.

Inside the harbor, sixty or more sailing ships were anchored near the beach. Every ship was secured with a strong rope to a tree with a stem anchor behind her. When the captain gives the order to sail away, the crew will untie the rope securing her to the tree and pull on the stem anchor line. Their ship will then swing around and be free to sail with the offshore breeze. Mobareek and Taleb Ali did not anchor near shore among the ships of the fleet. Instead, they steered to a deep blue hole in the middle of the lagoon. We dropped our heavy anchors to the sandy bottom. Here we were sure our ships could not drag their anchors, even in the strongest gale.

The next morning, we put our empty waterskins into four canoes, and crewmen paddled to a small waterfall at the north end of the bay. As we approached land, the smell of smoke was strong in the air, and many plumes of smoke rose over the hills. The natives were burning debris swept down by the flash floods during the heavy monsoon rains. It was time to clear the land and plant new crops.

We beached our canoes near the waterfall. The pool of fresh water under the falls was overflowing into the sea, but it was covered with decaying vegetation and a white foam. Our crewmen dug a large hole near the pool, and soon it was filled with fresh, clean drinking water, filtered through the sand. After filling our waterskins, the young men stepped under the waterfall to bathe and play. Every day some of our crew would go to this waterfall to bathe and wash their clothes.

While the young men were playing in the river and enjoying the sparkling waterfall, I took a long walk on the wet, cool sand of the beach. The entire beach was in the shade of coconut palms and *tembu* trees loaded with clusters of white and yellow blossoms with sweet perfume. The coconut palms leaned out over the sea, attracted by the sunlight reflected from the lagoon. Some of their ripe coconuts had fallen into the sea. Winds and currents would cause them to drift to faraway atolls where they would grow to mature trees, providing drinking water and food to humans in need.

On the beach of fine white sand were a few big black rocks, higher than a tall man, smooth and shining with a metallic sheen. Where did they come from? Did these rocks roll down from the hills? They were too big to be pushed by the flash floods. Were they smoothed by the waves of the sea? No, they were too high on dry land. I was wondering about the mystery of the black rocks and enjoying a fresh sea breeze that rolled away the smoke hanging in the air when I was startled by a loud scream of unmistakable terror. There were two girls in the sea. One of them was screaming. Although they were swimming quite some distance from the beach, the water was shallow, and they could stand on their feet.

I ran into the shallow sea, and when I reached the screaming girl, she shouted, "No! Help my friend! I am safe!"

I swam over to the second girl. She was paralyzed with fear, her face pale, her eyes closed, and her hands clasped around her right knee, pulling her leg up to her chest. Around her left leg, a large sea snake was entwined! The snake's tail touched her foot, and its head was moving near her waist. I held the girl's arms and pulled her backwards toward the land. She kept her eyes closed and did not utter a sound. Over and over again I told her, "You are safe. The snake will not bite you. Breathe hard." She did not respond. I pulled her as fast as I could, keeping her head out of the water.

As soon as I got the frightened girl onto the sandy beach, the snake slithered back into the sea. The girl watched it with terrified eyes. Then she sat down, her eyes downcast, crying uncontrollably. Her younger friend did her best to calm her, kissing her head and hugging her, talking to her in a soothing voice, until she calmed down. Finally she stopped sobbing. I held her hands, and she looked up at me, her eyes the color of dark green emeralds, shining with tears. All the fear had gone away. There was nothing but calm and trust. She spoke softly in a musical language that I could not understand. The younger girl, the one who was screaming, spoke Greek. "My mistress wishes to thank you from the bottom of her heart."

I looked at her, and she must have noticed that I was very surprised. I had recognized her accent. "Are you from Alexandria?" I asked.

She answered, "Yes. My name is Bresis. I have served my mistress for three years. I learned her language, but I suppose my accent from home is hard to lose. My mistress comes from the hills far to the north of India. Her name is Nedra. And what is your name?"

I said, "You can call me Hiro. I am the captain of these two trading ships that you can see far out in the lagoon."

Bresis seemed to be sixteen years old or younger, and Nedra, whom she called her mistress, seemed to be twenty-two or twenty-three years old. I said to Bresis, "Please tell your mistress that these sea snakes don't bite people. They like to entwine themselves on swimmers' legs, but they will probably not hurt you, even if you handle them.[70] You can swim here without fear." Nedra looked up at me and smiled. I guessed that she understood Greek even though she did not speak it. Or perhaps a comforting tone of voice is understood everywhere.

I leaned back on one of the big black rocks and watched the girls walking away toward the south end of the bay. They turned around and waved goodbye. In the distance I could see the governor's house, white and shining in the sun.

Back at the waterfall, the crew was ready, and we returned to our ships. I told them of my encounter with Nedra and Bresis.

Adoo and Seenara were always close to Galen, anticipating his every need. Seenara was eager to learn Adoo's language, and he spent much time teaching her. Every time she pronounced a phrase correctly, Adoo kissed her and put a sweet date into her mouth. Galen asked him, "Why are you doing this, Adoo?"

He said, "If I put the sweet in her mouth, she will not forget."

Galen laughed at his naïveté. "Please, Adoo, don't make me laugh. My ribs hurt so much. I think at least two are broken." All the time we were in Serendib, Galen did not leave the ship.

Mobareek told me, "We have to visit the governor. His men notice every ship entering or leaving this harbor. He already knows we are here. Besides, he is the only man on this island who has rubies and sapphires for sale."

Taleb explained, "The people here don't need to work hard in mud pits digging for gems. The sea is full of fish and the trees loaded with fruit. The only man who can make them work is their chief priest, the 'king of the island,' as he likes to be known. All gems go to him and from his hands to the governor. The Greek governor has about a hundred soldiers with him and helps the chief priest defend his coastal domain against the king of the highlands."

---

[70] The olive sea snake (*Aipysurus laevis*) is found in the Indian Ocean and will entwine itself around a swimmer's legs. It has a powerful venom that it uses to hunt.

The next morning, Mobareek, Taleb, and I went ashore to visit the governor. Adoo came with us, carrying a bag full of silver coins. Taleb advised us not to offer any gold coins or the man might think that we were very rich. We passed through a small town built on a low hill and surrounded by a drainage ditch to divert the rainwater to the lagoon.

In the marketplace, we encountered Che, Marcus, Ari, Justin, and some of our crew buying baskets of fish and fruit. They had stopped buying from the women vendors and were watching a strange-looking man. He was a beggar, tall and bald-headed. His torso was nude and hairy with a barrel chest. I thought he must be the son of a foreign sailor because the men of this island are not bald, and they don't have hairy chests.

The beggar was walking slowly, his red eyes bulging and frightening, afflicted by some terrible disease. In his right hand he held a flat stone, and every few steps, he would stop and strike himself on the chest with the stone. A dull thud reverberated in his ribcage, and he reinforced this sound by grunting out loud, "*Hah, hah, hom, hom,*" repeated over and over again.

I asked Taleb Ali, "What is he saying?"

Taleb smiled. "If you don't give me rice, I will curse you thrice."

"Give me rice, or I'll curse you thrice." And he bashed his chest with the flat stone. "*Hah, hah, hom, hom.*" There was a trickle of blood flowing down his hairy chest to his waist and dried blood on his chest.

The young children ran to their mothers, screaming, "*Riri Yakka, Riri Yakka!*" The women left their cooking fires and came out to give the beggar small baskets filled with rice and fish. They dared not approach him but gave the food to a young man following him, probably his son.

Taleb Ali was smiling. He looked at me and said, "These people believe in a powerful demon called *Riri Yakka*. This demon can hurt them or help them, so they must placate him with gifts. They believe in many spirits and demons, both good and evil, and their chief priest plays on their fears. I will take you to see how they worship their gods in their Temple of a Thousand Columns."[71]

As we approached the south end of the harbor, in the most sheltered corner of this wide lagoon, I could see a thick wall in the shape of a great square that had been built in the sea at low tide. The square was filled with earth and gravel. A narrow causeway connected this wall to land, and several buildings and houses had been constructed of coral rock, bleached white by the sun.

Flowering vines were climbing over the white walls, and large trees shaded the courtyards. There was a private dock for small boats. This was a perfect place for the Greek governor and his soldiers. It was cooled by the sea breezes and far enough from land to be safe from flying insects.

The soldiers ushered us into a reception room to meet the governor. It was a beautiful place, well built with huge windows and verandas for cross-ventilation. Many seashells were embedded into the walls, and the flowering vines growing against the white stone walls gave a marvelous effect. There was no other place like this on the island.

The governor walked into the room. His large frame loomed in the doorway. He wore a simple tunic over his chest, but it did not cover the curly black hair on his sloping shoulders. All his men were clean shaven, but he had a well-trimmed black beard. The governor was a military man. Though he wore no insignia of rank, I could see how his soldiers stood at attention whenever he approached them. There was no doubt of who was in command here.

He greeted us politely, and smiling, he said, "What news from Alexandria?" There was iron behind his smile. Nothing, absolutely nothing, could make me reveal Che's true name to this man, even though I knew he was a good friend of Julius Caesar.

I told him, "Antony and Cleopatra are dead. Octavian is now master of the Roman world."

---

[71] The Temple of a Thousand Columns was destroyed by the Portuguese in the seventeenth century. The stones were reused to build a fort.

He was not surprised. "Yes, I know. A fast ship arrived here a few days ago. I hope the Roman governor of Egypt keeps the trade with Serendib alive."

"I hope so, too. We all need it. And speaking of trade, we would like to buy rubies and sapphires. I know we are late, but we can pay a good price, and if there are any pearls left, we will buy them also."

"Yes, you are late," said the governor, "but if you wait for twenty days, I am sure the natives will dig out some more gems."

The governor stood up and walked to the large window. "I can see your two ships anchored in the middle of the lagoon, away from the crowd. Let me give you a ride back in my own boat." I thanked him and understood that he wanted to inspect our ships, and he found a polite way to come aboard without offending us.

We had a comfortable ride back to our ships in the governor's fast boat. Twelve Greek soldiers handled long, sweeping oars, six on each side. Each man had a leather pillow to sit on, and their corded forearms showed that they were used to this exercise. Once on board, the governor recognized Galen and went to him with outstretched hands.

Galen apologized for not rising to greet him. "I broke my ribs in a storm, and I have to rest for a few weeks." The governor sat next to Galen, and they talked for a while. He never asked Galen, "What brings you to Serendib?" However, Galen volunteered, "I am here to collect medicinal plants."

The governor rose to his feet, inspected the ship and her crew, and noticed Marcus, who stood out because of his fair skin and Greek looks. "And who is this *Greek* boy?"

Galen quickly replied, "He is my private servant."

Our crew was standing respectfully, and the governor spoke a few words in Greek to each man. They responded, greeting him in Arabic using the dialect of Red Sea fishermen, which of course he did not understand. I was pleased to see Ari, Justin, and Che act like true sailors. When the governor spoke to them, they said a few polite words in Arabic. They also looked like sailors. Their eyes were red because they swam daily in the salty sea, their hands were rough from handling ropes and oars, and their skin was tanned a deep brown color.

Marcus was the only boy whose fair skin could not stand exposure to the sun and had not browned under the ocean's sun, and I realized then we should have tried to disguise him better. When the governor spoke to him in Greek, asking some questions about Alexandria, the man's intense curiosity was obvious.

Before leaving, the governor invited us to attend a farewell banquet for the captains and navigators of the fleet getting ready to sail back to Egypt. "I will expect you in my house in six days before sunset."

After the governor left our ship, I sat down next to Galen. Mobareek and Taleb joined us. Galen said, "Hiro, did you notice his suspicion when he spoke to Marcus?"

"Yes, and he mentioned a fast ship that sailed into this harbor a few days before us. I wonder if that ship brought the governor an order to arrest the son of Caesar and Cleopatra?"

Galen said, "I am sure he is worried about his ill-gotten treasure. How can he convince the Roman government to allow him to live in Alexandria with his wealth when they can simply confiscate it? I think the Roman governor of Egypt will close this trading post and concentrate his efforts on the grain shipments to Rome. This trade with India will be left to the Arabian sailors and merchants. They will take the gems and ivory of Serendib and the aromatic resins of Yemen and send them across the desert on camel caravans to Syria and Palestine, and then by sea to Rome."

Mobareek said, "Since we have to wait till the governor collects some gems, we should careen our ships and dry their bottoms one at a time."

The next morning, everything in the *Sorceress* was transferred to *Sword of the Sea*, and at high tide, the empty ship was pulled out on the beach. The crew got busy scraping and cleaning the bottom. A crowd of curious children gathered on the beach and enjoyed the show. They were handsome young children with wide, intelligent eyes.

I was standing in the shade of an old tembu tree watching Che, Ari, and Justin working with the crew to pull the ship out of the sea and onto dry land. This voyage had changed them. Their bodies were much stronger, and their whole demeanor was that of strong, self-assured young men. They were not boys anymore.

Two young women stepped out of the crowd. I recognized Nedra and Bresis. Each wore a piece of loose, colorful silk wrapped around her body, and each had a crown of fragrant flowers and ferns. Nedra had three lotus flowers in her hand, one pink, one yellow, and one blue. She rested the flowers on her cheek and then offered them to me with a smile of strange sweetness, full of trust but mixed with something else, which was poignant and sad. I asked the girls to sit near me in the shade and watch our boys working on the ship.

Ari, Che, and Justin came over to my side. I introduced them. "Here is the girl who had the sea snake around her leg." The boys looked at Nedra and Bresis with undisguised admiration. The conversation flowed easily, Bresis translating for Nedra. After a while it was time for the girls to leave us. I held Nedra's hand and looked into her emerald green eyes. I thanked her for the flowers, speaking slowly, hoping that she understood what I said. And once again, she gave me her unforgettable smile.

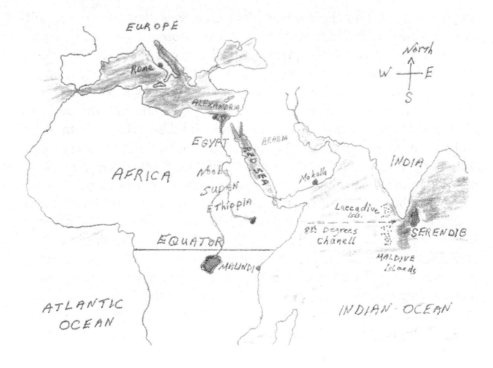

EUROPE

North
W — E
S

Rome

ALEXANDRIA

EGYPT   ARABIA

AFRICA   Nooba   RED SEA   Mokalla   INDIA

SUDEN

Ethiopia

EQUATOR   Laccadive
Isls.

9½ Degrees
Chanell   SERENDIB

MALINDI   MALDIVE
Islands

ATLANTIC
OCEAN   INDIAN OCEAN

CHAPTER 20: The Black Stone

Taleb Ali called me to his side. "Hiro, tomorrow we have a moonless night. Let me take you to the Temple of One Thousand Columns. The boys should come with us. We will witness a strange ceremony."

The next day before sunset, we went by canoe to a head of land, a small, sandy peninsula jutting into the sea. More than two hundred canoes were already there, with people coming from every village on the coast. The sand was clean and soft. The natives had cut down all the coconut palms because the seabirds nesting in them were defiling the place and the noise they raised at night disrupted the solemn ceremony. A thousand columns of coral rock stood upright in a great circle, each about fifteen feet high and three feet thick. As the sun sank lower on the horizon, the natives planted flaming torches into the ground, one for each column. After sunset the crowd sat down in complete silence. We could hear the small waves lapping at the shore, and on a night of dead calm like tonight, voices carried far and wide.

The flaming torches made the circle appear like a thousand columns of light, rising straight up to the sky on this dark night. We sat in the first row to get a good view of the ceremony. Taleb Ali warned us, "Don't approach the altar."

I told him, "I cannot see what is on the altar."

He whispered, "Be patient. The Greeks are not the only ones who know how to perform on stage. Soon the priest will illuminate it. This man is their king, and he rules the coastal villages. The high forested interior is ruled by another king. The Greek soldiers and their governor help ensure that the king of the highlands remains only the king of the highlands."

After a short wait, the high priest walked in holding a flaming torch in each hand. He planted them near the stone altar, and now I could clearly see that it was a black rock just like the rocks I saw on the beach. On top of this rock rested a large tray of pure gold. Inside it was a small conical black stone the size of a large melon surrounded by gem—rubies, sapphires, and pearls, all shining with different colors, their lights playing on the shining small black stone.

The king priest wore a robe of red silk and on his forehead a diadem of gold studded with red rubies. He understood the importance of mystery and distance to preserve the awe of his people and the power of the black stone. No one was allowed to approach the altar except the high priest. He stood between the two flaming torches and spoke in low tones, the volume of his voice rising gradually. His people were spellbound.

I felt a reluctant admiration for the priest. He was a great orator. His gestures and the expression on his face, his whole demeanor, were those of a great leader. He held the crowd in the palm of his hand, and he could sway them any way he wanted. He modulated his voice, savoring every syllable.

Of course, I could not understand a word, so I turned to Taleb Ali. He whispered, "He is recounting the story of the black stone. It fell down from the sky in a fiery trail on a dark, moonless night. The metallic stone landed here on this sandy peninsula. His grandfather, who was chief priest and king of the lowlands, witnessed this event. Many people who are still alive today saw this flaming rock falling from the sky." And so, believing was easy. There must have been another world up there, the abode of the gods. The demons lived down here, among us, on this earth.

When the priest finished his speech, there was total silence, and six pallbearers walked in carrying the dead body of a young man on a sort of stretcher made of bamboo. The body was not covered, and we could all see that he was too young and too handsome to die. The dead man's family were sobbing and wailing hysterically, and their sorrow and pain were overwhelming. I felt for these people.

The pallbearers set the body on the ground at a decent distance from the altar. The priest advanced in slow, majestic steps and ordered the dead man's clan away from the body. They kissed the dead man's hands and feet and moved away. Their wailing stopped.

The priest produced a fearsome mask and wore it on his face. He was now king of all demons, *Vezamuni* himself. He stood near the dead body perfectly still, a chilling menace in his very immobility. He called in the demons, and one by one they appeared, answering their king in low, respectful tones. "O!! *Vezamuni*. O!! *Vezamuni*," they chanted.

The first to appear was the most feared of demons, *Riri Yakka*, and we immediately recognized the beggar we had seen in the village. He wore a hideous wooden mask representing the evil one. He danced around his lord and master, and *Vezamuni* scolded him with a loud and hectoring voice. "Did you make this man ill? Did you kill this man? *Riri Yakka!!* I will torture you with fire!!" He then picked up a flaming torch and singed the skin of the beggar. Then *Vezamuni* called another demon, scolded him, and burned him with the flaming torch just as he did with *Riri Yakka*. One by one, the evil demons came close to the priest and got their punishment. "I will torture you with fire. Bring this man back to life!!" The demons danced a frenzied dance, coming nearer and nearer to the dead body. The silent crowd rose to their feet, unable to control their excitement. They chanted, "O! *Vezamuni*. O! *Vezamuni*," and shook the earth with their stomping feet.

The priest advanced toward the dead man and blew air into his mouth over and over again. The chant was getting louder and louder. The noise was a deafening roar, enough to wake up the dead, and *the dead man did wake up!!*

With a little help from the priest, he sat up, his eyes open. The priest slapped him hard on his back between the shoulders a few times, then retreated majestically to his black stone, and he laid both his hands on it. The frenzied crowd surged forward toward the black stone, yelling and shouting, "Aah!! *Vezamuni!!*" They wanted to touch their king. I saw the fanatical expressions on their faces, and for one dreadful moment I thought the priest had lost control. But he did not flinch; the man had a core of steel in him. He roared his warning, and the crowd stopped as if by an invisible fence. He threw up his head and looked imperiously around him. The crowd slowly moved back and returned to their canoes, back to their villages

I had no way of knowing the king's thoughts at this moment, but everything in his posture betrayed the fact that he was drunk with power. He was king, priest, and oracle all in one. The resurrected man's family lifted their son on their shoulders and walked away. They would toil happily in the mud pits, digging out rubies and sapphires for their king. He would pile the gems around the black stone, and the gods would descend at night and take them away.

After the crowd dispersed, I approached the black stone. I knew in my heart that I should not do it, but I wanted a closer look at this stone sitting in a gold tray filled with brilliant rubies. The priest stood there, his hands on the stone and his shoulders squared. He gazed at me with massive composure. I am sure he recognized that I was a foreigner. I looked into his eyes and felt the power and sheer presence of the man, and I could not move any closer to his black stone.

Back on our ship, I described everything we had witnessed in great detail. Galen's eyes narrowed as he was thinking. "Hiro, are you sure the young man was dead?"

Before I could answer, Adoo said, "Yes. I saw his dead body right in front of me and heard the wailing of his family."

Galen said, "This may be a mystery. But there is an explanation, even though we don't know it."

The entire crew was gathered around us, listening intently and marveling at the story. Young people love stories with miracles and magic.

Mobareek said, "It is time to rest. Tomorrow at high tide, we will push the *Sorceress* back into the sea, and the day after tomorrow, we will pull *Sword of the Sea* out to dry."

The next morning, we were making ready to push the *Sorceress* back into the sea. The same crowd of cheerful children gathered to watch us. They found foreigners and their wonderful ways to be irresistible entertainment. Nedra and Bresis also showed up every morning. They stood near me in the shade. Bresis noticed that my attention was drawn to two small boys. She explained they were brothers, sons of a fisherman. The younger boy, about five years old, had a pet bird, the biggest, fattest goose that I ever saw. The goose followed the young boy wherever he went, and he in turn followed closely behind his brother, who was about ten years old. The older boy waded into the sea towing a raft of bamboo behind him. The small boy swam after his brother, and the white goose followed him. Whenever he got tired, he threw his arm around his pet goose. The bird supported him easily and swam after his brother.

The older boy had many fish traps in the shallow water made of split bamboo. Any fish he caught went into a basket on top of his bamboo raft. The boys and their goose went far away down the coast, and soon we could not see them.

Adoo, sitting in the shade, was digging his heels forcefully into the sand. Inactivity was almost torture to him. "I am going to follow the coastline in our canoe," he said, calling out to Che, Ari, and Justin, hoping to spark some enthusiasm and get the young men to go with him. But they refused to go. They were talking to Bresis and basking happily in the sunshine of Nedra's smiles. Adoo laughed his boyish laugh and said, "The boys won't explore with me. Will you, Hiro?"

I laughed. "I must confess I cannot blame them. But I will join you, Adoo."

So we jumped into a fast canoe. The water near land was calm and flat. We hugged the coast, our canoe flying.

Beyond the waterfall, at the north end of the bay, we found the two brothers and their white goose on the beach. The small boy was jumping up and down, waving his arms frantically. We went to them and found the older boy crying, his ankle bleeding from an ugly wound and his leg swelling rapidly. I lifted the wounded boy into the canoe, and his brother sat near him, holding the pet goose. Adoo picked up their basket full of fish, and we hurried back to *Sword of the Sea.* Adoo climbed up on deck. I lifted the boy up, and Adoo carried him to Galen's side. Then I helped the younger boy up onto the deck with his goose and his fish basket.

Taleb Ali could understand their language, and he asked the boy, "What happened to you?" The boy explained that he had stepped on a stingray when he was checking his fish traps. Taleb said, "We must get the poison out of the wound quickly." He ordered the crew to boil some water in a pot. Taleb held the boy's ankle in the steam above the boiling water, taking care not to burn the skin. The venomous mucus from the barbs of the sting ray sticks to the wound. However, the hot steam will melt it away. Taleb kept cleaning the wound with pieces of cloth dipped in the boiling water. The pain in his swollen leg was too great. However, when he lay down on his back, he could tolerate the pain and stopped crying.

After this treatment, the boy could not stand up. Galen said, "Taleb Ali, today I have learned something new from you. Let me see the fish in the boy's basket." Taleb reached into the basket and lifted a large *drimma*. Galen said to the boys, "Don't you know this is poisonous? Every fisherman knows he will die if he eats this fish."

The older boy said, "We never eat these fish. We sell them to the priest."[72]

The idea came to me in a blinding flash. The king priest wanted the poisonous liver of this fish—what for? Before I could say anything, Galen said, "Now we know how the priest 'raises the dead.' The liver of this fish contains a powerful poison. If he dries it and grinds it to a powder, one of his helpers can put it in the food of his victim. A healthy young man is chosen because if he feeds this poison to an old man, he will surely die. A healthy man will fall into deep sleep, his body completely relaxed and his heartbeat feeble and very slow. After twenty hours, the priest can wake up the young man. Obviously, the priest found the right dose by experience and experiment. I wonder how many victims died before he mastered his theatrics? If fate had not intervened today, we would never have found out how the priest performs his 'miracles,' and this young boy might be dead."

---

[72] This poisonous puffer fish of the family *Tetraodontidae* is found in shallow water and grows to a length of one foot. It can blow itself full of water or air into the shape of a ball. To this day in Haiti, the voodoo priests use the poison of this fish to turn their victims into "zombies," brain-damaged men drugged into catalepsy and speechlessness.

CHAPTER 21: Elephants and Ivory

Taleb Ali had many friends on this island. Wherever we went, someone would step forward and greet him. He said, "Hiro, I cannot find any ivory. We are late, and the traders sold all they had to the fleet. You will have to go to the highlands to buy ivory from the Mahoots. I cannot go with you. The trail is too steep and my knees too old. However, I will find a guide who will show you the way."

Mobareek said, "The forests of the highlands are deep and untouched. I will go with you. I need four perfect masts for new ships."

Taleb warned us, "You must take thirty armed men with you just in case you encounter armed gangs of thieves, who are ruthless and know the forests well. They prey on merchants and travelers, and they give the loot to their leaders to enrich their temples."

To reach the land of the Mahoots, we followed a rough track that snaked up over the hills and through the green jungle. In many places we walked on a thick mat of fallen leaves. Higher and higher we climbed, sweating heavily. The humid air was rich with the penetrating scents of the jungle. It was the smell of rotting fruit. Gigantic trees loaded with ripe, wild figs were dropping their fruit all over the trail. Fortunately, the trail ran alongside a small river, and at every stop we cooled ourselves in the running water.

Late in the afternoon the cloud cover broke, and in the gentle evening sunshine we saw a wide, open plateau. We followed our guide to a village of about forty large huts, each big enough to shelter a whole family. This was the village of the Mahoots, who tamed wild elephants, collected ivory, and harvested fine woods.

It was a gentle landscape, infinitely soothing with the elephants bathing in the river or resting in the shade of ancient trees. Giants of the forest and sacred to the Mahoots, the tame elephants wandered into the jungle in the early evening to feed on leaves and shoots. We could hear the noise they made while foraging and a deep rumbling sound coming from their chests as if they were talking to each other. At first light the elephants came back into the clearing, and the Mahoots fed them fruit, tubers, and sugar cane for a sweet breakfast. By midday the heat was intense, and the working elephants entered the river to cool themselves. Nothing could induce them to get back to work.

The young Mahoots riding their elephants controlled them with well-placed kicks behind the ears, which the elephants barely felt. Driving an elephant seemed to be childishly easy, but the reality is that the Mahoots spent many months taming the young elephants until they became docile, obedient, and friendly.

We explained to their leader that we wanted to buy ivory and wood logs. Mobareek paid them in silver coins and then gave their leader an extra gift, a small leather pouch filled with golden coins. The man received this gift with pleasure and surprise. Mobareek turned to me and said, "These poor people have to pay the king of the highlands, and they will judge a stranger by one quality only, his generosity. We will now be given the choice ivory and the finest logs of wood."

We slept in a hastily built lean-to. The next morning, the Mahoots invited us to ride into the jungle on elephants' backs. No doubt this was the best way to view the ancient forest. As we rode high above the ground surrounded by an endless variety of big trees and climbing vines, colorful birds and troops of monkeys were at eye level, noisy and entertaining.

The elephants were following well-beaten paths that crisscrossed the forest. The Mahoots had created these trails over years in their search for valuable trees and herds of wild elephants. Mobareek was looking for *saag* trees, valued by sailors for their oily wood (teak). He wanted four trees, perfect without defects, with trunks free of branches and at least thirty feet long. Finally, he found a tree that he liked. The Mahoots cut a deep ring in the trunk, and then Mobareek took an axe and cut deep into one side of the tree. When he finished, he said, "This tree must not fall to the ground. If it does, the impact will case internal cracks that separate the rings of wood from each other and weaken the strength of the tree. These ring shakes are not visible from the outside. If it falls onto a neighboring tree, then we will cut the straight trunk and slowly lower it to the ground."

A young man climbed the tree and attached four strong ropes high up on the trunk. Four elephants stood where Mobareek indicated. The ropes were tied to a harness around the elephants' shoulders, and the Mahoots, sitting on the necks of the powerful beasts, urged them forward. The animals pulled with all their might to please their friends and masters. With a loud crack, the tree fell down.

We cut four trees to make perfect masts for new ships. The elephants dragged the logs back to the Mahoot village; then they went into the river to cool off. When they came out of the cool water, they had their reward: sugar cane and bamboo shoots. After debarking the logs, the Mahoots would drag them down to the coast. That would take two or three days. The next day we had a load of choice ivory, and six elephants took us back down to the coast. Our young sailors had an unforgettable ride. We never saw any thuggees in the jungle of Serendib.

When we reached the sea, the jungle giants waded in the shallows, then swam right out to the deep blue hole where our ships were anchored. The riders were awash in seawater. The elephants swam submerged, with only their eyes and trunks kept in the air. For Galen, Adoo, and Seenara, it must have been quite a sight to see us returning on the backs of swimming elephants.

We quickly unloaded the ivory, and Mobareek gave each Mahoot a golden coin. They turned back, and on the beach I could see the bulky forms of these intelligent elephants and their Mahoots waving their hands at us with gentle benevolence.

CHAPTER 22: Dirge for the Dead

An hour past midnight, I sat up and saw Che standing at the bow, gazing at the horizon. I walked over to his side. "Che, why can't you sleep?"

"I had a terrible dream."

"Tell me all about it."

"I saw Marcus in the ocean drowning, struggling to save himself, and I was unable to reach him no matter how hard I swam. Finally, when I stretched out my arm to grab him, I saw his body drifting without a head. The dream was so vivid, I got up and walked over to look at Marcus sleeping in his usual place on deck."

"Are you worried about him?"

"No, I have no reason to worry about Marcus . . . but I have never dreamed about him before."

"Try to get some rest."

It was a calm, clear night, and I went back to sleep, leaving Che alone on the ship's bow. Midmorning, a Greek soldier came aboard to remind us that the farewell banquet for the departing fleet would start just before sunset, and all navigators and captains were invited to attend.

Adoo chose to stay with Galen aboard the *Sorceress.* Mobareek, Taleb, and I got into a large canoe and paddled to the governor's compound. Ari, Justin, Che, Marcus, and Atiya followed in another canoe. When we reached the governor's private dock, our boys insisted on carrying Atiya with his beloved simsimiyya in his hands. Laughing, they said, "Atiya, you're the king of musicians. We must carry you on our shoulders." They were an effervescent group of young men, eager to enjoy the party.

The banquet was to be held in the open air. We entered a courtyard illuminated with many torches. There were more than a hundred captains and navigators sitting in groups. Mobareek made his way through the crowd, cool and unhurried, with natural grace. He was an overpowering presence with his massive shoulders and the vast expanse of his chest. People stopped talking and turned their heads when he passed. Every navigator from the Egyptian fleet recognized Mobareek and saluted him.

Hails of welcome and a friendly greeting came from every table. I followed in his regal wake as he slowly made his way to a dais at the far end of the courtyard. Seated on this dais was the governor and a few of his officers, and to his right I recognized Nedra and Bresis. We saluted the governor and seated ourselves at a table near the elevated dais.

I told Mobareek and Taleb, "Take a good look at this beautiful young woman. She is the one who had the bad scare with the sea snake."

Mobareek asked me, "The one near the governor?"

"Yes. Her name is Nedra."

"Hiro, you never said she what a great beauty she is!"

"The young woman next to her is her maid, Bresis. I wonder, is Nedra the governor's wife or his concubine?"

The tables were laden with a variety of foods. It was a memorable spread. Young island girls were circulating between the tables, filling the guests' cups with wine. Nedra and Bresis were serving the governor and his officers. But I lost all interest in food and wine. I could not take my eyes off Nedra. She was beautiful in the torchlight, dressed in a robe of white silk, a tiara of pearls on her head, and in her hands a musical instrument with six strings.

After the meal, Atiya played his five-stringed simsimiyya. When he stopped for a rest, I was surprised to see Nedra step down from the dais. She walked over to Atiya, sat down next to him, took the simsimiyya into her own hands, and played it magically. Her radiant beauty and the melodies she coaxed out of the instrument made the crowd stand up and cheer.

Our boys, Ari, Justin, Che, and Marcus, gathered around Atiya, and he played the songs of the Red Sea and songs from Yemen. Most of the guests knew the words, and they joined in the singing and hilarity.

Nedra and Bresis served more wine to the governor and his officers. They all seemed to be half drunk. Then Nedra walked gracefully to our table. She refilled our wine cups, smiling at me her sweet, mysterious smile. Then she seated herself between me and my friend Mobareek.

I looked at Nedra, her glorious brown hair falling on her shoulders, her green eyes luminous in the torchlight. I offered her the cup of wine that she had refilled for me. She took a sip and put it down on the table. Mobareek looked at us with utterly serene, humorous eyes. "Be careful, Hiro. This is no ordinary wine. It is a potent drink. The natives make it from sweet fruit."

The crowd was singing, Atiya was playing his music, and the men were clapping their hands to the rhythms of a hilarious song. Mobareek was singing in his deep, resonant voice, and I joined him. Nedra moved closer to me, and I felt the back of her hand brushing against my thigh. I changed the words of the song, and to Mobareek I sang:

Take out the torchlight. I don't need any light tonight.
Put out the torchlight my friend. Help me tonight!

Mobareek never stopped singing. He just reached over my shoulder and took the fiery torch away from me and extinguished the flame.

We were in the shadows, and I reached down and took Nedra's soft hand in mine. The gentleness of her touch and the nearness of her fair beauty sent a great wave of longing over me. I kept her hand in mine and felt her fingers entwine around my own.

I continued to sing with the happy guests. The drummers were playing as loud as they could. I looked at the governor and his officers, and they appeared to be drunk. Many guests were on their feet getting ready to leave. They crowded around the dais to say goodbye to the governor. I was sure he could not see us, so I walked out of the courtyard, holding Nedra's small hand in mine.

We walked slowly away from the singers and musicians, out onto the causeway flooded with moonlight. We stood there silently admiring the reflection of the moon on the sea, the image of the goddess of love. I took both her hands in mine and kissed Nedra's beautiful face gently and unhurriedly. I could no longer hear the drummers or the singing. In an instant, there was no noise, just the two of us standing in the moonlight with the fragrance of her jasmine garlands rising around us. Life was incomprehensibly sweet.

I kissed Nedra again and again. I could not understand her words, but I loved her melodious language falling from her lips like kisses as she whispered in my face. I was filled with a calm resolve. *I must get this girl out of here. I will do it. I must.*

Bresis came running on the causeway. The magic spell was broken. She took Nedra by her arm, and they both hurried back without saying a word to me. I walked back to the dock crowded with old friends, navigators, and captains saying goodbye to each other, happy to be going back home to Egypt, the Arabian ships returning to Yemen, to the port of Mokalla, or the harbor of Aden.

Taleb Ali and Mobareek were waiting for me. I asked them, "Did you see our boys?" Taleb replied, "Their canoe is here. They must be here somewhere."

"I wonder what the boys are doing?" said Taleb.

We did not have to wait long. Ari, Justin, and Che came to the dock carrying Atiya. Che had a worried expression on his face. "I cannot find Marcus. Did you see him?"

"No. Was he drunk?" I asked.

"No, he was sober and singing with us. Then he disappeared in the jostling crowd."

"Maybe he went to the village with one of the dancing girls," said Taleb.

We sat down and waited for Marcus. Hours passed, but he never returned. Taleb said, "Let us go back to the ships, and at first light, we will send the crew to search the villages."

We went back to our ships. I stretched out on deck, but sleep would not come to me. The bright moon had a perfect ring of light around it, a beautiful halo that indicated a change of weather tomorrow.

Che could not sleep, either. He paced the deck for some time, and then noticed I was awake. He sat down nearby and whispered, "I am worried, Hiro. I told you about my bad dream. That was a warning. I should have kept my eyes on Marcus last night. I am sure he is in great danger."

I was at a loss for words that might calm Che. Finally I said, "Try not to worry. Tomorrow the entire crew will go to the villages and look for him. I would not be surprised if he showed up at sunrise."

At first light, Che woke up the crew, and after a hasty breakfast, forty young men went to the small town on the coast and the villages surrounding it looking for Marcus, shouting his name.

As I expected, the weather changed, and we had a strong offshore wind blowing from the east. Many captains took advantage of this and sailed out of the harbor to the open sea. I watched them raise sails and listened to their chanting. By early afternoon, more than half the fleet had sailed out on their way home.

Che and the crewmen returned. Che sat next to Galen, exhaustion and worry all over his face. "We did not find Marcus. We went to every hut and every house, shouting his name."

Galen replied, "We will not sail out of this harbor till we find him."

Che thanked Galen and managed to smile through the tired lines on his face. He had a meal with the crew and then fell asleep.

Before sunset I saw Bresis running on the beach, waving her arms. I jumped into a canoe and took Adoo and two strong crewmen with me. We reached the beach in no time. Bresis was sitting on the sand, distressed and crying. I knelt next to her and put my hands on her shoulders. I was tense and worried. I knew beyond doubt that something horrible had happened.

"Bresis, tell me, why are you crying?"

"I overheard the governor talking to his officers this morning. Your friend, the Greek boy . . . " She had to stop. Tears were flowing down her face, and her body was shaking.

I held her shoulders. "Yes, Marcus. What happened?"

"I heard the governor say, 'Galen, the queen's physician, is here, and with him a well-fed Greek boy. If the boy is Cleopatra's son, his head will be my gift to Octavian.'" After a while, she calmed down and said, "They tortured him, and he admitted that he was the son of

Caesar and Cleopatra. Then they cut his head off and sent it to the new emperor on one of these ships!"

I was stunned. I sat down next to Bresis and held her for a long moment. I was trying to think clearly, but that was impossible. The warning dream had come true.

"Bresis, no one must see you talking to us. Calm yourself. Go back and pretend you know nothing. Don't come to us unless you have something very urgent. Go now, and stay with your mistress." Bresis washed her face in the sea and walked back on the beach toward the governor's compound.

When the crew heard what Bresis had said, all merriment stopped, and instantly there was a chilling emptiness in our hearts. Che and Justin, who were closest to Marcus, reeled from the news. Che fell to his knees and wept bitterly. When he had drunk his fill of his own tears, he sat down, holding his head in his hands, his body rocking back and forth, and he let himself sink into deep misery. Justin remained stunned, trying to comprehend what had happened, unable to grieve fully.

The entire crew gathered around Che and Justin to show their compassion. They sat in a tight circle, totally silent, respecting their pain and sorrow. The young men loosened their turbans and let the fine cloth fall down over their faces. They did not want to be seen in their moments of weakness.

They sang a sad dirge that brought tears to their eyes:

What is life without a friend?
What is life without a brother?
Sadness and pain without end!

What is life without a father?
What is life without a mother?
Sorrow and pain without end!

Cry for the orphan without a father!
Cry for the child without a mother!
Cry for your lost friend!

The slow, sad lament stirred up a nest of memories, sad memories. They repeated the song over and over again. Every man was crying, not only for Marcus but also for his own departed loved ones. Each man had his private pain and hid his flowing tears behind his turban. No one could resist this continuous lament, this sad, monotonous dirge, the voices rising and then falling down to a low whisper, then up again to a high, shrill note of pain. None could resist, even Mobareek, who had tears rolling down his iron cheeks. Who knows what sad memories this strong man kept hidden in his breast?

Galen and I retired from the larger party to digest the news of Marcus's brutal death and assess our situation. Galen quietly anguished, and I knew that he, like I, was burdened with Marcus's fate.

"Galen," I said, "we could not have known."

He nodded quietly. "Thank you, Hiro. And Justin and Ari, how will they be?"

"I do not know, Galen, as they are in shock, especially Justin. I will take them now for a long walk on the beach."

Galen looked at me and, as if seeming to understand my own anxiety in helping my sons through their grief, told me quietly, "It will take time. And as they have no mother, they must talk to you, so let them."

I breathed deeply, and sadness engulfed me.

CHAPTER 23: Sati

At the far end of the bay beyond the waterfall, there was a green hill about one thousand feet high. A cool mist was swirling on top of this hill. Che told us he wanted to climb the hill to be alone to think about his friend's short life and about his own.

Adoo said to Galen, "Let him go. Among my tribe, when a man is stricken with grief, he walks into the desert alone for a day and a night. Thirst, hunger, and fatigue will overcome his misery, and he returns resigned to his fate."

Galen said, "I understand. But he must take some drinking water."

Adoo picked up a small waterskin. "I will go with Che to the foot of the hill to mark the place where he starts his climb. If he is late returning, it will be easy to track him." Adoo took Che by the arm and in a kindly voice said, "Come, Che, let us go. I will fly a yellow flag on top of the mast. If I take it down, you must return as fast as you can." Both Che and Adoo climbed into a canoe and headed for the green hill.

We gathered around Galen, and I told him about the warning dream. He said, "Yes, these things will happen. Many parents dream about their children being sick or in danger. If millions of mothers have such dreams, some are bound to come true. I must say, this is a coincidence."

I said, "But this case is different. This was the only time Che ever dreamt about Marcus, and the dream was not vague. It was a precise description, a body at sea without a head! And the warning was only one day before the murder."

Galen answered, "Such dreams happen only once or twice in a lifetime, so we cannot study them. How can you learn about an incident that happens only once in your life?" Galen looked at the young men listening to him. "Beware of people who pretend they have an explanation. The truth is, we do not know."

Adoo returned to the ship and raised a bright yellow flag high on the masthead. Then he joined our circle and sat down near me. Taleb spoke up. "I know every one of you is thinking of revenge. We want to punish the governor, but I say it would be wiser to leave the island now, and we can think of a plan to punish him later."

I told Taleb, "We cannot leave until Che returns." And I was thinking to myself, *I will not sail until Nedra and Bresis are safe on board.*

Taleb looked at Adoo and said in a loud, clear voice for all to hear, "The Greek governor thinks he killed the son of Cleopatra! He also believes that the queen's son would have escaped out of Egypt loaded with a great treasure. No doubt he will try to get his hands on it. Adoo, the crew must be alert and have their weapons close at hand. Mark my words, you will see the governor's ugly face very soon."

Mobareek added, "Taleb is right. His soldiers are mercenaries. They don't want to fight. All they want is to go back home to Alexandria. However, if the governor convinces his men we have a treasure on our ships, they will attack us."

A whole day passed with no sign of the governor or his men. At night we were alert, ready for anything, but no one came close to our ships. All night I was thinking of a plan to take Nedra and Bresis off this island and back with us to Alexandria, but how could that be done? Adoo was near me, and on an impulse I confided in him, "Adoo, I don't want to sail away and leave the girls Bresis and Nedra on this island. I hate the idea of leaving them here to serve the governor."

He laughed his broad laugh and said, "I know. Mobareek told me what happened to you at the banquet. Don't worry, Hiro. We can find a way to take them with us. And once we sail away, who will catch us? Who in Serendib has a ship fast enough?"

The next morning, we were surprised to see six elephants and their Mahoots on the beach. A crowd of natives, children, and adults were gathered around the gigantic beasts. Adoo was leading the crew in their military exercises. I interrupted him. "Adoo, I am going ashore with Mobareek to meet the Mahoots. Keep exercising the crew, and stay alert."

Taleb Ali, Ari, Justin, and Mobareek joined me, and we went ashore with swords in our belts. Mobareek picked up his heavy axe. He was sure the elephants had dragged the logs he wanted and had brought them down to the edge of the sea. On the beach, Taleb Ali greeted the Mahoots. They seemed amazed at the sight of our ships. Taleb explained that we wanted their elephants to drag the logs to our ships after Mobareek cut them to the right length. The Mahoots untied the logs, and one man tried to lift Mobareek's double-headed axe, but it was too heavy for him. The Mahoots were small men, and they marveled at the size and weight of this axe.

Mobareek towered above them like a colossus. He raised his axe and struck the log with great vigor. The crowd was curious and silent. There was something very rewarding in watching this giant at work. The natives formed a semicircle around us. There was no one between us and the ships. Mobareek had cut three logs and was working on the last one when the crowd parted, and the governor came walking toward us, followed by about twenty armed Greek soldiers.

I told Mobareek, "Don't stop. Keep working." Then I held Ari and Justin by their wrists. "Quick. Go to the ships, and get Adoo and the whole crew with their weapons." I gave the boys a friendly push toward the canoe, and then I turned to meet the governor.

Mobareek stopped working, and the governor said, "I heard six elephants were on the beach, so I came to see what is going on." He looked relaxed and confident. I smiled at him, pretending I knew nothing of his evil deeds.

"As you can see, we are preparing extra masts for our ships."

"When are you sailing away?"

"We are waiting for two missing sailors. They must be in one of the villages. You know how the boys follow the girls." I looked straight into his eyes, trying hard to keep my voice friendly.

"Only two of your men are missing?"

"Yes, and as soon as they return, we shall sail away."

It seemed to me that the governor was pleased with himself, believing I did not know about the foul murder he had committed. There was a brief silence. I could see six canoes racing toward us, their crews stripped to their waists, and I knew their weapons were hidden in their canoes.

The governor saw them, but he had no way of knowing they were armed. He said in a pleasant voice, "Before you leave, I want to come aboard with my men to inspect your ships."

"You are welcome aboard, of course, but why bring your men?"

Before he could think of an answer, the six canoes hit the beach, and Adoo, with thirty-six armed sailors, surrounded us. The surprise was complete. The governor and his twenty soldiers were trapped.

I looked at our young men covered with sweat, their muscles glistening in the sun, and felt a surge of pride rising in my breast. The daily training Adoo gave them had turned them into fighters, and now they were eager to avenge the death of Marcus.

Adoo stepped forward. "Order your men to drop their weapons."

There was a sudden change in the governor's attitude. From a stupefied man, he became an angry officer. His voice was loud and hectoring as he shouted at us, "What is the meaning of this? You will be captured and tortured." He looked at the young crew trying to scare them. "When I am finished with your leaders, those among you who are still alive will envy the dead!"

Adoo, his whip in his right hand, his left hand on the hilt of his sword, swaggered forward toward the governor. He wore his lazy smile on his face, but there was a dangerous light in his eyes. "You are wasting your breath. Not one of my crew understands your Greek!"

The governor walked toward his soldiers, anger distorting his ugly features, and he cursed them as cowardly sons of whores. He knew his men would not fight for him. He took a sword and a wooden shield from one of them. Then he faced me, only a few steps away.

"You say you are a naval officer. Come and fight like one!" He was no coward, and he had decided not to surrender. His voice was loud and threatening. "Come, my guest! You too will die. It will be quick. No one will hear you cry!" There was an arrogant challenge in his voice and words, and faced with the sheer brutal force of the man, few would stand up and fight him hand to hand. His fierce eyes were filled with anger and hatred. The thick hair covering his shoulders and chest was now covered with sweat. I could see he was determined to kill me. No man could defeat this monster except with great strength or great speed, neither of which I had anymore. I circled around the man slowly, and as I did so, I saw Mobareek take off his turban and wrap it around his left forearm. He was getting ready to fight. Our eyes met, and he read my silent appeal for help.

Mobareek finished wrapping his turban around his left forearm. Then he nodded his head calmly, and I saw his face being transformed, the lines hardening and a dangerous look coming into his eyes. He stepped forward, his great axe in his hands, and a roar like that of a wounded lion came out of his massive chest.

The governor turned to face Mobareek, and I saw fear in his eyes. The Greek had a wooden shield tied to his left forearm and a sharp sword in his right hand. Mobareek walked slowly toward him, his axe swinging around his head, a loud rumble coming from his throat. He was like an angry volcano about to explode.

The Greek stepped forward, his right arm raised for a strike, and at the same moment, the axe head flashed in the sunlight and crashed into his shield, right through the wood. Mobareek pulled the man toward him, the axe firmly fixed to the shield and the shield tied to the Greek's forearm. I saw Mobareek gripping his axe handle with two hands, pulling his enemy toward him. The man let himself be pulled, hoping to strike Mobareek with his sword. As his heavy body moved forward, Mobareek stretched his leg and tripped the governor. He fell down flat, his face in the wet sand, and Mobareek's fist crashed down on the back of his neck at the base of the skull, killing him instantly.

Mobareek stood over him like a colossus made of stone until he was sure his enemy was dead. Then he walked toward me and said, with great dignity of voice and gesture, "It was a good fight. Thank you, Hiro!"

A rush of emotions overwhelmed me, and I could not answer him. Strange that Mobareek should thank me. He had just saved my life. Later on I understood; he had thanked me for the opportunity to kill this brute.

The governor's body lay in the sand. He was the victim of his own greed and pride.

Military men have a certain way of talking to their soldiers. They use a tone of voice, words, and gestures that civilians never use. And now I faced the Greek mercenaries and spoke as an officer should. "Listen carefully. Mark Antony is dead. The queen is dead. Alexandria now has a Roman governor. Your salaries will not be paid. The Romans will ignore this trading post. You must elect one of you to be your leader. Go and find the governor's treasure, and your leader will divide it among you. There are a few ships still in the harbor. They will take you back to Egypt."

There was a ripple of satisfaction in the ranks of the soldiers. They looked at each other, smiling, knowing their troubles in this distant land were over. They could return to Alexandria loaded with silver. The mercenaries left the body of their dead leader and their weapons on the beach. We collected the weapons and returned to our ships.

I looked back and saw the crowd of natives surrounding the dead body growing bigger every minute. There was no wailing. They were sullen and silent. No one lamented the fallen governor. Adoo, who had an endless store of proverbs, said, "The victorious warrior must have his reward before the sweat dries on his brow." Then he called the crew, and Galen pressed gold coins into every man's hand.

I took Adoo by his arm and said, "Thank you. Your men were marvelous. They all love you, Adoo. Why, I don't know!" But of course I *did* know. His kindness and his concern for the crew made him like an older brother to them.

Adoo, laughing, brought down the yellow flag. "I will bring Che back. I will be the first to tell him that the murder of his friend has been avenged."

Ari and Justin joined Adoo, and two hours later they returned with Che in their canoe. I looked at him as he stepped on deck. His face looked as boyish as ever, but the dark lines of exhaustion around his eyes told an eloquent story of pain and lost innocence.

Che heard in great detail how we trapped the governor and his men, and how Mobareek sent him down to Hades. Che wanted to go ashore to view the dead governor, but I restrained him.

The silent natives did not touch the body. They were waiting for something or someone. The priest king arrived and gave the order.

Then they lifted the dead man on their shoulders and followed the priest to the small town.

Taleb Ali, wise in the ways of this island, advised us, "We should go ashore and invite the Mahoots to be our guests and sleep on board tonight. Tomorrow, if the native crowds grow ugly, they can help us with their elephants. Let us go."

So we went ashore, Mobareek, Taleb Ali, and I. The Mahoots had a great admiration for Mobareek. He had just killed the enemy of their king. They gladly accepted our invitation to sleep on-board ship, and our crew made huge balls of boiled rice mixed with sweet dates for the elephants. The crew was fascinated with the sight of the elephants swimming, bringing our new masts to the ships.

Galen paid the Mahoots handsomely in silver coins, and everyone seemed to be relaxed and happy, all except me. I was worried about the girls, and so I told my friends, "I must go to the governor's compound and bring back Nedra and Bresis. They are not safe there among the drunken mercenaries." Adoo immediately volunteered to go with me.

Mobareek said, "Take half the crew with you, well armed, and go by sea to avoid the crowd."

It was near sunset. As we were getting ready to move, we saw a human figure in the dark water. The swimmer came close to our ship, and Adoo reached down and pulled her up. It was Bresis, tired and wild eyed. For a while she could not talk. The poor girl was breathing heavily and crying at the same time. Seenara put her arms around Bresis and tried to calm her down. I held the girl's hand. "Bresis, what happened? Where is Nedra?"

She had a desperate look in her eyes. "The priest took her away. She could not escape. They will burn her alive on the funeral pyre." Bresis was maddened with grief. She was tearing her own hair. "Please save her!" She kept repeating the same words until she lost her voice.

"Calm yourself, girl," I said. "Where can we find Nedra?"

She answered in a hoarse whisper, "Tomorrow in their Temple of the Black Stone at sunset, the governor's body will be cremated, and Nedra has to die on the funeral pyre even though she was not his wife, only a concubine."

Adoo took me by the arm and pulled me away from the wailing Bresis. "Listen, Hiro, the priest will have to bring Nedra alive to the funeral. We will snatch her away from him right there in the temple!"

Adoo said these few words with total confidence, and Mobareek said, "Don't worry, Hiro. The elephants can cut through the hostile crowd. The Mahoots will be glad to help us because the priest is the enemy of their king."

Both these men had a marvelous effect on me. Their presence of mind and great self-assurance calmed me down. My heart stopped racing, and I could think clearly again.

Taleb Ali held my arm and spoke earnestly. "Be careful, Hiro. If you kill any natives, the crowd will be wild with anger." Taleb closed his eyes for a moment as if he were deep in thought. Then he said, "Our ships will be ready to sail. Take thirty armed men with you on the elephants' backs. I have already explained our plan to the Mahoots. They will bring you back safely."

Adoo asked for volunteers. Every man stepped forward, and he selected the best among them. "Now, go to sleep. I will need your strength tomorrow."

This was one of the worst nights I ever endured. Restful sleep would not come to me, so I stretched on deck next to my wise friend Galen, and we talked far into the night. "Galen, what madness is this, to burn a girl alive on her husband's dead body? What do these people believe?"

"Diodorus Siculus witnessed this horror in the Punjab when he was traveling in India," said Galen. "In some quarters there, a virtuous wife must throw herself onto her husband's funeral pyre. They call this barbaric custom *Sati*.[73] I believe there is a poignant tale associated with it, of a young princess who was overwhelmed with grief when her husband died in battle. No one tried to stop her when she threw herself on the funeral pyre to be with her beloved husband in another life. In

---

[73] Akbar, the Muslim mogul, ruler of India, tried to abolish the custom of *Sati,* or burning widows alive on the funeral pyre of their husbands, around 1582. Lord William Bentinck, the British governor-general of India, supported by the Hindu reformer Rammohan Ray, abolished Sati in 1829.

fact, the people admired her great love, which was stronger than the fear of death and stronger than the love of life."

"And yet the custom in those quarters in India where it is practiced is anything but poignant," I said.

We talked till the early light. Finally, at dawn, I fell into a much-needed restful sleep.

In the afternoon, the Mahoots were ready. We rode the elephants, sitting comfortably in the *howdag*, which was made of wood and split bamboo in the shape of a great basket. The elephants proceeded slowly to the site of the Temple of a Thousand Columns.

We arrived an hour before sunset. There was a look of unreality about the stone columns reaching up into the sky and throwing a thousand long shadows over the clean, white sand. We sat quietly on the elephants' backs, observing the scene. The wind was blowing hard from the land, and the sunset was red and angry. There were no children in the crowd of spectators, only adult men and women. Many were carrying gongs. Near the black stone, a pyre of wood was piled up in a manner that would allow the fire to explode. The body of the dead Greek was placed on top of the wood. Men were pouring oil on the body to help it burn quickly.

The natives kept their distance from the elephants, and we sat patiently, our weapons concealed in the howdag. Some men set fire to the wood, and a long-drawn wail arose from the women in the crowd. The men beat their gongs louder and still louder. The king priest appeared, walking toward the flaming pyre with Nedra beside him. She was dressed in her finest clothes, and my first thought was that she was drugged. Adoo, sitting next to me, kept whispering in my ear, "Stay calm; stay calm. Wait for the right moment. Wait until I tell you." My heart was thumping in my chest. I depended on the judgment and fighting instincts of Adoo.

The Mahoots started their elephants moving slowly toward the flaming pyre. The priest was on the other side of the fire. When he saw us, the expression on his face became menacing. The great tangle of his eyebrows bristled fiercely. He put his arm around Nedra's waist, supporting her, his eyes mere slits in a stony visage. She walked beside him like a woman in a trance. Adoo shouted in a loud voice over the din of the gongs, "The elephants will not come too close to the fire! When they stop moving, jump!"

The wind was fanning the flames toward the priest, and the terrible heat stopped him. He wanted Nedra to take the last two steps on her own. Nedra stopped moving. The fear of death was still strong in her young heart. I could see the priest urging her forward, pushing her with his right hand on the small of her back. It was as if all the forces of darkness were pressing upon me.

The elephants stopped, and Adoo roared, "Jump! Get the priest!"

I ran around the flaming pyre, and from the corner of my eye, I saw Adoo sailing over the flames. He landed in front of Nedra, between her and a horrible death. She fainted, and he held her. At that very instant, I was upon the screaming priest. I hurled him into the flames, and he did not stop screaming until he died. The vision of his face surrounded by flames is burned in my memory forever.

Our armed sailors were around us. The frightened, superstitious crowd was running away. I climbed up to the howdag. Adoo, with the help of our crew, lifted the unconscious girl up, and I held her in my arms. The Mahoots were chattering away. We did not understand what they were saying, but it was obvious that they were happy. I am sure they approved of what we had just done. The second enemy of their king was burning in flames. They drove the elephants as fast as possible. When we were opposite our ships, the great beasts waded into the shallow sea. When they reached the blue hole, they swam to the ships, only their heads and trunks in the air. It must have been a marvelous sight for our friends on board: Elephants swimming! Mahoots yelling! Excited sailors shouting!

Strong, friendly arms were outstretched to help us on board. We were surrounded by joyful, young people, and happiest of all was Bresis. But Adoo was not rejoicing. He was moaning in pain, the energy depleted from him. And now, for the first time, I noticed burns on his back.

"Great gods, Adoo! Your back is burnt!" Galen spread balm over Adoo's burns.

Then he turned his attention to Nedra. He examined her carefully. Then he called Bresis and Seenara to his side. "Your comfort will also be Nedra's medicine until peace returns to her soul."

I sat down next to Adoo. "Adoo! My friend, how can I ever thank you enough?"

He briefly flashed his invincible grin and held my arm in a powerful grip. "Remember, Hiro. With this arm, you pulled me and Seenara out of the slave ship!"

CHAPTER 24: Atoll of Pearls

Compassion was foremost in Seenara's character. She offered food and drink to Nedra and Bresis. They drank some water but did not touch the food. Then Seenara washed Nedra's face, arms, and feet with cool water. It would take a few days for Nedra to overcome the horrors she had gone through. The crew built a small tent of sailcloth on the stem deck to shelter the girls from rain and sun, and to give them some privacy. Seenara and Bresis sat near Nedra, hugging her and comforting her as best they could.

Galen called Bresis to his side. "Nedra needs the healing powers of sleep. Give her this potion to drink. It will make her fall into deep sleep, and when she wakes up tomorrow, talk to her and try to make her talk." Galen looked at me. "And you, Hiro—you must try to distract her. Look how pale she is. Poor girl!"

The crew gathered around Adoo and sat down in a tight circle, eager to hear the story once again. Adoo recounted every detail in his inimitable way, how they went through the dense crowd riding the elephants and how they snatched Nedra from the priest. The young crew was silent, enjoying every detail of this adventure.

When Adoo finished the story, Taleb said, "I am glad you did not take the black stone or the jewels. This would have enraged the people, and we would never be able to return to this island."

Taleb stood up and stretched his stiff muscles. Then he said to Mobareek, "The natives might attack us before sunrise. They have poisoned arrows and firebrands. I say we leave this island now."

Mobareek stood up and said, "Let us go. We have a strong offshore wind and no dangers in our way. Taleb Ali, you lead the way."

The crew smartly pulled the *Sorceress* close to *Sword of the Sea.* Their captain stepped on board, followed by Ari and Justin. The boys liked to sail with Mobareek because he let them steer as much as they wanted. The cheerful, strong voices of our young crewmen filled the air as they pulled the heavy anchors out of the blue hole. They chanted Mobareek's own song:

Sword of the Sea and the Sorceress,
You pierced my heart, Sword of the Sea!
I built you and I shaped you,
And I cut down your tree!
And now you beat me and defeat me,
O Sword of the Sea!

The drummers were beating an exciting rhythm. The young men were stomping their feet on the deck and clapping their hands, getting ready to raise the heavy yard to the top of the mast. *Drum Tom Tom—Wal-Sahera, Drum Tom Tom—Wal-Sahera.* Taleb and Mobareek let the ships drift with the wind for a short distance, then gave the signal to raise sail, "*Sheraaa!*" Up went the huge, white lateen sail and the powerful wind drove our ships out to the open ocean at great speed.

I was steering. Taleb Ali, standing next to me, pointed to a star low on the horizon. "Hiro, this is your course to the Atoll of Pearls. If we stop there, you can buy some of the best and biggest pearls you ever saw."

I said, "Let us go to that atoll since we cannot buy rubies or gems from a slain governor."

It was a clear night with a few clouds. The wind was singing in the rigging, and the sea was almost black, swooshing under the hull. I looked up at the sky, and there was the Red Planet, Mars. "Taleb," I said, "look up. Ares, the red-eyed god of war, is near the star Anti-Ares, the red heart of the scorpion."

He said, "Yes, I see them. There might be war in our future." Then Taleb laughed his hearty laugh. "To many people, these are omens, but to you and I, that is nonsense." Then the old navigator wrapped himself in his camel-hair blanket and stretched on deck. He gazed at the heavens for a long time before he fell asleep.

I was wide awake. The excitement of the day would keep me up all night. There was silence on deck. Almost everyone was asleep, and I reflected on the kind providence that had decreed that an old navigator from Mokalla would save the life of Che, the son of Caesar and Cleopatra. We had been ready to trust the Greek governor. Taleb Ali saved us from that blunder, which would have left a heavy load of shame and regret on our shoulders forever.

At first light, Taleb Ali was up and looking at the bright navigation stars on the eastern horizon. "This is the beginning of winter," he declared. "The whales will return to these warm seas to give birth and to feed their young for five months until they are strong enough to migrate with them."

The very next day, we saw a pod of whales spouting. Taleb brought the ship close to the whales, keeping the sun behind us so we could take a good look at these gigantic creatures. Everyone was excited and animated. Some crewmen had never seen whales that close. Taleb shouted, "Watch the leading whale! Look closely, Hiro. This one is pregnant. The other three following her are adult females. If we are fortunate, we will witness the birth of a whale today!"

The sighting of these whales lifted Nedra and Che out of their deep depression. Nedra was no longer absorbed in her own misery. Her attention was concentrated on the whales moving majestically at a slow speed alongside our ship, their great flukes propelling them forward with easy, powerful strokes. They spouted a fountain of water high into the air, higher than the deck of our ship, to clear their blowholes before every breath.

As the hours passed, the whales seemed accustomed to our two ships moving silently beside them. At noon, with the rays of sunlight penetrating the clear sea, the leading whale, the mother-to-be, arched her back and lunged forward. The other whales attending her stayed close beside her, one on each side. The pregnant whale turned on her side and heaved mightily. Blood was flowing out of her body, and in this red cloud we saw her newborn baby.

The whale attending the mother lifted the newborn on her tail flukes and tossed him high into the air so that he could take his first breath. The effect of this scene on Nedra was like magic. She became her true self, laughing and chatting with Bresis, her cheeks and lips red as roses. She held my arm and said in Greek, "Marvelous, really marvelous."

I was surprised. "You can speak Greek?"

Nedra answered in a halting manner. "Bresis taught me. I can understand if you speak slowly."

"You are very lucky. Very few people have seen the birth of a whale."

We watched the mother whale lifting the newborn on the pressure wave created by her huge body moving through the sea. The little one swam above his mother's head.

Our ship was very close to the whales when Taleb said, "We have to move away. I don't want to disturb them." He steered *Sword of the Sea* away from the giants of the sea, and he looked at me, smiling. "You know, Hiro, the *bettan* are our kin. They breathe air like us. They find their food in the sea like us. We never harm them. That would bring bad luck. In summer they disappear. No one knows where they go, but they return every winter to give birth in these warm seas. How do they find their way in this vast ocean? Sometimes I wonder, do they also look at the stars?"

Nedra, Bresis, Seenara, and Adoo sat down next to me in the shade of the great sail. The wind spilling out of it kept us cool and comfortable. Atiya joined us and entertained us with his music. After a while he handed his simsimiyya to Nedra. She took the instrument and sang a beautiful song. Bresis translated the words for us, and I asked Nedra to sing the song a second time. She played the melody and sang in the language of her people about her faraway childhood home:

> *When I was a small child, I was a slave girl,*
> *and I wished I could die.*
> *I was sure my soul would live in a strong little bird,*
> *a brave bird that can fly*
> *Far away to the mountain, the tall green mountains*
> *that touch the clouds and the sky.*
> *I will find my mother's home in the valley, and I*
> *will be happy living in a tree nearby!*
> *Every day I will see my brothers and sisters!*
> *They will feed me, I will sing for them, and they will never cry.*

Nedra finished her poignant song. There were tears on her red cheeks, like dewdrops on a rose. I took her small hand in mine, and she told us her story, how her mother and father had sold her during a famine to save her life. "I was a young girl when they sold me. The pain of that day will never go away. I remember the face of my mother crying, holding me close to her heart, wailing, 'What will happen to you? My beloved child, what will happen to you?' and my father sitting on the ground, his head and face covered so no one could see his shame. I was so young, I could not understand what was happening to me. The people who bought me made me a domestic servant and taught me how to sing and play music. I was treated well. They didn't want me to look tired or sick. My young body had to be sold without a scar to bring a higher price.

"When I was sixteen, I was sold to the Greek governor. The first night he beat me with a thin cane all over my body. I cried and screamed, and he said, 'Now you will be obedient, and you will not run away.' I learned a few words of Greek from Bresis, but I never let anyone know because I did not want to talk to the governor. If I did not have Bresis next to me, I would have killed myself. She is my only friend."

"Look around you, Nedra," I said. "You are surrounded by friends."

She turned her head and looked at our crew. Every one of them had a friendly smile for her. She held my hand tightly like a trusting child, and she looked up and smiled her mysterious smile. This time there was no trace of sadness on her face. It was a sweet smile, full of happiness and trust.

At sunset, Taleb Ali was steering, and he called Che to his side and let him steer the ship. I watched Taleb instructing Che and talking to him for a long time until the sky was dark and the bright navigation stars were visible. Then Taleb walked across the deck and sat down by my side.

He said, "Che will be a great navigator, possibly an explorer. The love of the sea is growing stronger in his breast every day. I can see it in his eyes."

"What were you talking about?"

Taleb lowered his voice, like a conspirator. "I talked to Che about Sondosa. Do you remember the dancer with a blue-green tattoo in the Garden of Paradise?"

"Yes, I remember her. Che wanted to marry her."

"I reminded him of Sondosa and promised to introduce him to her father. If Che marries her, he will stay in Mokalla."

"How could you promise him that? Do you think a young girl like her will wait?"

"Hiro, there is something that will delay her marriage. You will find out soon enough when we visit her father." Taleb laughed and slapped me hard on my shoulder. "Now, my friend, what is the excuse for stalling your marriage?"

"Do you think I should get married?"

"Hiro, Galen told me of how you mourn your wife, and I am deeply sorry. But you are in this world, and in this world, you must live." Taleb was not smiling anymore, and he moved closer to me and held my forearm. "Hiro, if you don't marry Nedra before your eventual return to Alexandria, you will regret it forever. I saw how you looked at her when she finished her song and how she looked at you when you held her hand. If you let her slip away, these brief tender moments will haunt you always. It is your turn to steer. Think about my words, and don't hesitate."

I steered the ship the second half of the night as I thought of my late wife, my children, and my strong feelings for Nedra. The sound of the gentle wind against the sea's surface eased my thoughts.

Adoo eventually came and stood next to me, and we took turns at the tiller. We talked about many things, but our conversation always returned to Nedra and Seenara. Adoo was looking forward to a happy return and a good life with Seenara in his own country, surrounded by his own people. I remember his words clearly. "Hiro, I would like to live in Alexandria, near you and Galen, but I know Seenara will be unhappy in the big city. She would be alone, without friends and without family. In my land, Nooba, she will be surrounded by my clan and my family. There will always be someone to help her raise her children, and if perchance I should die, Seenara will be safe among my tribe."

I told him, "Seenara is a brave young woman. She stayed with you even though she could not understand your words. Adoo, you must never forget that she left her own people to be with you."

After a while, Adoo smiled at me and spoke softly. "Nedra is a rare beauty. Don't hesitate, Hiro. Marry her! If you don't, you will regret it for the rest of your life."

I laughed. "Taleb gave me the same advice, and he used your exact words: 'don't hesitate'!"

"Taleb is a wise man. You should heed his advice."

Before sunrise, we turned the ship over to Taleb and Che, and we surrendered ourselves to deep, restful sleep.

The next day, Taleb Ali was steering *Sword of the Sea*, and he called Che to his side and showed him a white cloud tinged with green light. He said, "This cloud is sitting above the shallow lagoon in the center of the Atoll of Pearls. Every day around noon, the lagoon reflects the green light up to the clouds. Steer for this cloud as long as you can see the green." Taleb looked at me and said, "We will be there in less than three hours."

Just as Taleb predicted, we reached the atoll in the afternoon. The wind was favorable, and we sailed close to the coral reef, followed by the *Sorceress*. The sea was a deep blue color, and the barrier reef arose from the depths like a great wall made of coral in the shape of an immense horseshoe, enclosing a shallow green lagoon and a safe anchorage that could shelter a hundred ships like ours. On top of this coral atoll, we counted six sandy islets covered with coconut palms. Obviously, the pounding waves ground up the coral, and the big storms and strong current formed these sandy islets on the atoll.

We entered the sheltered lagoon through a break in the reef. The *Sorceress* followed, and both ships sailed into the lagoon riding a rushing current. When the tide rose in the ocean, water flowed into the lagoon, and when the tide fell, water flowed out of the lagoon to the open sea. No sailing ship could move against this current; she must wait till the tidal stream reversed itself.

Our ships anchored in shallow water, and we waded out to meet the local people. It seemed as if the entire village was waiting for us. The arrival of two sailing ships to this lonely atoll was cause for celebration. A festive mood spread among these smiling pearl divers. An old man stood in the midst of the crowd. He was head and shoulders above the rest. When he saw Taleb Ali, he stepped forward and hugged him like a long-lost friend. He seemed to be fifty years old, but Taleb assured me he was over seventy. His name was Kareem, which means generous, and the hospitality he showed us was unforgettable. All the adults called him Kadi (Judge). He was the leader and judge of this small tribe, and now he insisted that our entire crew be his guests this evening.

I worried that we were too many people arriving at the atoll without warning. However, Taleb assured me, "We are only seventy-two. Kareem can feed two hundred! They might be poor, but they are never starving."

We gathered near Kareem's large hut. Soft mats made of coconut fronds were laid out for us on the beach. I was glad to see our crew bringing gifts for the children, small jars of honey and sweet dried fruits. Young men and women retrieved live fish and lobster from large baskets left in the shallow water and weighted down with stones. That was how they kept fish alive when the catch was abundant. They obviously had enough to feed the whole village.

Food was served on leaves of the banana plant. Kareem and his guests were the only people served on a table. This table was nothing but a very old canoe turned upside down. It was riddled with countless holes and cracks. However, it was a work of art with intricate carvings and decorations made with mother-of-pearl shell inlaid into the wood. I noticed Galen admiring this old canoe, moving his fingers slowly over the ancient carving, touching the mother-of-pearl, nacre, inlaid with great care and infinite patience into the dark, hard wood.

After the feast, there was a dance for our entertainment. Before the dance began, each one of us was presented with a necklace of small colorful seashells. Taleb Ali had many friends among the older men.Every one of them greeted him formally and presented him with a necklace of seashells.Before long, Taleb had at least twenty necklaces around his neck. He was beaming with pleasure.

Two groups of dancers faced the spectators, girls on one side and boys on the other. In the open space between them, a small girl, not older than six years, sat down and played in the sand. She was busy building a sandcastle. The dancers weaved around the little girl without breaking her sandcastle or bothering her in any way. That was only one example that showed the kindness and gentleness of these pearl divers, who lived here isolated from the world.

Around midnight, the dancers were getting tired, the singers' voices were soft and hushed, the torches burning coconut oil were dying, and it was time for us to leave our generous host. We thanked Kareem and returned to our ships. A few sailors decided to sleep on the soft sand near the edge of the sea. The next morning, we found them pale and tired. Hundreds of small hermit crabs had crawled all over them at night and deprived them of restful sleep. The sun was just rising out of the sea, and some young children were collecting hermit crabs to use them as bait on their hooks. Parrotfish loved this bait and swam up to the children fishing in shallow water. Every time a fish got hooked, there was much laughter and hilarity, and of course, the fish were kept alive in baskets resting on the bottom of the sea.

We watched the children fishing and swimming, and suddenly they stopped playing and marched silently toward a large old tree. We followed this procession and found Kareem sitting in the shade under that tree. There was no bell or any other signal to call the youngsters. They knew they had to gather around their teacher, Kareem, every morning, and there was no escape. We sat down and listened to him instructing the young people sitting around him in the shade. There was no attempt at reading or writing. Kareem could neither read nor write, but he had a store of wisdom, and he passed his experiences to the youngsters in the form of stories. Boys and girls were wide eyed and attentive. He warned them of dangers in the sea by recounting stories of adventure and misadventure, and he instilled in the minds of his young audience the code of proper behavior.

When the lesson was over, Kareem stood up, and the children ran back to the sea. He laughed and invited us to join him. "I am going to that islet you can see at the far end of the lagoon. I will try to bring back some sea turtles so we can feast on red meat tonight."

We crossed the lagoon in two fast-sailing canoes with round bottoms and shallow draft. Each canoe had a huge outrigger to balance the pressure of the sail. We were a group of five: Nedra and Bresis, Taleb Ali, Mobareek, and I. Four crewmen handled the fast canoes and, like all good sailors, made a race of it. The warm sea spray kept us wet all the way, and the girls, Nedra and Bresis, were laughing and excited. I marveled at how the crew bounced the outrigger over coral heads that obstructed their way.

When we landed on the sandy islet, I was surprised to see forty large huts, sturdy and well built, standing in the shade of coconut palms. However, they were empty. There wasn't a soul in sight. Kareem explained the mystery. "Every family has two huts, one on our island and a second on this sandy islet. If a big storm hits the atoll and the waves threaten to wash away our homes, we cross the lagoon in our boats and stay here on this sheltered side until the storm passes over our heads."

I asked Kareem, "Kadi, where did your people come from? Why did they choose to live here?"

He said, "Our grandfathers were pearl divers from the south of Yemen. They found wives in India and decided to live here. We are poor people, but there is no hunger and no war, and we are far away from oppressive princes and kings."

Kareem led the way, and we followed. He skirted the edge of the sea looking for turtles that come out at midday to rest in the sun on the sandy beaches. The young pearl divers ran ahead of us, eager to find a few large turtles.They were moving away from our group at a fast pace. We could hear them shouting, and we could see them waving their arms. "Come over here! Come quick! Run, run!" Kareem and Mobareek walked at a faster pace. I ran toward the young hunters with Nedra and Bresis running by my side.

The divers had found two dugongs,[74] a male and a female, mating in the shallow water. When we came close to them, the female rolled away to deeper water and escaped, but the huge male, over ten feet long, was left in a bed of brown seaweed. The water was too shallow

---

[74] *Dugong, dugon,* of the order *sirenia.* A marine mammal, it reaches 11 feet in length and feeds on turtle grass and seaweed. Dugongs are associated with the myths of mermaids and sirens in the sea.

for him to swim away. The receding tide left him trapped in this shallow pool.

The hungry humans dashed into the shallow water and laid their hands on the dugong, laughing and joking. They waited for us, and when we were close to the animal, I could see that the male dugong had given up the struggle to escape. His huge brown body rested on the seaweed, and the expression in his eyes was one of fear. His head was square and ugly, bristling with huge whiskers, the kind of face you would not like to see when you were swimming in the lagoon. But in spite of his ugliness and huge size, he was a harmless animal.

One of the hunters pulled out his sharp knife and shouted, "Judge, shall I kill the dugong?!" Kareem nodded his head. The young man tried to cut through the thick skin around the dugong's neck and a trickle of blood was flowing.

Nedra screamed, "No! No! Don't kill him!" She ran to Kareem and grabbed his arm. "Stop them. Please, don't kill him."

Kareem saw how anguished she was. He understood that she could not see the slaughter of this huge animal, and he shouted an order at the young hunters. They obeyed him, washed their knives in the sea, and came walking toward us slowly.

Mobareek spoke. "This sea bull has enough red meat to feed the whole village, but we will let him live."

Bresis and Nedra collected some fallen coconut palm fronds and laid them on the dugong's ugly head to shade his eyes and protect him from the sun's burning rays. The young hunters could not understand why the judge had ordered them to spare the life of this bull dugong, but he dismissed them. "You must learn to eat the fruits without killing the trees." Then Kareem walked beside me and said, "These young hunters cannot control themselves. They want every turtle or dugong in sight." Of course, I knew the truth. Kareem had saved the dugong to please Nedra. He could not stand by and watch her cry.

On the way back, I walked between Mobareek and Kareem. The judge put his hand on my shoulder and asked, "Nedra is a kindhearted girl. Is she your wife?"

I looked at Kareem and my friend Mobareek. They were both smiling broadly, eager to hear my answer. "Not yet, but she *will* be my wife."

The judge said, "Then marry her on our island according to our customs. She is young, beautiful, and kindhearted. What more do you want?"

That evening after our meal, Galen asked Kareem, "Kadi, will you sell this table—I mean this old canoe we are using as a table?"

Kareem said, "This old canoe full of holes and cracks? It is useless!"

"Yes. I would like to take it back to Alexandria to remind me of this voyage and your island."

Galen presented Kareem with a small pouch filled with gold coins. Kareem was thoughtful for a long time. Then he said, "I cannot believe anyone would want this old leaky canoe. I am sure you are trying to find a way to help me. You don't really want this. Look at all the cracks!"

No matter how hard Taleb tried to convince him that Galen admired the workmanship on the old canoe, Kareem just could not believe it. "If you like it so much, you can have it . . . a gift for you."

"A rare gift," Galen replied. "I thank you."

Then Taleb spoke about pearls. "Kareem, we came to your atoll to visit you and to buy pearls. Do you have any large pearls?"

"You shall have the best. I always keep the biggest and most perfect pearls for good friends."

Then, to everyone's surprise, Kareem announced he would organize a wedding feast for Nedra and Hiro. "Kareem, you should wait till I ask Nedra whether she wants to marry me!" I said.

"Ask her tonight. She will say yes. I saw how she holds your hand and the way she looks at you."

"You are not the first, or even the second person, to tell me this."

Late in the afternoon before sunset, when the colors were changing on the lagoon, I took Nedra's hand and walked with her at the edge of the sea. There was a strong, warm wind blowing, invigorating both body and mind. The song of the wind in the palm trees was pleasant to our ears, and the shining green leaves moved rapidly, scattering the light of the setting sun in every direction.

I asked Nedra, "Do you know who your people are? Do you remember?"

"I heard many stories when I was a young girl. My people are the Turkmans of the Black and White Sheep. They were horsemen and warriors. No tribe could defeat them in war. The drought drove them south into the green valleys of Kashmir. In the summertime, the green hills would be dotted with black and white tents. The high peaks of the mountains would be white with snow, and in the winter, they built small stone houses facing the southern sun. They were a happy people until the rains stopped falling and the small rivers stopped flowing. This is all I remember."

"Nedra, I can take you back to your people. I would like to see your green valleys dotted with black and white tents."

She was silent for a while, her hand holding mine tightly. I asked her, "Do you want to go back to your beautiful green valley, to your family and your childhood home?"

Nedra stopped walking. She didn't say a word but looked straight into my eyes. I kissed her passionately. She was relaxed and smiling happily. "I am happy with you, Hiro. My home is far away."

Trembling that I was finally prepared to propose to her, I asked Nedra if she would consider a life with me. She smiled and, with a gentle kindness that seemed to understand my thoughts, said softly, "Yes, Hiro, but will you be happy, too?"

"Yes, Nedra, I truly will."

"Then I want nothing more, dear Hiro."

The next morning, I found Kareem in the shade of his favorite tree, waiting for the children to come to him for their daily lesson. "Kadi," I said, "you can go ahead and build the wedding hut."

"I am glad you did not waste time, Hiro. Otherwise, I would have been tempted to make a stack out of old, leaking canoes on the spot where your hut should be as a monument to your silly hesitation. Give me three days; a beautiful hut will be ready for your wedding. I will prepare a great feast for the occasion."

I thanked him and left as the children were running from all directions toward the great tree.

Every morning I took Nedra in a small boat, and we watched the pearl divers collecting the mother-of-pearl oysters. Their canoes were steady with two outriggers, one on each side. The paddles were painted white so that they would reflect the sunlight. If by chance a canoe drifted away in a strong wind, the divers would drop a small anchor and signal for help with their white paddles. A sailboat would go and tow them back.

We swam and played in the sea next to the divers. They always chose to work the beds of turtle grass. Here the oysters had a weak anchor to the plants' roots, and it was easy to pull them out. Oysters found in the coral reef had a very strong attachment and were hard to pull out, so the divers never gathered them and left them to spawn their eggs into the lagoon. As a result, there was a constant supply of small oysters growing in the beds of turtle grass. The grass was thick and green, about as wide as a finger and one foot tall. Turtles loved to feed on it, and so did the dugongs.

On the third day I saw a pair of dugongs feeding. We approached them carefully. When the bull surfaced to breathe, I saw a scar on his neck. He was the same animal Nedra had saved with her tears.

The wedding was held in broad daylight around noon on the beach. A large group of children gathered with drums and gongs. They made the most incredible noise. How could such small hands produce all this thunder?! Taleb explained their customs. "Every adult man or woman has to attend your wedding, and the children are making all this noise to call every soul from the six islets on this atoll."

When everyone was present, they feasted and sang songs, and the children were now quiet. Judge Kareem made a speech. I could not understand a word of what he said, but everyone was roaring with laughter. Finally, the judge walked over to me. I stood up to greet him. His face shone with benevolence and kindness.

"And now, Hiro, you must go to your wedding hut. Your wife will be there waiting for you."

"Where is this new hut? I cannot see it!"

"Over there," said Kareem. He pointed to a faraway islet sitting on the coral reef about a mile away. "It is one of our traditions. You must swim to it."

I waded into the lagoon and swam toward the islet. A small flotilla of boats and canoes accompanied me. In the leading boat I saw Nedra and Bresis with Taleb Ali, Mobareek, and Adoo. The islanders in their boats were laughing, and the women were singing. It was a marvelous sight. I thought to myself, *This is a fine tradition. All the young men on this atoll must be powerful swimmers, or sad and lonely.*

The flotilla of boats reached the sandy islet before me. As I came closer, I could see the new hut and Nedra and Bresis with a group of women standing in the shade. The men were at the edge of the lagoon. Most were in the water up to their knees, and all, without exception, were laughing and smiling. I thought this was a great reception. When I stepped on the sand, there was loud cheering and clapping of hands. However, I was not allowed to be near Nedra. I had to sit with the men.

There was more dancing and singing. Then Judge Kareem stepped into the open space between the men and the group of women. He gave a speech in their dialect, interrupted many times with laughter. I asked Taleb Ali, "What is he saying that is so funny?"

Taleb laughed until tears came to his eyes. "He said that the rule about the man swimming to the islet on his wedding day is a fairly young tradition. In fact, it was invented today!"

The old man had a great sense of humor, and I didn't mind in the least. My name will be remembered on this atoll for a long time. The kind and jolly people jumped into their boats. They left me and Nedra all alone on the islet.

After five days filled with bliss and joy, Adoo and Bresis came to us in a fast sailing canoe and took us back to the village. Nedra hugged Bresis. "I am sad to leave this beautiful little islet and our small hut."

Bresis said, "There will be other beautiful places in your future, I am sure of it."

We had our last meal with Kareem. His one-hundred-year-old canoe was hoisted aboard the *Sorceress*. The old chief came aboard, kissed Nedra on her forehead, and presented her with a large, perfect pink pearl. "This is a rare pearl," he said, "from the *bosr*."[75] He turned toward me. "I hope you will return, Hiro, with my friend Taleb."

I presented Kareem with a useful gift, thirty sharp knives, and Galen gave him another small pouch filled with gold coins.

The *Sorceress* and *Sword of the Sea* rode the tide, flowing out of the Atoll of Pearls to the open sea. For a long time we could see these gentle people waving their arms. Che stood beside me and said, "I hope I will come back to this atoll someday."

I told him, "Che, you will be a great navigator, and there is a good chance you will return. Who knows? Perhaps I will be on your ship!"

---

[75] *Bosr:* A giant *tridacna clam* found in tropical coral reefs.

CHAPTER 25: In the Valley of Ostriches

At night, while Adoo was steering *Sword of the Sea,* we heard an ominous sound in the sky, like a distant drumroll. Taleb Ali sang out, "Adoo! Can you hear the gale coming from the west? Adoo! Can you feel the wind?" And in a low voice, only I could hear, "Oh, how I feel sorry for the young men on dry land, far away from the blue!"

A wave of excitement surged on deck. Our crew was preparing for rough weather. But there was another reason for their high spirits, their shouts, and their songs. They all knew this powerful wind from the west would drive the ship faster and faster toward the red light tower of Mokalla. Many among this crew had young wives waiting, and those who did not get married were hoping to find brides this time because of the generous rewards Galen had given them.

Taleb, as always, was an impressive man, even as he sat down among us, with his bare torso and massive head. At night he always wrapped his turban around his waist like a sash. As I watched him tightening the cloth like a belt, he laughed. "Keep your back warm at night, Hiro! You are no longer a young man." Then he cleared his throat, as if he were trying to find the right words.

"We must have a new name for Caesarion. When I introduce him to Sondosa's father and to her brothers, I obviously cannot say he is the son of the kaiser of the Romans and the queen of Egypt. His enemies must never find him."

Galen said, "A name chosen carelessly can condemn a man to low rank or ridicule. We have to select a name that has been and will always be illustrious."

I was about to suggest a name, but I stopped when I saw Taleb knocking his fingers on the deck nervously. We waited for him to speak. He said, slowly and deliberately, "I have been thinking about this for many days. There lived in these lands a heroic warrior who was also a great poet. In his youth he was a slave, the son of a black slave girl. His father was a powerful chief. He became a free man because of his valor in many battles defending his tribe. Then he fell in love with a young girl of noble birth. He could never marry her, but he composed love poems, beautiful love poems that bards will recite till the end of time."

Galen put his hand on Taleb's shoulder. "What was his name?"

"Antar. I will adopt Caesarion, and he will be known as Antar, son of Taleb Ali Zol."[76]

I looked at Galen. He was smiling. Thanks to Taleb, we had found a name for Caesarion in the brief time before the gale winds filled our sails. Now the strong wind was upon us. Mobareek steered the *Sorceress* closer to *Sword of the Sea*, and both ships were racing each other once again like two wild horses heading for the red harbor of Mokalla. Taleb, standing close by, said in a low voice, "Hiro, don't you pity the young men on land who will never know the excitement of the sea?"

As soon as our ship passed the red light tower of Mokalla, Taleb exchanged his turban and his shirt for perfectly clean clothes and a new cape. He asked me and Antar to do the same. He said, "We must go to the meeting room and let the navigators and captains know that we are back. Every captain does this before going to his home." Then he jumped out onto the sandy beach.

I followed with Che close behind me. Mobareek was waiting for us, resplendent in a golden turban and a silken cape he had acquired in Serendib. He smiled broadly and slapped me between my shoulders. "The *Sorceress* beat you to the harbor."

I replied, "That was easy. You had a young crew eager to race home to their wives."

Taleb Ali laughed. "Hiro and Adoo had their wives on board, so they won the race before it started!"

We walked briskly to the meeting place under the light tower. When we entered the three-sided room, it was crowded with captains and navigators. Both Mobareek and Taleb were well known here.

---

[76] *Antar* is a reference to *Antorah ibn Shaddad*, an Arab knight and poet, who lived from circa 525–608 AD, well after the events in Hiro's story.

Taleb introduced me and Antar to his friends. "This is my friend Hiro from Alexandria on the White Sea, and this young man"—he held Caesarion's hand in his own—"is my adopted son, Antar."

Antar carried himself with great dignity, and when we sat down surrounded by navigators eager to hear our news, Antar kept silent, listening to their conversation, absorbing their jargon and their peculiar manner of speech.

As we walked back on the sandy beach toward our ships and the waiting crew, Mobareek was sure no one could hear us. He put one giant arm over Taleb's shoulder and his other arm over my shoulder. "Every crewman saw me kill the Greek governor in Serendib. When our ships are back in Egypt, some of the sailors will talk because that's what sailors do. I don't know what the new government will do. Better that I should stay here with Antar and build new ships for him and for you, Taleb."

Taleb and Antar were stunned. However, I was happy for Mobareek. That was a good decision, and it was a comforting thought that Antar would begin a new life here with these two great men watching over him, guiding him and teaching him all he would need to know.

This day will remain in my memory as the turning point in Caesarion's life. From then on, he would be known as Antar, son of Taleb Ali Zol. A future of adventure and riches awaited him. With a little luck, he would also have love and happiness.

We settled comfortably in Taleb's huge house—his fort, as he liked to call it. Our sailors rested on the ground floor in the guest rooms. Some slept on-board ship. No ship was ever left unattended in this harbor. Mobareek gave permission to the married men to go and stay with their wives. Galen paid them handsomely, and we did not see them for many days.

On the first floor, I had a huge room with a grand view of the green mountains. Nedra was happy here. There was grace and serenity in this house. Adoo and Seenara had a room to themselves, and Mobareek was given another room. Taleb had a large bedroom, and his grandchildren insisted they had to sleep in the same room. Of course, he told them great stories of adventure and magic at bedtime. It was a pleasure to see the joy of the old navigator playing with his grandchildren.

In the morning, as we sat in the garden having breakfast, a young boy, not older than nine years, came running to his grandfather, complaining that his wooden sword was broken. Taleb found a palm frond and cut it to the right length. Then with a sharp knife, he fashioned the broad end to be the handle of a sword and made the blade with one sharp edge. The boy watched him, eagerly awaiting his new sword; however, Taleb hung the sword from a branch of a lemon tree and told the boy, "You must wait until I make the sword hard or it will break again." Then he walked into the kitchen and came back with some oil, already used once for frying. Taleb let the oil cool and poured it carefully over the sword. He repeated this about ten times. Then he told the little boy, "Tomorrow, when the oil dries, you can play with your sword."

After carefully oiling his grandchild's play sword, Taleb looked at me and said with mock seriousness, "Prepare for war if you want peace." Then he turned toward Antar. "Sondosa's father, Sheikh Zaki, is expecting us. Let us go and pay him a visit."

Sheikh Zaki and his four sons welcomed us to their house. It looked very much like Taleb's fort except that it was five stories high, with huge airy guest rooms on the ground floor. Mobareek, Galen, Taleb, Antar, and I were seated on comfortable pillows arranged against the walls. Colorful carpets covered the entire floor. The large windows were open, and the air carried the scent of jasmine into the room. Songbirds and fruit trees filled the extensive garden surrounding the house.

The anxiety Antar felt was swept away by the friendly atmosphere. Sondosa's father welcomed us with the ceremonial politeness of his country. He was a tall, dignified man with a high-colored face and a grey beard. He sat down and talked to Mobareek and Taleb. He inquired about our voyage to Serendib and showed great interest when we told him that trade with Egypt might stop, which meant that there would be more trade going to Rome via Mokalla and the harbor of Aden. I noticed his four sons sitting beside their father, silent and respectful, their hands perfectly still, resting in their laps.

Sondosa's father gently ordered his sons, "Tell your sister to serve us wine and fruits." Two boys left the room to bring us the wine. I noticed Antar, sitting next to me, glowing with happiness, like a man who is sure something marvelous is about to happen to him. Would Sondosa remember him? Would she like him? Her father said, "Now you will see my beloved daughter."

The two boys returned with trays of fruit. Their sister followed with wine and golden drinking cups in her hands. Antar looked up at a tall, big, powerful young woman. She was not ugly, but she had an air of effortless command about her that would send any man running for his life! Antar was entirely unprepared for the shock. A look of alarm spread over his face. He grabbed my hand and whispered, "Who is this woman? Where is Sondosa, beautiful Sondosa?" He let go of my hand, and his arms fell to his sides as he leaned back against the wall. Antar had the air of a young man to whom the future is of no account.

I noticed Mobareek looking at the girl and smiling. When she filled his cup with wine, she smiled back. He drank his wine quickly, and as she refilled his cup, her air of effortless command fell away from her face. Even her voice changed. She smiled sweetly like a young woman who had finally found a man she can admire, a man much bigger and stronger than she was, a man who could command her respect. She sat down, gazing at my friend like a thirsty desert traveler looking at a cool, green oasis. Mobareek smiled at her once again and said, "May I have more of your sweet wine?" She served him, her hands shaking lightly, the golden cups rattling on the silver tray.

On our way back to Taleb's fort, Antar was crestfallen. We walked at a slow pace. Taleb Ali, chuckling softly to himself, said, "Antar, my boy, I told you Sondosa would be waiting and unmarried. I knew all along that her father would insist her older sister must get married first. Some clans hold to this ancient custom, and if nobody marries the elder sister, then her first cousin is obliged to marry her." He was silent for a moment. "Of course, that cousin would be allowed a second wife if he wants one, but the first wife will have a husband, a house, and a child. Come to think of it, it is not such a bad custom after all."

Antar asked, "Do you mean I have to wait until somebody marries her gigantic sister?"

Mobareek surprised everyone when he said, "I can solve this problem for you. I will marry the girl. I think she likes me!" Mobareek was a man of quick decisions followed by action, as befitted the character of a great sea captain. He patted Taleb on his shoulder. "Taleb, will you go back to her father tomorrow and find out if he will accept me and if his eldest daughter will marry me?"

The next day Taleb Ali went all by himself to visit Sondosa's father. He returned with the good news. "Sheikh Zaki welcomes you, Mobareek, to join his clan, and his daughter will welcome you herself on our next visit."

"I told you she liked me! When will our next visit be?"

"After two days, we will visit their house. Antar will then see the beautiful Sondosa. We will employ these two days to pull the ships up on dry land and move the treasure to my fort."

Adoo and Mobareek gathered the available crewmen, and they took everything out of the ships. Our treasure of gold and silver coins, pearls, and ivory was stored in Taleb's fort. I was glad to see Antar, Ari, and Justin working hard with the crew. This voyage had matured them. They did not shrink from hard labor, and there was an easy friendship between them and the crew with absolutely no pretense of difference in rank.

Galen divided the treasure among us with characteristic generosity. He gave me a portion of the golden coins and then a large bag full of silver coins. "This is for the crew, which will sail back to Egypt with you." He presented Mobareek with a generous gift of gold coins and then two bags filled with silver coins. "This is for two new ships as fast as the *Sorceress*."

Mobareek thanked Galen with a few gracious words. "Antar will be by my side the whole time I build them, learning the art of shipbuilding."

Taleb received a bag of golden coins for himself and an even heavier second bag. Galen said, "This is for Antar. Give it to him when he reaches twenty years of age."

Then Galen walked toward Adoo. "My faithful friend, now that you love the sea, will you be happy living on the banks of the River Nile?" Without waiting for an answer, he gave Adoo a heavy leather bag filled with silver coins.

Adoo showed his surprise. "This is too much for me!"

"Indeed it is too much for any one man, Adoo. But I know you will share this treasure with your entire clan." Then Galen added, smiling at Adoo, "Will you build a few riverboats and come to visit me in Alexandria?"

"With all this silver, I can build two seagoing ships and return to Mokalla to visit Mobareek and Antar!"

Galen replied, "I will gladly sail back every winter with you to see Antar, Taleb, and Mobareek. I might convince Hiro to join us!"

On our second visit to Sondosa's father, Taleb and Galen were dressed in their finest clothes. Antar, walking between them, looked every bit the young prince that he was. As for Mobareek, he was resplendent in his green silk mantle with thin threads of gold running down from his shoulders to his hands. He looked like a king. What a pity he did not have a large fleet to command!

Sheikh Zaki and his four sons received us with gracious words and florid phrases. They knew the purpose of our visit. Taleb Ali had prepared them. His adopted son, Antar, wanted to meet Sondosa, and Mobareek was going to ask Sheikh Zaki for permission to marry her older sister.

We had a pleasant conversation. Marriage was never mentioned nor the money dowry, which the husband would pay, nor the presents, which would be presented to the bride. Taleb Ali would negotiate all this without our presence.

Sheikh Zaki dismissed his four sons. We were alone in the huge reception room. Sondosa's father solemnly said, "Taleb already told me his adopted son, Antar, is the son of a king, murdered by his enemies, and that Antar's true identity must remain secret. You have my solemn promise that after I hear his true name, I will never mention it as long as I live."

Galen approached Sheikh Zaki. "Do you give us your oath that if your daughter Sondosa accepts Antar, he will be her husband?"

Her father said, "If Sondosa is willing, upon the honor of my clan and my own honor, I promise that Antar will marry her."

Galen spoke to the sheikh in a soft voice. "Antar's dead father was the kaiser of the Romans, and his mother was the queen of Egypt!"

In spite of his great self-control, astonishment and surprise forced Sheikh Zaki to stand up. He repeated several times, "The son of the kaiser of the Romans! The son of the kaiser of the Romans!" Then he took Taleb's hands in his own. "Taleb Ali, I have known you for many years. You are an honorable man. Do you swear that this young man is the true son of the queen of Egypt and the kaiser of the Romans?"

Taleb replied without hesitation. "I swear to you by my honor that this is the truth. Antar Ali Zol is Caesarion, the son of the queen of Egypt, Cleopatra, and Julius Caesar!"

The sheikh's face was alight. To these people, nothing, absolutely nothing, was more important than noble lineage. He regained his self-control, sat down, and clapped his hands. His four sons appeared as if by magic. "Serve our guests wine and fruit." The boys hurried to obey, and when they returned with trays laden with sweet fruits, their two sisters followed with golden cups and fine wine. The older girl was blushing. She knew Mohareok had asked permission to marry her. She sat beside him and served him fruit and wine, and they talked in hushed tones that only they could hear.

Sondosa looked at Antar with a level gaze, full of puzzlement and wonder. I watched Antar, his chest rising with strong emotion. His eyes were sparkling. He smiled at the beautiful young girl. "Do you remember me?" She looked at him with her steady gaze without any sign of recognition. He tried to remind her. "In the Garden of Paradise, when you were dancing, I scratched your leg!"

"Yes, of course! But why are you so sunburnt?"

"I was at sea for a long voyage. Now I have returned to see you. I have never forgotten your beautiful face."

Sondosa smiled sweetly and sat next to Antar, serving him wine and fruits. Galen and Taleb moved closer to Sheikh Zaki. I followed their example. The room was very large, and the girls could speak freely without being heard by their brothers or their father.

Our conversation with Sheikh Zaki took an unexpected turn. He talked of war. A great battle was to be fought between his tribe and a neighboring tribe.

"Five days from today, the battle will be waged in the Valley of Ostriches. Our opponents have accepted our challenge." I noticed Sondosa's father did not use the word *enemies*. He was smiling and seemed totally relaxed and confident.

Taleb said, "We will watch the battle. I am sure you don't need our help."

Before leaving, Sheikh Zaki spoke to Antar and Mobareek. "You have my permission to visit my house any day except the day of the battle, when we obviously won't have time for entertaining guests. However, our young warriors will be more than happy to put on a good show. You should be there to see how they fight!"

When we left Sondosa's home, Antar was wrapped in a mantle of euphoria, and Mobareek walked with a light, energetic step. Taleb seemed happy and excited, but for a different reason. He grabbed my arm. "Hiro, I haven't seen a battle in ages. This will be marvelous, believe me! Now we have to start preparing for that day. The Valley of Ostriches is almost ten miles out of town. We will need to rent some camels."

On the day of the battle, we started before sunrise on camelback, riding toward the Valley of Ostriches. We moved in two groups— Galen, Taleb, Mobareek, and I, followed by Adoo, Antar, Ari, and Justin. When we reached the valley, we picked a low hill and settled down to watch the battle.

The Valley of Ostriches was quiet and peaceful . . . but of course the two armies had not yet arrived. I asked Taleb, "What is this war about?"

He said, "Our young shepherds were here with their goats and sheep when some hunters from the other tribe stole a few sheep and cooked them on their campfires. They were after ostriches for their feathers. Didn't you notice, Hiro, that every man decorates his spear with ostrich feathers?"

"Grilled lamb? That is reason enough to go to war?"

"Yes. And when our young men steal a few camels from the other tribes, they challenge us to a battle, and we are glad, because without these battles, Hiro, how will our young men learn to fight? How will we separate the brave from the cowardly and avoid complacency?"

It was strange to me that tribes would fight over a few sheep, but then here I was in this land shielding a fugitive from Rome who would be killed on a ruler's whim.

The sun arose in a sky of unsullied blue, and I felt the heat on my neck. I sprinkled water on my turban. Taleb Ali did the same. "I hope we get a strong breeze from the sea this afternoon," I said.

Taleb replied, "When the land gets hot, we will have a cooling breeze from the ocean. Look, the warriors are coming! They will meet in the widest part of this valley."

About two thousand horsemen streamed into the valley. The air was thick with cries of joy. It seemed as if nobody here cared whether they lived or died. The atmosphere was that of a festive show. I looked around me in disbelief at the happy, excited warriors on horseback. Taleb Ali, next to me, was relaxed and smiling, not a trace of worry on his face. He said, "Hiro, I have not seen a marvelous show like this in a very long time!" So this was their war, a grand show, where every man performed for the welcomed diversion and excitement.

The army on horseback formed a long line in the shape of a crescent. The leader in the center, their emir, held a large black flag. The emir on the right wing had a green flag, and the emir on the left wing raised his red flag. The opposing army rode into the valley with resounding shouts of joy. They, too, formed their long line of battle in the shape of a crescent. If an army were quite large, it would try to close the two horns of the crescent and surround its enemies. Here, however, the armies were small, about two thousand horsemen per side, and there was only limited space for maneuvering.

Behind our line was a small spring of fresh water. Some of our young men were busy building a basin of clay and stone to be filled with running water for our warriors and their horses to drink.

The enemy's cavalry were sure we would not attack them until they formed their battle line. Now I saw a small group of about thirty warriors on horseback riding toward the center of our line, their

223

swords sheathed and their leader shouting, "We come in peace! We are thirsty!"

Our emir, holding the flag of our center force, raised his face to the heavens and puffed out his cheeks. There was total silence in the valley. Then he said, "Let them drink. The battle has not yet started!"

The enemy horsemen advanced without fear, drank their fill and watered their horses, filled their waterskins, and returned to their side. I could not believe my eyes, but gradually it dawned on me that these people were fighting according to time-honored rules. Every man present understood that there was no glory in a victory over a thirsty and tired opponent.

The enemy battle line was divided into three forces, just like ours: one in the center, a force on the right wing, and another on the left wing. Each force had a commander, or emir, holding up a flag so his men could gather around him and hear his orders in the heat of battle.

The horses were restless, whinnying and snorting as if they sensed that a life and death contest was about to begin. The young warriors in their showy, many-colored cloaks were real horsemen, able to dominate their steeds, soothe them, and make them obey. These horses were raised in the tents with the children and treated with utmost kindness. If an owner fell to the ground, his horse would stand still next to his master. This was a scene to gladden a warrior's heart. I tried hard to remain an uninvolved spectator, but that proved impossible.

Now the battle started, with the time-honored ritual of hand-to-hand combat. Three warriors on horseback advanced between the armies and challenged our men to produce three champions of equal rank, for they would not fight freed men or slaves. They boasted of their past glories, and they boasted of their generosity and courage. The two armies quieted down. The men wanted to hear what these champions had to say. One of these warriors rode a black charger and wore a black turban on his head. His torso was bare, covered with hideous scars, and he rode his horse up and down between the lines, declaring:

A curse on all cowards,
trembling with fear!
Black Derrar, they call me.
I am still alive, still here!
All my body is scarred by the edge of a sword
or the point of a spear.
To die in my bed, old and crushed,
is my only fear!

I asked Taleb, "Who is this man?"
"He is the champion of his tribe."
"He is not a black man. Why do they call him Black Derrar?"
"Because in battle, he always wears a black turban and rides a black horse. And he always fights with his torso nude. He knows the sight of his ugly scars frightens his enemies."

There was an eerie silence over the valley as three champions from our side rode out to meet Derrar and his two comrades in man-to-man combat. They boasted of the valor of their tribe, the power of their swords, and the liberality of their hands. One of our champions, wearing a red and gold turban, drew his sword and recited these famous lines:

Look for me between the lines of battle, brother!
When the waves of war crash into each other!
And the spray of blood rises high in the air!
Look for a man with a Sharp Indian[77] in hand!
Fighting like a lion defending his lair!

One by one, the champions in the open space between the two armies recited their poetic verses, boasting of their courage and skill in battle and glorifying their own tribe. Then they attacked each other on horseback.

They showed great skill attacking and defending. There was no bloodshed, and the six warriors dismounted and fought on foot. I noticed they never used the point of their swords. Shouts of encouragement filled the air. The warriors watching this combat were

---

[77] In Arabic poetry, "Sharp Indian" refers to a sword made in India.

restless and excited, eager to start the battle. This went on for some time until one of our champions dealt a tremendous blow to his opponent that sent the man's head flying in the air. This so enraged the enemy that they drew their swords and charged our line with a loud roar reverberating off the canyon walls. The battle raged, and whenever an enemy horseman rushed through our lines, he would turn back and join his own troop before our men could take him prisoner.

The battle raged until sunset. Then the armies disengaged. We found Sheikh Zaki and his four sons and joined them around their campfire. The enemy was not far away. We could hear their laughter and smell their stewing pots. No one thought of posting guards! A night attack was unthinkable; whoever did that would bring dishonor upon his tribe. Warriors and horses were tired, thirsty, and hungry. Almost everyone was covered with fine yellow dust. It was time for a hot meal, pleasant conversation, and a night of rest under the stars.

Sondosa's father asked me, "Did you enjoy the battle, Hiro?" He was smiling contentedly. His tribe had taken many prisoners today. Each of them would be ransomed.

I said, "I admire the skill of the warriors," which, while true, was not the entire answer. I had seen enough fighting in my service in the queen's navy to wish never to see more battles.

The sheikh spoke in slow, deliberate words, addressing himself to his sons. "The warriors we fought today are our neighbors. If we kill too many of them, we will be planting hatred in their breasts and a desire for revenge that will be passed on from generation to generation. If a foreign army of Ethiopians or Persians invades our country, our neighbors will fight on our side. That would then be serious war with no prisoners taken, no quarter given. You see, Hiro, it would be foolish to weaken our neighbors. That is why we distrust commanders who harbor a strong desire to punish."

I asked Sheikh Zaki, "I did not see any archers today. Why?"

He laughed. "Arrows cause too much damage. Even stray arrows might injure our horses. We use archery only against foreign invaders. I assure you, Hiro, every man here is an expert with his bow."

Taleb Ali explained the rules of the game. "The aim of every warrior is to take a prisoner, not to kill, and every side will pay ransom to free their prisoners. If a man is very poor and no one offers to pay his ransom, his captor will shave his forelocks and let him go. If the prisoner is lucky, he might even get to keep his sword."

The next morning, there was a beautiful sunrise. The cloud formations in the east were colored orange and gold, the kind the Badu called "tail of the fox," and the clouds on the western horizon were colored pink against a light blue sky. A strong, cool breeze was blowing in from the ocean, and it lifted our spirits. It was a peaceful scene. Both armies were preparing to return to their homes. On our side, two men were killed and eleven wounded. On the enemy side, four were killed and thirty wounded.

I walked up into the valley with Mobareek at my side. Taleb Ali walked ahead of us. We came to a spot where the dead warriors were buried, wrapped in their cloaks in simple graves, covered with a few heavy stones to keep jackals away.

There was a man kneeling between two graves, crying. We stood at a distance, respecting his solitude. Taleb Ali said, "He is one of the great poets in our tribe. Without him, our heroes would be lost to eternal night, their names forgotten, their deeds unknown."

The poet stood up between two graves, majestic in his loneliness. In a loud, sad voice he cried, "Where have you gone, my friends? Where have you gone?"

The echo, bouncing uselessly off the canyon walls, answered him: "Friends, gone, gone, gone!"

The lament of the poet still held a wistful quality, which filled us with sudden sadness. We walked in silence to join the army heading back to the town of Mokalla. This beautiful Valley of the Ostriches was peaceful once again, and with the next flash flood, the rushing water would bring seeds from the desert bushes, and the fanlike plain would become green for a few weeks. The goat herders and shepherds would be here from both tribes, and some young hunters would steal a few sheep and another battle would take place. This cycle of war and peace would be repeated.

CHAPTER 26: The Falcon

Mobareek was engaged to Laila, Sondosa's sister, on the night of the new moon. Their wedding was set for the night of the full moon. Between their engagement and the wedding were fourteen nights of song, dance, and feasting. Many people in this community believed that good fortune came to those who start their new lives with the growing crescent of the moon.

The women celebrated in Sheikh Zaki's private garden, and men were not allowed inside the garden walls. The sound of the women's singing and rhythmical dancing was irresistible to young boys, and they clambered up the garden walls, taking turns climbing on each other's shoulders. They inhaled deeply of the jasmine perfume and jumped down, smiling and laughing.

The men celebrated in open fields. Huge tents were set up for the guests with the sides rolled up to let the breeze through. Every afternoon there was a show: horse racing, camel racing, archery, and swordplay contests. In one of the races, sixty young warriors on their Arabian horses galloped through a field of watermelons. Each man held a lance in his hand and tried to pick up a melon on the point of his lance. The thundering of the horses' hooves and the shouts of the warriors quickened our pulse. At the far end of the field, every man held up his lance dripping with red melon juice instead of his enemy's blood. It was a stirring show, followed by feasting, dancing, and singing that went on until late night.

The fourth day was devoted to falconry. Each falconer wore a glove on his hand to protect him from the falcon's sharp talons. The noble birds of prey were hooded to keep them calm. Their hoods were proudly decorated with feathers. The falconers were fanatically devoted to training and flying their birds. Their great pleasure and real motive was to watch the wonderful aerobatics of their falcons, not to put food on the table.

One by one the falconers stepped into the center of a great circle of enchanted spectators to show off their skill and the obedience of their trained birds. The falconer would sit on the ground and wait patiently for the crowd to quiet down. Then, in the total silence, he would stand up and remove the hood from the falcon's head and give his bird time to look around. Then with a sweep of his arm, he would toss the raptor up into the air. The falcon would circle and climb higher and higher and higher until most of the spectators could not see the bird. Then, from a tremendous height, the falcon would obey its owner's signal and dive back to earth, wings folded, hurtling down like a rock falling from the sky, gathering speed faster and faster, everyone wondering when the bird would slow down and whether it would crash into the rocks. Near earth, the falcon would open its wings gradually, slowing down and responding to its trainer's whistles. The noble bird would circle above the crowd and land gracefully on its owner's forearm. A shout of admiration would arise from the crowd. The falcon got his reward immediately—a piece of fresh liver red with blood.

I was enjoying the show. Taleb was near me, and Antar was standing between us. A falconer stood a few steps away from Antar. When his turn came, he removed the hood from the bird's head. I fancied that the falcon was looking at us with its large, bright eyes. The falcon flew so high that we could not see it anymore. Antar asked Taleb, "Do you think the falcon flew away, never to return?"

Taleb replied, "We have to wait and see. Some of them prefer freedom and life in the wild."

The falconer seemed unperturbed, and he calmly took off his turban. It was of an unusual color, orange with yellow stripes, and he twirled it around his head in widening circles. The man could not see his falcon, but the falcon saw him and came from the heights at an unbelievable angle, almost straight down. A shout of admiration rose up from the crowd. The falcon circled above our heads, and its owner whistled to bring it down. At this very moment, Antar impulsively stretched out his right arm, and the noble falcon perched gracefully on his forearm!

The falconer was not upset and saluted Antar. "My falcon never did this before! It is a good omen for you, my boy." Then he took his bird of prey onto his forearm, well protected from the sharp talons with a leather glove, and the falcon got its reward.

I looked at Antar's arm. Blood was flowing out of the deep holes in the flesh dug by the falcon's sharp talons. Antar quickly covered the wounds with his left hand so the sight of blood would not upset the guests. He lowered his forearm and kept the pressure on the wound with his left hand. I touched Antar's shoulder. "Are you all right?"

The faintest smile played on his face. "Yes. This is nothing, nothing at all."

Later, Galen looked at the wounds on Antar's forearm. He said, "Your 'good omen' had dirty talons. The wounds might fester. Let me clean them." Immediately, Galen enlarged the wounds with his knife and filled them with honey. He said, "Honey will prevent deep wounds from festering if you use it without delay." Galen had to use a golden needle and silk thread to close the wounds. Antar did not utter a sound, but I noticed the pallor on his face. He recovered quickly enough to insist on going back with us to Sheikh Zaki's tent to enjoy the music and singing.

In the largest tent, Mobareek feasted and entertained his close friends. Adoo, Galen, and Taleb sat next to him. I sat across the table from Mobareek with Antar at my side. The bride had to stay with the women in their private garden, and Sheikh Zaki sat at a separate table with the tribal leaders and elders. After the meal, music and singing lasted until late after midnight. The singers were women, slaves, with heavenly voices. They sang behind a wide curtain.[78] The musicians accompanying them were also behind the curtain. That arrangement had many advantages, allowing all to enjoy the music while the guests could focus on each other, and the singers and musicians could relax and perform their art without worrying about performing in front of watching eyes. These women singers were called *Al-Keyan*, and the best among them became famous. If someone wished to give a gift to a

---

[78] In Europe, many princes had their private chamber orchestras, and the musicians played behind a curtain while the prince and his guests dined. Until Mozart's time, the musicians playing for the princes were treated as servants.

king who had everything the human heart could wish for, he or she would present him with one of these famous keyan.

That night, there was a silvery moon low on the western horizon, sinking slowly, almost touching the sea. One of the keyan sang a beautiful poem describing the new moon. She repeated every verse several times with different inflections of the words and variations of the melody. The men were drunk with the good wine and the heavenly voice. The air in the big tent was loaded with perfume. I leaned back and closed my eyes like the guests all around me. I let myself drift with the song. I wished that the poem were longer and that this music would never stop:

> *Sing for the new moon, so young! So slender!*
> *The words, the eloquent words! Do you remember?*
> *Like a boat made of silver!*
> *Loaded—nay, overloaded—with amber!*
> *Sing with me! Your voice so soft and so tender!*

Two days after Mobareek's wedding, on the night of the full moon, Sheikh Zaki led us to the sacred Mountain of the Gods. He rode his black Arabian stallion flanked by two bodyguards, and we followed on horseback, Antar, Adoo, and I. After about two hours, we were close to the mountains, and Sondosa's father stopped for a rest. He called Antar to his side. "My son, do you see these two high peaks? The Mountain of the Gods is between them, but you cannot see it from here."

We rode on for some time, and suddenly the sacred mountain was visible, a low tabletop mountain about four thousand feet high, sitting between two high peaks, each about ten thousand feet high. We dismounted at the foot of the mountain. The two bodyguards took our horses and gave us heavy cloaks of camel hair to keep us warm and three waterskins but no food.

We climbed an easy trail for about an hour, and then it changed into wide and easy steps cut into the rock. I could hear Sheikh Zaki breathing heavily. He was not a young man anymore, and he was pushing himself. I called out, "Let us rest for a while." I asked Sheikh Zaki, "How did your people cut these steps into the mountainside?"

He smiled at me. "These steps were cut into the rock by strong young men in a time of peace and plenty. They worked in rotating groups of four men working shoulder to shoulder. They cut into the rock using heavy mallets with a serrated edge made of the best Indian steel. The entire community supported the workers on the mountainside. That is how these steps were created."

Adoo stood up and removed his turban. It was over twelve feet long. The proper length for a turban is twice the owner's height. He folded his turban four times. Now it became a wide, strong belt, and he said to Sondosa's father after bowing to him politely, "Sheikh Zaki, if I may, this will make your climb to the top easier." He wrapped the cloth around the old man's waist, then took the two ends of the long belt, one over his right shoulder and the other under his left arm, and tied the ends above his chest. Adoo smiled at the old sheikh. "Now lean back against this belt and let me tow you up these steps."

We kept going up the mountain, Adoo leading and Sheikh Zaki one step behind him. He seemed comfortable and was not breathing hard anymore. I looked around me. The trees were stunted, dry, and twisted. This low mountain did not get much rain. It was in the rain shadow of the two mountains towering high above us. We kept climbing higher and higher. The steps were wide and easy. We were close to the top when the wind hit us with great force. It was blowing hard between the two high peaks, driving small, black, fast-moving clouds before it. They constantly changed their forms like a herd of wild shaggy beasts galloping in the sky. It was an exciting scene, but not a raindrop fell on us.

When we stepped onto the flat top of the mountain, we were filled with admiration for the people who had dragged three awesome statues of their gods up there. Their war god was carved from black marble and stood twelve feet high. He had two large, angry red rubies for eyes. In his right hand was a real sword made of steel, three times the size of a warrior's sword, and in his left a lance with a shining point of gold reflecting the sunlight.

To the left of their war god stood the goddess of wind and rain, ten feet tall, made of green marble. She was leaning forward as if about to take off and fly, her long hair streaming behind her over her two wings. She wore a necklace of green emeralds, large perfect gems sparkling in the sunlight.

To the right of the war god stood the goddess of fertility and renewal of all life. She was made of white marble, glowing in the sunlight. In each upturned hand she held a large white egg the size of an ostrich egg. I admired the beauty of her hands and fingers and the gentle expression on her face. Her girdle was festooned with eggs the size of goose eggs, made of colored stones. She wore a necklace made of the largest pearls I have ever seen, the size of bird eggs.

We approached the gods slowly, leaning against the wind coming at us with great force from the gap between the two high mountain peaks. As we stood under the statues, an insistent droning sound that could not be ignored came from their heads. *Hum, hum, home—O, fey fey, you you, home . . .*

Sheikh Zaki asked, "Antar, my boy, can you hear the gods speaking?"

Young Antar replied quickly without thinking, "Yes. What are they saying?"

The sheikh answered, "You have to look into their heads to understand." Then he called Adoo. "Adoo, please help Antar. Lift him up so he can look into the ears of the wind goddess."

Antar stood barefoot on Adoo's shoulders and looked into the large ears of the goddess. He shouted above the wind, "There is a tunnel connecting both ears!"

Sheikh Zaki shouted back, "Now look into her mouth!"

Antar did and then looked down at us, laughing. "There is a tunnel opening at the back of her head, concealed by her hair."

Adoo let Antar down gently and said, "Now we know how these gods sing their songs."

"It seems this is one thing the gods share in common with men," I mused. "The more empty their heads are, the more noise they make!"

We sat down to rest on a huge slab of flat rock. Antar was sitting next to me. He rubbed the brown, smooth stone streaked with black with the palm of his hand. "Why are these flat rocks burnt black and brown?"[79]

Adoo replied, "This must be the fire of the gods that strikes down from the sky when they are angry." Adoo had a streak of superstition in his makeup. I never found out how much he believed or disbelieved.

Adoo looked at the statues with admiration. He said, "The gods are beautiful, even the war god, so solemn and majestic." Then he sang a few lines in the dialect of his land, Nubia:

Tell me, who can save you in your darkest hours
on land and at sea?
To whom do you pray in fear and supplication?
And when at last you are saved, whom do you thank?
Where do you lay down your offerings and gifts?
Tell me, do you know the wondrous names of the gods?

We sat silently at the feet of the gods, wrapped in our heavy camel-hair cloaks, trying to get some shelter from the howling wind. The gods never stopped their insistent humming, like the droning of a million bees.

There was a moment of awe when the moon rose out of the ocean and bathed the statues in a cold glow. We suffered silently from hunger and cold but never mentioned food because we had none. Sheikh Zaki broke the silence.

"I know you are cold and hungry." He put his hand on Antar's shoulder and said, "When we bring our young boys up here to face their gods for the first time, they suffer more than we do because they climb the mountain barefoot." We were eager to hear more, and he continued, "Tired, hungry, and cold, they experience an unforgettable night, and everything we teach them on this sacred mountain stays etched in their memory forever."

I asked the sheikh, "What do you teach the young men in one night on this flat, windswept mountain?"

He was very serious when he said, "They learn that a day and a night without food will not kill them. That alone is valuable. But most

---

[79] A dark patina of iron and manganese oxides, known as "desert varnish," will sometimes coat large rock surfaces in the desert.

important of all, with their stomachs empty and their minds open, the young boys memorize prayers that will fortify them in times of great danger. They have to sit down cross-legged facing the gods, and we make them chant the prayers over and over until sunrise."

Even after a sleepless night, Sheikh Zaki still had a serene look on his high-colored face. At sunrise, he walked around the gods, trying to get the stiffness out of his cold legs. Out of the valleys, a falcon appeared and circled over the heads of the gods. The rays of the rising sun gave him golden wings.

Sheikh Zaki called out, "Antar! Keep your eyes on the falcon!" The noble bird climbed higher and higher until it was nothing but a barely visible dot in the sky. Sheikh Zaki stood by Antar, his hand on the young man's shoulder to be sure that he got his full attention. "Can you still see the falcon?" he asked.

"No, not anymore," replied Antar.

I approached to listen to what the sheikh was saying. He said, "From your land, there is a myth that teaches that the sun god will turn the falcon into a ray of golden light, but you and I know otherwise. So, too, it is with these statutes. Where the gods really reside we know not, but our myths help us teach our children about our gods."

Sheikh Zaki was smiling, and then he said to Antar, "Taleb Ali told me how the falcon landed on your arm." He shook his head and slapped his thigh twice. "Incredible . . . the noble bird preferred you to his trainer. This is an omen of future greatness and good fortune. I hope to see you as a great leader among our people. When the time comes, remember this trip, and return and climb this mountain to be alone in your thoughts. When you descend from the mountain, the gods will put eloquent words in your mouth, powerful words that will move armies of men to follow you to war and to obey your laws in peace."

We stayed on the mountaintop and fell asleep in the warmth of the noonday sun. After a much-needed rest, we slowly descended the steps. The two guards were waiting for us with food and water. After a light meal, we rode our horses. Sheikh Zaki led the way on his black stallion. Just before sunset, we stopped and turned around, all of us at the same moment as if compelled by a powerful hand. We sat patiently in our saddles watching the Mountain of the Gods change colors from reddish brown to pale violet to a light grey color.

It was the third night after the full moon, and we rode all the way to Mokalla in the brilliant moonlight, every man silent, pensive, and lost in his own private thoughts.

The very next day, two giants paced majestically through Taleb's garden gate. They were Sheikh Zaki's bodyguards, leading the sheikh's black stallion between them. We stood up to greet them. One of them said in a booming voice, "A gift from our chief to Antar Ali Zol!"

Antar stepped forward. "I am Antar. I will walk to your chief's fort to thank him a thousand times. He has bestowed upon me a great honor." Taleb Ali looked stunned.

The second giant gave Antar the bridle, saying, "Take good care of him. His name is Edhem El-Gabar."[80]

I was glad that Antar was a great horseman. Horses know whether their rider is inexperienced; yes, they know. It would be a pity to spoil such a marvelous stallion. I told Antar, "Take care where you gallop with this horse. Choose the ground carefully."

Taleb recovered his composure and spoke with unalloyed joy on his weathered face. "Antar, my boy, the chief just gave you his favorite horse. The admiration he must have for you!"

Antar replied, "What valuable gift can we give Sheikh Zaki?"

Taleb took Antar's hand in his right hand and my hand in his left. "Come and sit down," he said. "There is nothing we can do or give. He has conferred a great honor on our prince. Don't you see, Hiro, the real gift the sheikh has just given our young man is fame? The entire tribe will be talking about this!"

Antar looked at us, asking, "Don't you think that at least we should give a gift to his daughter Sondosa?"

Taleb said, "Wait for me here," and he went to his rooms. When he returned, he was carrying a box made of fine wood, inlaid with

---

[80] *El-Edhem* refers to the color. A blue-black stallion is called *Edhem*. *Gabar* describes the character of a war horse, powerful and unbeatable.

mother-of-pearl shell. "Here is a gift I prepared for Sondosa. I knew Antar would need one soon!"

Antar asked eagerly, "May I see it?"

Taleb gave him the box. "Present this to Sondosa after you thank her father."

Antar lifted the lid. We were dazzled by the brilliance of the jewels—three necklaces, one of green emerald, the second of blue sapphires, and the third made of red rubies.

We changed into our fine clothes and walked to Sheikh Zaki's home to thank him. It seemed to me that Antar was walking with a lighter step, faster than usual. He had not seen Sondosa's beautiful face for seventeen days. She had stayed in her father's house, helping with the preparations for her sister's wedding.

The three of us, Antar, Taleb, and I waited in the great reception room, the same room where Mobareek had seen his wife, Laila, for the first time. To my great surprise, Mobareek stepped into the room with his wife. He looked like a happy man starting a new life and a new family. He hugged me, almost crushing my ribs, and then gave a warm hug to Antar. With Taleb he was even more gentle, kissing the old navigator on his shoulders. I told Mobareek all about our night on the Mountain of the Gods and about Sheikh Zaki's gift.

He smiled. "Yes, I know. Everyone is talking about the sheikh's generosity."

As we were talking, Sheikh Zaki walked into the room with Sondosa. She sat down near her father, smiling at us with a mysterious radiance about her that affected Antar in a way I had not seen in him before, no doubt from love he had never experienced until now. He waited politely until Taleb, the eldest, saluted the sheikh first. Then I saluted the chief. "Sheikh Zaki! Edhem, El-Gabar will bring honor and fame to young Antar!"

The sheikh seemed pleased that we understood the effect of his generous gift. Then Antar walked up and bowed politely. "May I present this gift to your daughter Sondosa?" Her father nodded his head approvingly. Sondosa opened the box, and her eyes widened. She showed the necklaces to her father and to her sister, Laila. I was pleased when Sondosa said to her sister, "Please choose the necklace you like the most. Three are too many for me!"

Before we left, Antar stood before the chief and said simply, "Sheikh Zaki, El-Edhem will always be your horse. I will take care of him, and no one will ride him except you and me."

The next ten days were happy in spite of the fact that Taleb kept reminding me every morning, "The winter storms are not far off. As soon as the east wind blows, you must sail back to Egypt."

Antar and Sondosa rode their horses daily on the wide open beach. She was always accompanied by one of her brothers. Her horse was a purebred Arabian, white without a blemish, the color of ivory.

At low tide, they galloped on the wet pressed sand, Sondosa's glorious hair flowing behind her and the horses' long manes waving in the air. At high tide, the horses' legs kicked up a spray of seawater. An Arabian horse's graceful step galloping at half speed is called *traheel*. I was enchanted by the picture of graceful movement and high energy, and the two young riders full of the joy of life.

I decided then and there to teach Nedra how to ride. She learned surprisingly quickly, but of course she was a descendant of the Turkmans, the greatest horsemen on earth. It came naturally to her, and Taleb presented her with a beautiful mare. Every morning in the cool, pure air of the sea, we joined Antar, Sondosa, and one of her brothers in riding on the wide, lonely beach.

One morning, Antar came galloping toward me. He looked remarkably young and was bursting with joy. He gave me a great bellow. "Hiro! She said she wants to marry me!"

Back in Taleb's fort, Antar begged the wise old navigator to go to Sondosa's father and fix a date for her wedding. Day after day he begged, and Taleb refused again and again. I could not understand why. Finally he gave in and visited Sheikh Zaki to talk about Antar's wedding to Sondosa. He returned late in the afternoon and sat down in his garden. We gathered around him, Antar eager for the news.

"Did Sheikh Zaki fix a date?"

"Yes, he did," said Taleb, his hand on his forehead in a gesture of resignation.

"When will it be?"

"After one year."

Antar was stunned. Taleb kept talking to him to ease the blow. "My boy, you don't know the customs of our people. Sheikh Zaki is a great chief. He cannot marry his daughter to a stranger. He knows and we know that your father was the ruler of an empire and your mother was the queen of Egypt. But all his people, his tribe and his clan, will never know your lineage." Then in a gentle, soothing voice, Taleb said to Antar, "You have to wait, my boy, until your fame spreads and you are honored by Sondosa's whole tribe." Taleb Ali looked at me. "Hiro, my friend, the truth is, I was surprised that Sheikh Zaki did not say Antar must wait three years. But he likes my son."

I walked with Mobareek in the Red Harbor of Mokalla. He liked to spend time with his friends, the shipbuilders and navigators. We stopped near our ships, the *Sorceress* and *Sword of the Sea.* My friend said, "Your crew is getting restless. They are eager to go home to their wives and children."

I said, "I know. We must sail as soon as the east wind blows."

We stood together, looking at our graceful ships. Mobareek put his arm on my shoulder. "Hiro, don't sail through Bab-El- Mandab at night." He looked at me and smiled. "If you have to wait for the south wind, stop at Zabargacf [Emerald Island]. The girls will enjoy picking up the green stones. It is like finding one's own colorful seashells on the beach instead of buying them."

I told Mobareek, "Don't worry about us. I will lead with *Sword of the Sea*, and Adoo with Ari will follow with the *Sorceress.*" Then I laughed. "Mobareek, you had better build two fast ships because next year I will come back and race you again."

The wind from the east sprang up at midnight. I could hear it in the palm trees. Taleb Ali, as usual, was out of his house long before sunrise looking at the stars. When he returned, the sun was still below the horizon.

The old navigator woke me up gently. "Hiro, the east wind is blowing. It will get stronger by tomorrow."

We watched the sunrise together and sat at his table for breakfast. Taleb looked at me with serene eyes. "Hiro, who knows whether I will see you again? Who among us knows his own *maseer* [destiny]? Write a few words for me to remember you by."

Taleb gave me a piece of soft leather and a feather quill. He put a pot of black ink on the table. I knew he would hang my lines on his wall and that the calligraphy was as important as the words, so I took my time and did my best:

Some friendships will never be forgotten,
And some loves will never die!
Like our brotherhood and our love
For the mountains, the sea, and the sky!

Mobareek stepped on board *Sword of the Sea* carrying his son, Atiya, on one powerful arm and in his other hand, his son's simsimiyya. "Here he is, Hiro. Take care of him until he finds his way in the city." And to his son he said, "Atiya, if you want to return and live here with me, Hiro will bring you back."

Mobareek kissed Atiya and said simply, "I wish you happiness."

The crew came forward to salute Mobareek. One by one, every man kissed his forearm and said a few words of thanks. It was my turn to say goodbye to him. He hugged me once again, crushing my ribs. I wanted to thank him for everything he had taught me and for saving my life, but powerful emotions clutched at my throat, and the words never came out.

Galen, Adoo, and the girls kissed Antar on his forehead, and the crew gathered around him to wish him happiness. The young men really loved Antar, and every one of them hugged him and kissed his shoulders. Ari and Justin took him aside, and they had a long conversation together.

Taleb had kind words for everyone on board. When he stood before Galen, he did not say a word. He just held Galen's small hands in his big hands and kissed them. The expression on his kind lined face said it all.

At last, just before we raised our sails, I looked at Antar standing between Taleb Ali and Mobareek, now a strong, bronzed young man whose fate was still being written, and behind them the Red Harbor of Mokalla. I walked toward my friends, all three smiling, and I hugged them all. Taleb looked at us through his serene eyes, a smile gently appearing on his wrinkled face, and said, "Hiro and Antar, yours is now a bond that will not be forgotten."

Then I led Antar aside and spoke softly with him. "Antar, my duty to my queen is now complete, but my friendship is yours forever."

He could not hold back his tears, and he asked me in a soft voice, "Will you return for my wedding, Hiro?"

"Yes, Antar! I promise I will return at the end of summer, when the north winds blow strong and steady, and the seven stars lie low on the horizon."

> *'Tis all a checkerboard of nights and days,*
> *Where destiny with men for pieces plays;*
> *Hither and thither moves, and mates, and slays*
> *And, one by one back in the closet lays.*

—Omar-Al-Khayyam (Rubaiyat of Omar Khayyam by Edward Fitzgerald, first edition [1859])